HOBOKEN

Marcus Reichert is the author of the novels *Verdon Angster* (1995) and *The Miracle of Fontana's Monkey* (1997). He is also a painter whose work is held in collections internationally. In 1979, he wrote and directed the film *Union City*, now recognised as the first *neo-noir*, which is in the permanent archive of the Museum of Modern Art, New York. *Displaced Person: Poetry, Pornography & Politics* (Selected Writings 1970-2005) and *Art & Ego: Marcus Reichert in Conversation with Edward Rozzo* (2007) are published by Ziggurat Books.

Dom Gabrielli is a poet whose *The Eyes of a Man* (2009) is published by Ziggurat Books International. He studied literature at Edinburgh University and prepared for his doctorate in Paris and New York. In Paris, Gabrielli's passion for French literature and thought led him to begin writing, translating, and teaching. His published work includes translations of Battaille and Leiris.

HOBOKEN

*A Novel
by
Marcus Reichert*

Introduction by
Dom Gabrielli

ZIGGURAT BOOKS
International

Hoboken Copyright ©1999 by Marcus Reichert
Introduction Copyright © 2009 by Dom Gabrielli

All rights reserved. Except for brief passages quoted in a newspaper, magazine, radio, or television program, no part of this book may be reproduced in any form or by any means, electronic or mechanical, including photocopying and recording, or by any information storage and retrieval system, without permission in writing from the Publisher.

Front cover photograph: Amos Chan
Copyright © 1979 by Marcus Reichert
Back cover: Portrait of Marcus Reichert
Copyright © 2007 by Edward Rozzo

UK office: 27 St. Quentin House, Fitzhugh Grove,
London SW18 3SE, England
Editorial office: 6 rue Argenterie,
30170 St. Hippolyte du Fort, France
Enquiries: zigguratbooks@orange.fr

Printed by Imprint Digital, Upton Pyne, Exeter

Distributed by Central Books Ltd.
99 Wallis Road, London E9 5LN, England
Tel UK: 0845 458 9911
Fax UK: 0845 459 9912
Tel International: +44 20 8525 8800
Fax International: +44 20 8525 8879
email: orders@centralbooks.com

Visit the author's website: www.marcusreichert.com

First Edition

ISBN 978-0-9561038-4-0

for Rosalie Siegel

REICHERT'S HOBOKEN
Introduction by Dom Gabrielli

I was at New York University during the first Gulf War, studying literature and the cinema. I spent days and nights going to the cinema, loitering at the back of jazz clubs until the small hours, attending improvisation readings, and roaming the streets from Alphabet City to Brooklyn, the Village to Central Park, Little Italy to Soho, Chinatown to Times Square. I have to admit: I never went to Hoboken. My ears became fine-tuned to the vernaculars of the street, to the grammatical innovations rising in circles from the tarmac like curls of smoke. I liked to think of myself as a vessel filled and emptied at will. I spent a lot of time copying styles, writing reams to nobody in particular. I was pushing toward a strange and positive energy which I sensed simultaneously inside *and* outside me. Ahead of me lay my liberation. I learnt about writers and film-makers who had invented new forms and renamed old ones. I digested a whole series of these narratives, but no Reichert.

Some names are destined to escape such narratives, not only because the writer or film-maker (or poet or painter) doesn't have the pretention to try to encompass what went before, or overshadow what will follow, but because he is himself a pocket outside history, a nomad signifier outside any tradition. Reichert is one of these and that's probably why I didn't find him at New York Film School or Columbia University or the Metropolitan Museum. He is an exception among exceptions, magician of the disappearing act along a life trail upon which he is not master but pupil to his sensibility. To outwit boredom Marcus Reichert has perpetually renewed himself, and to accomplish this has used a multitude of media. He has always run from fame and kept his production at the centre of his activity. Take for instance the film *Union City*, the Crucifixion series of paintings, the divinely funny novel *The Miracle of Fontana's Monkey*; who can claim, as Reichert can, to express himself with equal ease in images and words? But it is essential to understand that *sensibility* is the thread that connects all Reichert's work, uniting it across media and form.

Hoboken, an *exercise de style*, is a study in senseless criminal behaviour. More tellingly, it examines how the so-called *innocent majority* who are desperate to conform choose to overlook the sickness growing on their doorstep and end up sacrificing their children because they don't have the courage to speak up and protect them from evil. These are the onlookers, the voyeurs, the people who allow criminality to flourish. Reichert the Freudian moralist meets Reichert the anthropologist: this is an epitaph for an exile – for the central character of Diego Ildefonso, Spanish immigrant – but it is also a description in minutiae of a sick society in the process of being inexorably dismantled, character by character.

Reichert pulls us into the mire. He scans this *société sombre* with the objectivity of the lens he once mastered. The story, set in the spring of 1977, is propelled from the start in the tradition of the crime thriller. A multitude of crimes, a multitude of the guilty, a minimum of guilt. The certainty that things are not going to get better but, in the manner of Greek tragedy, are headed for doom *and* fast. Reichert, with omniscient efficiency, depicts the innards of a society of ordinary people on the verge of implosion. His characters are without intellectual passion, without a sense of achievement. They are left to play with their instincts. Sex and violence predominate but with a horrendous realism reminiscent of the terrifying musings of the Marquis de Sade. We look in vain for hope, but this world is condemned and this particular tribe will auto-destruct. Reichert's novel was not written to make friends and we soon understand why *Hoboken*, completed in 1999, hasn't been published in America.

Hoboken asks to be read in one or two sittings, its crescendo opening into an impossible purgatory. It is not an ostentatious work of art. It is a revolutionary object because it is perfectly readable and most intentionally so. Hilarious, disgusting, pornographic, and poetic, here the novel becomes an act of sabotage. *Hoboken* will remain a vicious indictment of the greedy decades of brutal late capitalism, when even Jesus was another product to market through a sinister triumvirate of media, politics and religion. These were times when America had lost its coordinates, emptiness loomed at every street corner draped in slick images of an impossible future.

Paris – Brindisi
4th June 2009

HOBOKEN
APRIL 1977

For banishment have many good men braved
Who in their souls refused to conscience evil,
While evil held the fatherland enslaved.

Far better to accept such fate and travel
Than carry on among a folk depraved
And bear the hatred of the blinded rabble.

Count August von Platen Hallermund
(1796-1835)
as quoted by Thomas Mann in his Diary
21.11.33

ONE

Before his parents rose, Roland Ildefonso usually stood by the living-room window that had the best view of the square, his gaze inevitably drawn to the WWI cannon that had been enshrined there under a canopy of poured concrete. Like many children, Roland had an imaginary friend. His was named James. As they watched an early bus passing in the empty street below, a fly alighted on the window-pane before them. Roland quietly engaged James in an exchange similar to many they'd had.

"Flies aren't like us," he said.
"They're different, aren't they?" James replied.
"Very."

Roland heard his father singing in the shower. He always sang in the shower, and always in Spanish or Italian. In the morning, his father often complained of a ringing in the ears. He said it was due to permanent damage done his eardrums by bombs dropped on his Uncle Isidro's restaurant when he was nine, only a year older than Roland.

Dolores, Roland's mother, passed silently behind him, through the darkened living-room and into the kitchen.

Roland wished they would drop bombs on Hoboken, like they had on Guernica. He wished it with all his might, so that he and his father and a handful of other courageous men could rush down to the square and man the cannon and, as his father's friend Gus put it, *blow the Commie bastards out of the sky!*

Dressed immaculately as usual, Diego Ildefonso strode into the kitchen. His son followed.

"You look nice," said Dolores.
"I look like I feel," Diego replied.

She waited. He wasn't about to elaborate. As she returned to squeezing her oranges, he went to stand behind her and breathe in the fragrance of her damp hair. Roland, who was lingering in the doorway, blushed.

"Shall we plan on eating early?" she asked. "It would be fun to get to the fairgrounds before they turn the lights on."

Roland observed their behavior at an angle in the large mirror over the sofa in the living-room. He observed his own behavior too. The boy he saw in the mirror, fair of complexion and deceptively delicate, now turned to smile endearingly at his mother and father. Diego went to him, touched his face, and kissed him on the head. His mother followed his father into the back hallway. A long moment passed before Roland heard his father go down the stairs and off to work. Every morning it was the same.

It was spring and Dolores Ildefonso longed for a lawn with daffodils, an enchantment she remembered vividly from her childhood in Trenton. At thirty-seven, and having been married contentedly to Diego for nine years, she had only this one wish. An only child, she had often gardened with her father, who considered bulbs one of God's finest creations. He called them "instant flowers." Once when substitute teaching, Dolores had managed to convey this ingenious concept to her third-graders and it had fascinated and delighted them. Today, while Roland ate his breakfast – scrambled eggs, one long spicy sausage, a slice of white toast smothered in store-bought grape jam, and a large glass of milk – Dolores thought about the daffodils.

Roland knew his mother had a kindly face. Sometimes it was beautiful too, especially when she wore lipstick and smiled. Billy Nolan's mother's face was like a statue. It was very pale, and her hair fell without curving at all, straight down along her cheeks, which were peppery, like a pitted stone. Looking at Val Nolan always made Roland feel funny in his stomach.

The telephone at the Ildefonsos' rang every morning but Sunday between 9:00 and 9:30 – Val, on her second cup of coffee. This morning when the telephone rang Dolores was already sorting through Diego's and Roland's socks to see which needed mending.

"How's it going, Val?"

"My Billy's got a rash."

"Where?"

"Where do you think? He still leaks in his drawers. Things form in there. Then his testicles get contaminated. Something like that, anyway."

"Diego broke Roland of that when he was only four."

"I wish Tommy-Tom had any inclination to do that about Billy. What'd he do?"

"He made him go around the house without any pants on."

"That sounds OK."

"It forced him to use the toilet."

"Huh?"

"Otherwise he would have been wetting all over the place."

"Like a dog."

"Not exactly."

Dolores often found Val's comments perplexing. It was as if Val subconsciously resented her rapport with her son.

"I'm thinking about getting a job," said Val. "Something in hosiery. I've got good legs. Your Diego says I've got good legs, and he ought to know."

Dolores was now thoroughly annoyed with herself for answering the telephone. The agitation Val demonstrated on coffee was often disconcerting. When drinking alcohol, she could be positively chaotic.

"Nobody can spend all her time doing next to nothing around the house," Val went on.

"I find there's always something to do," Dolores responded, wearily.

"Yea, and the man goes out and has his fun with younger women. You probably wouldn't know about that, about those girls who hang out at The Jewel. Most likely, they wouldn't be interested in Diego."

"Those are drag queens."

There followed a lengthy silence. Val's face floated up vividly before Dolores, but it wasn't the face Dolores now knew, it was the face Val had had before the energy had gone out of her. She was standing on a patio by a swimming pool, resplendent with Japanese lanterns, and she was grinning. Eighteen, and her face was like the face of a wild angel, illuminated from within and wickedly disconcerting to behold. It was about to happen all over again. Val was about to make a mess of things. A senior in high school, Dolores had just moved to Teaneck, had met Ray, Val's older brother, at a dance in Fort Lee, and more than liked him. Val was drunk. Everyone stared and Tommy-Tom, up from Hoboken and not about to suffer their snobbish scrutiny, slunk off to find another beer. Val pressed herself to Ray, clutching his hand to her skinny thigh. There she was, again, flirting with her own brother in front of all of Dolores's nicest friends, pressing herself against him and smiling up adoringly into his eyes. Before long, Dolores and Ray wouldn't be welcome anywhere, not in the homes of the nicer people, and all because Val insisted on making Dolores her friend.

Val mumbled something. It sounded like the word *repellent,* but Dolores knew it couldn't be. Val was lighting a cigarette. She claimed she only smoked outside the house, in the evenings, when she went out on the town with Tommy-Tom, but Dolores knew she lit up the moment she was alone with little Billy.

Diego Ildefonso made his way along Willow Street in the direction of Bernardi's Italian Restaurant. The sun had broken through the clouds and the buildings along the way shone with that mysteriously comforting yellow light Diego had come to associate with Hoboken on a good day. Glimpsing himself in the wide front window of Willow Street's only laundromat, recently defunct, the idle washers and dryers staring out from the darkness within, Diego liked what he saw: behind the big man in his smart clothes rose, several blocks away, the spire of St. Eleanor's Catholic Church, giving the bedraggled scene around him a majesty perversely reminiscent of the old world. Beyond this picture, lying unseen but undeniably gleaming, lay the Hudson River, and beyond that, the epic towers of the metropolis itself. Pausing to savour the dimensions of his universe, Diego sensed the imaginations of his fellow citizens, most of whom dwelled eternally in the warm shadows of their livingrooms, drifting through their television sets and deeper into the cosmos.

Fred Barbiche, who owned Pretty Feet with his partner Giles Petit-Pont – they also owned glitzy St. Martine on Lexington Avenue – had come over that morning from Manhattan to have a chat with his manager. He had been nice to Diego: usually nothing was sold on a Monday morning and the fat man had sold two matching pairs of baby sneakers to Mrs. Delano for the twins, Bonnie and Bobby, both little girls. The sneakers were adorable, with tiny broken eggs emitting yellow chicks scattered over a magnolia ground.

To celebrate, Diego was planning on having Bernardi's only Mexican dish on the menu, Yellow Mole, for lunch. He was particularly fond of pork and most particularly pork bones, and this dish had pork bones in abundance. It also had a hearty sauce made with guajillo chilies, tomatillos, zucchini, green beans, acuyo leaves, onions, and lots of garlic, which Diego loved. He steadfastly refused to give up his garlic at lunch even though he was obliged to then ruin what taste was left in his mouth by sucking a peppermint on his way back to the shop.

Today Diego chose a table by the front window. As he sat, he tucked his tie into the waist of his trousers. In imitation of his uncle Isidro, he wore braces rather than a belt. His suit was a roomy fifty-eight inches around the middle, which easily accommodated his tie without creasing it when he was seated. As the restaurant wasn't too busy, he insisted Bernardi keep him company while he ate.

When the Yellow Mole arrived, Bernardi sat himself at one corner of the table to watch. Bernardi was also a large man, but his weight was firmly lodged in his bulky shoulders and chest. Before long their communication consisted exclusively of glassy-eyed smiles. The head waitress Ramona, who harbored a secret affection for Diego Ildefonso, watched from the doorway to the kitchen. She often wondered why her boss treated the beautiful fat man with such deference, invariably concluding that it was because Mr. Ildefonso was political.

After ten minutes or so, Bernardi said, "A little *Frank* for the digestion?" meaning Sinatra on the restaurant's soundsystem, and got up, leaving Diego to his meticulous extraction of the pork bones.

"Succulent," said Diego, through the mulch between his teeth, and his host limped off happily, his left foot having been reduced to spaghatini by a land mine outside Agrigento in 1943. Diego and Bernardi had this in common: ghastly memories of the war.

As the Yellow Mole settled in Diego's stomach, he pondered the peculiarly unpleasant intricacies of the previous evening.

In the end, what was meant to be fun had been nothing but wearying. Sunday and as usual he'd had his two pals Gus Rozzo and Tommy-Tom Nolan over for spaghetti. Babs and Val and Dolores had all agreed that this was a safer situation than having the boys finish off the afternoon at some local bar, although it was Dolores who had to make nice entirely on her own. On these occasions Diego played the music he liked best. Of course only Dolores, listening quietly in the background, appreciated this. It had been an unseasonally hot night, utter stillness in the streets. At 231 Willow, seven blocks up from Bernardi's, if you listened carefully, you could hear the hi-fi playing Puccini's *Madama Butterfly*, the delicate strains eddying forth like a gentle breeze four floors above you. The heat had swarmed in from nowhere, the limp air murky with the overwhelming scent of humanity. At one point, feeling faint, Diego went into the bedroom and threw open the window. Across the way, a cat lay sleeping in the darkness under one of the parked cars. Even with the door closed, Diego could hear Gus and Tommy-Tom arguing at the other end of the apartment. They usually stayed late, drinking Diego's wine and talking – about work, about other guys they knew, about politics – but they'd drunk more than usual and the conversation had overheated. They were still carrying on when Diego finally left Dolores to her book, around eleven, and returned to the kitchen.

Black hair shining blue in the fluorescent light, Tommy-Tom stood slouching by the kitchen sink. "So, what is it?"

"So, what is what?" Gus snapped back. The diminutive Italian, the sleeves of the pastel orange shirt he'd worn to church that morning rolled above his biceps, stood up and leaned violently across the table, took up the bottle of Chianti, the seventh Diego had uncorked that evening, and refilled his glass.

"The fucking Knights of Columbus, what else're we talking about? It's a club to control things, all with guys who already think the same. Big fucking deal. I don't get it. What's to fucking control?"

Diego had been studying Tommy-Tom for the past few minutes. There was something wrong about Tommy-Tom, he concluded, and it wasn't merely his insolent manner, so unbecoming in a man whose virility and alleged maturity obviously meant so much to him. Diego waited, savoring the moment, watching Gus wonder anxiously whether to go on the attack or not: naturally, Gus was one of the *guys* Tommy-Tom was referring to, a guy who hadn't the guts, as Tommy-Tom saw it, to separate himself from what came easiest in life, like joining some dumb men's club. Gus had asked Diego to join, early on in their friendship, but at the time Diego hadn't realized the political potential in such an involvement.

"Try getting in on your own – then let's see what happens," stammered Gus, and began twitching his dainty fingers through the breadcrumbs scattered over the table. "I bet they don't want you, and not cause you're a fucking mick." He laughed to let Tommy-Tom know his Irishness really didn't matter, it was a joke as far as his pal Gus was concerned.

"Cause I don't fucking cooperate with nobody." Tommy-Tom directed this remark to Diego, then stared off into the Ildefonsos' living-room.

Following his glance, both Gus and Diego now saw the child listening in the dim light just beyond the doorway.

"What's your kid doing up?" Gus abruptly inquired of Diego. "Kid should be in fucking bed by now. It's – what?" He peered around the kitchen looking for a clock.

"Leave the fucking kid alone." The gangling figure by the sink smiled at the boy. "Come here, Rolex. Come over here and give your uncle Tommy-Tom a kiss."

"Roland?" said Diego, softly.

Tommy-Tom smoothed his hair, limp with lanolin, back with both hands. "Hey Rolex," he whispered, "gettin any pussy lately?"

"He's drunk," Gus cautioned Diego.

"Roland, what're you doing up?" Diego persisted, shifting his enormous bulk away from the table to wave his son back into the shadows.

"I want to know what the Knights of Columbus have to do with the communists," answered Roland, matter-of-factly.

"Get this," sighed Gus, and glanced up at Tommy-Tom, who shrugged. "The kid's brainy too."

Roland stepped fully into the doorway. "Hey Pop, aren't all these organizations fronts for counter-revolutionary activity?"

"What organizations?" whined Gus, and drained his glass. "Yea, yea, I know, our kids are all gonna be marching around Red Square – for Chrissake."

"Around Manhattan, but they'll be wearing suits and carrying brief-cases," said Diego.

"What about the girls," snorted Tommy-Tom, "what're they gonna be wearing, combat boots and nothin else?"

"Roland, go back to bed, before your mother wakes up," urged Diego.

"Yea, and tells us to go home," said Gus.

"She wouldn't," murmured Diego, "you know that."

"I know who's the boss in my house." Tommy-Tom stared blearily at Gus. "Me. That's who."

Gus looked at the bottle of Chianti. "Somebody should finish this."

"Yea, and somebody should do the fucking dishes. What'ya say, Captain?" Tommy-Tom, now gazing down into the sink, was addressing Diego.

Both men, Diego knew, had come to acknowledge him as their intellectual superior, in Gus's case, begrudgingly.

"Somebody should get this here tomato sauce before it gets hard," said Tommy-Tom.

"Dolores won't mind. Roland, go to bed. Tommy-Tom, please, just leave that."

"I gotta go," said Gus. Wobbling on his little feet, he picked up the bottle of Chianti and drained it. "Oooeee! Get ready Babs, you gorgeous piece of fuck-meat, here I come!"

"Shut-up," grunted Tommy-Tom.

"Oh yea-ah," Gus blurted back. With laughable determination, he then walked past Roland and through the living-room in the direction of the front hallway. "Go to bed, Roland," he barked, mimicking Diego, as he let himself out.

"I'm goin out the back so I don't have to give the fucker a lift," said Tommy-Tom. "Hey Rolex, shake it more than three times and you're playin with it."

"How many times do *you* shake it?" Roland called after him.

"So now you're a wise-ass too," was the last thing Diego remembered saying, as he scooped up his son and took him in to bed.

The strains of "September" cascaded over the shining surfaces of Bernardi's. Diego shifted his focus from the pile of bones he had amassed on what would have been his neighbor's napkin and concentrated his attention instead on the deliciously spicy sauce at the bottom of the dish before him; it adhered beautifully to the large pores of the baguette provided by Ramona. Without Bernardi there to distract him, Diego's thoughts turned once again, sadly, to himself. The sentimental music reminded him that he had awoken that morning in tears. What had he dreamt? He couldn't remember, only that it was somehow unbearably lovely. As always, he had found his enormous belly tucked into the curve of his wife's lower back, the underside of his girth resting, gently pulsing, on the lean rise of her buttocks. This was where his belly belonged, and would belong forever. He was fat, fat and now at forty-seven mundane in every way. Fat with sincerity and stale thoughts. Earnest to a fault. Fat with nothing new.

My stomach is full now, Diego concluded, and pushed himself away from the table, accidentally tipping it upwards, like a see-saw. The dish that once held the Yellow Mole slid onto the floor and shattered. The pool of yellowish gruel he had been soaking up splattered in tiny droplets over the immaculate tiled floor.

"Fucking oaf," he muttered, and reached for the fresh handkerchief he always kept in his breast pocket, his eyes wet with shame.

"My mother's looking after Dommie and the twins," said Babs Rozzo, when she ran into Dolores on the street that day, Roland by his mother's side. "I'm shopping for some new bras. I've grown."

"They say child-bearing will do that."

"Yea, child-bearing and bras that are too tight!" Throwing back her head, Babs let out a laugh. Gus and Babs Rozzo lived in a split-level on the western fringes of Hoboken. This meant they perceived themselves as being a lot more glamorous than some people. "Aren't you gonna take you-know-who (meaning Roland) you-know-where (meaning the fair) this year?" Cocking her head to one side, pin-curls bound in a huge scarf decorated in what appeared to be panda bears, Babs waited.

Dolores absorbed the spectacle. "We haven't decided about that."

"Well, let us know if you change your mind. We'd love to go with you. You know how Mikie looks up to Roland."

Dolores wondered why Babs allowed herself to be seen on the street in such a guise, her wide babyish face startlingly immature without make-up. Then it came to her: Babs's mother Ruthie. Ruthie had always done the same in anticipation of a big night out. Before evening events at church, Babs and her mother often presented themselves to the world, out shopping in tandem, in that condition. Dolores imagined it heightened the thrill, after hours of chatty exertions, of finally looking utterly ridiculous.

"Roland looks funny," said Babs.

How do I look funny? wondered Roland, waiting for her to elaborate, but instead Babs's attention was drawn to a new car passing in the street.

"You think Diego's ever gonna get that, you know, whatever it is he's always talking about?"

"We don't really need a car." Dolores smiled down at Roland, mildly embarrassed. There were times when she rued the night she and Diego had met Babs and her husband Gus, an old friend of Val's, at Bernardi's and brought them home for more drinks, the evening ending with Babs and Gus in their bedroom, on their bed, simulating love-making and laughing hysterically. That was ten years ago. The Rozzos had found the Ildefonsos entertaining, especially Diego, and took them everywhere, even on a canoe trip, just the four of them, down the Delaware River. Now there she stood feeling strangely sorry for this woman, and, deep down, she knew why: Babs hadn't a life of her own, never had and never would.

"Gus says he's gonna call Diego about that trip they're planning to Vegas. Ugh, I gotta go and get my boobies some relief. I'll call ya. Bye. Bye, Roland. What a great looking kid!"

Her hips rolling deliciously – Dolores knew that was what she was thinking – Babs sauntered on.

The evening air was alive with excitement. Blocking the long low slant of the sun, the Washington Street bus pulled up to the curb and the Ildefonsos got on. The three had eaten early and well on tuna fish salad, cold boiled potatoes, iceberg lettuce, one head cut into three tidy wedges, two similarly sectioned tomatoes, and blueberry pie with ice cream. It was a meal that Diego particularly disliked but ate without signalling his aversion as a gesture of affection for his wife: it reminded her of the summer holidays she'd spent as a child with her aunt and uncle on Lake Pocono. Roland always ate his supper in two identical installments, James obliged, naturally, to eat the second installment after Roland had finished the first. The dessert course was another matter altogether. James was only ever allowed to lick the plate.

On the bus, Roland and his mother sat chatting softly on one seat, while his father sat silently on the seat behind them. Like his son, Diego gazed out the window, the clamoring color on their side of the street now submerged in shadow. The doorways, most laid open and breathing in the cooling breezes, shone along the way like the spaces between a pumpkin's teeth. Diego wanted a cigarette.

"Look, it's the Rozzos," said Roland, turning around and tugging at his father's sleeve. The bus stopped and the Ildefonsos peered down, watching the nine Rozzos board the bus.

Dolores couldn't work out why some Catholics, like Diego for instance, were sensible about the number of children they had and some breeded in a sustained frenzy. It certainly wasn't that some Catholics were sexier than others, and it certainly wasn't that they simply adored children. No, it undoubtedly had to do with a single-minded commitment to the Church, a carnal dimension to life invoked in childhood. Luckily, Dolores had only one friend confined to this dimension. Babs, she accepted, was incapable of comprehending that she embodied a form of dimentiae distressing for any sane woman to behold.

"Where's the van?" she asked Babs as the Rozzos trooped down the aisle.

Babs swung her baby around, nearly striking the infant's head on the rounded metal edge of the seat in front of Dolores and Roland. "Ask the boss," she said, directing her words at her husband.

"Fucking spade ran into me on a bicycle," Gus declared, loud enough for everyone – conveniently all of the passengers on the bus were white – to hear. He pushed his eldest son Teddy, a skinny kid with a bad case of acne, on ahead of him.

Roland looked expectantly up at his mother.

"Mr. Rozzo means a colored man."

"A Negro," said Roland, with satisfaction.

"Yes, sweetheart." Dolores was staring at Alicia Rozzo, aged about fourteen, who had made up her face identically to her mother's. Babs looked like a surly Jane Mansfield, with the added dimension this evening of having dipped her head in a geisha's paint box.

Alicia caught Dolores's curious gaze and stopped to grimace at her, her face only inches away, like an insane person. Dolores glanced past her, blushing, at Gus Rozzo.

"You can fit here," said Diego to Gus, and shifted his cumbersome weight as far back in the seat as he could. Gus gave his son another push, insisting the boy move to the very rear of the bus, and sat next to Diego, his legs splayed out before him, obstructing the aisle. Gus giggled, making twinkle-toes by vibrating his little feet in the air: he had new shoes. They were two-toned snakeskin cowboy boots reduced by some smart-aleck designer to slip-ons.

"Different," commented Diego.

"Originals," Gus corrected him, "from Nudie's – you know, in Vegas."

"Too cool," said Roland. He had his pale head hung over the seat before the two men, balancing himself with a tightened fist on his father's knee.

"Dyn-o-mite," said Gus, and swung around to survey the lay-out of his family. He winked at Babs, who was gesturing in secret sign-language at him: she was asking his permission to breast-feed the baby. Gus opened his mouth wide and bit down slyly on his tongue to communicate the word *later*. "I love to watch her do that," he confided to Diego, who didn't know what he was talking about.

"So how long will your vehicle be out of commission?" asked Diego.

"Only a week. Or so the mother *says*."

"Who's doing it?"

"Freddie Friedrich, who else? He's the only one can match the paint. Fucker charges an arm-and-a-leg. He was telling me that they're talking about starting up a union of auto-body workers."

"I thought they had one?"

"I'm talking *body shop guys*."

"I've never seen them do it so that it looked like it was before," interjected Dolores.

Gus frowned at the back of her head.

"Mrs. Ildefonso, I was trying to listen to what my dad was saying," called Alicia Rozzo, from somewhere behind her father and Diego.

"That'll do, sweetheart," said Babs from across the aisle.

"But what my dad's saying is interesting. And I want to hear," insisted Alicia.

"At any rate," Gus went on, "it looks like some of these morons just won't let well enough alone. I mean, who needs a fucking auto-body shop union to jack up the price of repairs, which only jacks up the price of the goddamned insurance? Right?" He stared at Diego, screwing up his face to look aghast. "Oh right – I forgot!"

"Come on, Gus, you know we don't need a car."

Roland couldn't quite work out what was the matter with his father. Perhaps he only shouted back at Mr. Rozzo when they were at their house. His father looked sad.

"I told you before, National Finance will give you a loan. I know the manager there." Gus had lowered his voice but still spoke loudly enough for both Babs and Dolores to hear. Diego resented Gus's high-handedness. He stared at him, and kept staring at him, until Gus grew so nervous his eyebrows shot up involuntarily. "You want a car, you can have a car. You can do anything you fucking want, boss. That's all I'm saying."

•

"You'll never grow up," Roland said to James, as the two boarded *The Wild Mouse* for their first carnival ride of the evening.

"Maybe we should have gone on *The Snowball* instead," said James, obviously frightened to death of the stupid machine with its stupid safety bar which was being clamped over their thighs.

"It's not even as scary as *The Bullet,*" sneered Roland. "It's just like that tea cup thing. Remember? Only faster. You probably don't remember, you probably were too scared."

"I remember. At Dorney Park."

"Wait just a minute there, Roland," grumbled Babs. No matter what tone she used, Mrs. Rozzo always made Roland's name sound too sweet, as if she were addressing a little girl or, worse, a *sissy boy,* as Tommy-Tom Nolan liked to say. She wrenched the safety bar out of the attendant's hands and shoved Mikie Rozzo, who was just five, in next to Roland. "Watch him," she ordered and left.

As the curvilinear metal box in which they were sitting began to slide slowly outward on its long hydraulic arm and swing around in a series of uneven arcs, gradually elevating itself as it went, Roland stared down at the little boy. Mikie wasn't gripping the safety bar, he was banging his tiny fists up and down against it in a fit of gleeful excitement. He had orange wax, like a clot of gooey caramel, in his ear.

"Push his head the other way, James!"

"Huh?!"

Roland freed one hand from the safety bar, reached up awkwardly between himself and Mikie, and flicked the child's ear sharply with a spring-like finger. Mikie screeched and reared away from him.

"Now stay that way. I mean it, you little asshole!"

Throughout the ride, Mikie glanced fearfully over at Roland, who had shifted his attention once more to James.

"You see, he's only a child. Anyone can control a child."

"Oh, really? And what are you?"

"Nearly an adult."

"How do you figure?"

"I behave like a man."

"Yea, you play with yourself."
"So?"
The two continued to bicker, neither taking any enjoyment in the exhilarating elasticity of the machine's odd movements.

"Go with him," said Babs to Mikie, when the ride was over. She expected Roland to offer the smaller boy his hand. Sensing this, Roland thrust his hands into the pockets of his shorts. He walked on, ignoring Mrs. Rozzo, and Mikie was obliged to follow.

Most of the paint had been blasted from the shifting metal silhouettes by millions of snapping pellets, so that the cut-out shapes looked more like the battered tines of some archaic conveying machine than cute aquatic targets. Dolores watched as her husband and Gus shot at the ducks. They both had cigarettes stuck between their teeth. They pling-planged the last two ducks over on their hinges.

"Dead-eye Dicks, I'd say." Diego put down his rifle.

"You're opposed to be shooting one at a time," said the man running the game.

"That was all me anyways," chortled Gus, then threw an arm around Diego's broad shoulders.

"I always let him win," Diego assured the man.

"You bet," said the man, and reached for a chartreuse panda bear with a day-glo pink tongue, which stuck out like the tip of a dog's erect penis, or so it appeared to Dolores.

"Please don't offer it to me," she said. "You can give it to one of the kids. Or all of them, for that matter."

"Get outa here, I'm giving it to Babs!" Gus yelled over the din. "She loves fucking bears!"

"Smart move," said Diego.

"I'll bet she's feeding the goddamned baby right now," tittered Gus. "Kid gets all the tit. They gotta beer tent this year?"

"They always do," said Dolores, as she moved away slowly, distractedly, through the corridor of gaming stands.

"Last year it was Bernardi did the food," said Diego. "I don't know how he did it but he lost money on the deal."

"His food costs too much," declared Gus flatly and led the way, quickly overtaking Dolores, in the direction of the beer tent.

Eventually Diego caught up to her.

"The guy's got a nose for a drink," he laughed as he took her by the arm.

Dolores said nothing.

"I said he's got a nose for a – a beer," he insisted, coughing, momentarily out of breath.

"I know, I heard you," she whispered, making the effort, as she always did, not to spoil the occasion.

"The sign says *Miller's High Life!*" shouted Gus, fist raised high, thumb extended, not glancing back. The chartreuse panda bear was staring over his shoulder.

Alicia Rozzo was watching the older boys, boys who were old enough to drive cars, wrestling outside the portable lavatories. Rather than appearing formidably glamorous for her age, an illusion she was confident her meticulously rendered mask of cosmetics had accomplished, Alicia, at that distance, appeared forbiddingly grave and anemic. She had intended to change her tampon, but now shifted her emphasis, in anticipatory terms, from the delectable insertion of the cardboard applicator to the idea of intercourse itself.

"Look at the blood-sucking freak," called one of the boys.

Alicia glanced around.

"Suck me," called one of the others.

Alicia, always too quick to judge, could imagine herself sucking the first boy's penis but not the second's, an uninformed and biased attitude, especially as the second boy's father was the manager of the Chemical Bank in Jersey City.

"Go *suck* yourself," she called back, and scrunched up her face fetchingly.

Boldly, she now went where no sane girl her age would go: directly through the boys, in the direction of the Ladies' portable lavatory.

As she passed by, the boy who had called to her first said, "Real warm for April," and plucked at her blouse.

When she hissed back at him, he yanked her blouse from the waist of her black fake-leather skirt and out of her rayon panties. The tail of the blouse, upon which she'd been sitting on the bus, fell over the dark shape of her bottom. Down between her plushy buns had seeped the contents of her engorged tampon, leaving a wealth of menstrual discharge clinging to the fragile stuff of her shirt-tail. The boys stared.

Thinking they were only mugging, Alicia turned on the youngest.

"Aren't you Freddie Friedrich Jr.?"

The boy made a face as if she were talking nonsense.

"Your dad's fixing our van. You know, he *had* better do it right. And he *had* better not have any of those union guys mess up the job."

Friedrich Jr.'s face reddened, and then he began to giggle.

"You better get your rag fixed first," he said, and pointed at her bottom.

Alicia turned indignantly. She felt him gingerly lift the tail of her blouse with a finger or two and peered down awkwardly to see her menses soaking the gauzy sweep of fabric. Stamping her gold ballet slippers violently up and down at the heels, Alicia began to stutter.

To most of the boys, who moved closer, surrounding her like anxious insects, it sounded as if she kept saying *I must copulate...* They sniggered nervously. But only Friedrich Jr., who was now silent, actually heard her moaning refrain:

"It must be chocolate..."

To Alicia's surprise, her mother emerged from the Ladies' lavatory, baby on hip, walked directly over to Freddie Friedrich Jr., and slapped his face.

Tommy-Tom Nolan had found Gus and Diego and was making the most of it, buying them endless cartons of beer. His long black hair shining with oil, he stood slouching against the bales of hay brought in to preserve the playing field beneath their feet. He had dressed his gangling figure all in green, so that he looked like an overgrown leprechaun. As usual, Dolores found him repulsive. Although Tommy-Tom had at first only begrudgingly accepted her husband – a *foreigner* ten years her senior who used big words – he now followed Diego around as if he were a cross between Elvis Presley and Leonardo Da Vinci. For twenty minutes or so, Dolores had been yearning to locate Roland and set about gathering the Rozzo brood together. This Babs would require of her anyway, before the Ildefonsos could themselves leave the fair. Sometimes, when she studied Roland's luminous features, Dolores thought of the Rozzo children, picturing each face and dreading the moment God's turmoil would come to fill their eyes with despair. It was a numbingly sad admission but in many ways she worried more for Babs's children than she did for her own son.

Dolores wandered away from the beer tent. Walls of jostling flesh pressed in on her and she longed to stride from the confinement of the stadium, out into the night. The Christmas lights strung overhead hung so loosely they flapped in the breeze. The breeze rode well over the crowd, its currents free of the metal vats stinking of bubbling grease, free of the tangle of slick garments brushing annoyingly up against her, rich with the stench of perspiration, adrenaline, cheap cologne. The Ferris wheel loomed over the stadium. Its colored lights glinted like fireflies in a jar. More and more people were crowding in, to get on the thing before it shut down for the evening. But the Ferris wheel never shut down, it revolved endlessly in the darkness, even after the fairground had been emptied of everyone but the carnies. The crowd gathered at the base of the wheel had to be there for another reason. As Dolores drew closer, she heard one woman, her voice hushed but tinged with condemnation, say: *I certainly wouldn't entrust my little Bobby to another child.* And then another shout: *What kind of mother would do such a thing?!*

TWO

When Leon Huff, Hoboken's Chief of Police, heard Roland babbling to himself, his head swivelling on his shoulders, he assumed the boy was hysterical and allowed him to go home with his mother without questioning. Huff would visit the Ildefonsos the next day, when Roland was sufficiently recovered. Babs Rozzo refused to look at her son's broken body. She stumbled off in silence, clutching her baby to her breast, to find her husband. Alicia, who was already in a state of extreme agitation, was left to identify her brother. Although Mikie's face had been destroyed on impact, Alicia knew him by his shirt, a miniature Hawaiian-style one identical to his father's. When Babs returned to the base of the Ferris-wheel with Gus and Tommy-Tom and Diego, Mikie's body was already on its way downtown in an ambulance. Diego volunteered to take the Rozzos' remaining children home, but no one responded.

Staring down at the mixture of dust and blood at his feet, his face a quivering mass of black lines, Gus spluttered, "You should of left him, Huff. You should of left him for me to take."

"I'm sorry," said the Chief.

"Where is he?" wept Babs.

"He'll be at the morgue," offered Tommy-Tom. "It was a freaky type of accident. They'll have to *autopsy* him."

Babs's words riffled from her. "What's *that* mean? Gus?!"

A long silence followed. The men stared at one another.

"That's not true," said the Chief. "He'll be in the basement of the hospital. St. Mary's."

"What'll they do with him?" demanded Gus.

"They'll keep him there until you can make other arrangements."

"To bury him," added Tommy-Tom.

"I can give you the telephone numbers," said the Chief.

Pressing herself frontally against her father, her thumbs locking and unlocking convulsively through his belt-loops, Alicia now insisted on displaying her grief.

"He was my little brother," she sobbed.

"Yea, Mikie was real cute," said Tommy-Tom, and reached out his heavy callused hand and allowed his fingers to slide despairingly down the hair at the back of her head.

Shrugging him off, Alicia buried her face in the folds of her father's shirt and whispered, "Our family's in mourning now, isn't it, Daddy?" And Gus put his arms around her. Then, so that everyone could hear, she said, "I was molested, Daddy. I was."

Chief Huff watched as Gus took his daughter's face tightly in his hand, her lips puckering with the pressure, and in what struck the Chief as a particularly cold and lifeless voice said, "Who did what to you?"

"Freddie Friedrich's kid – he tried to stick his finger," she grunted, while twisting her head free of his grip. "That hurts!"

Alicia now pushed her father away, so that he stepped backwards onto his wife's foot.

"Oh God," whined Babs.

"Easy now," said the Chief, and put his arm around her. The Rozzo infant lay sleeping against her bosom.

"Do something about the Friedrich kid, Huff," Gus blurted. He clutched at Alicia's hand, but she was too quick, and darted behind Tommy-Tom.

"Yea, you'se should bring him in for questioning," said Tommy-Tom, grinning.

"What's so funny?" asked the Chief.

"Nothing," said Tommy-Tom. "That tickles," he laughed, blindly reaching around behind him, as Alicia pirouetted ungracefully away.

"I'm in mourning," she called over her shoulder, eyes dramatically slit. "And I'm *not* going home. I'm going down to St. Mary's with you to get Mikie."

"You're not going anywheres. Get her," said Babs, and shoved her husband in the direction of their unruly daughter, so that he shot forward, off balance, lunging onto his knees in the dust, his hands thrust out before him.

When Gus lifted his hands, everyone saw Mikie's blood sticking to his palms. Everyone, that is, except Tommy-Tom, who was staring at the dark stain on the tail of Alicia's slithery blouse.

The inside of Tommy-Tom's Pontiac Bonneville was metallic green. It reminded Alicia of a Christmas tree ornament. Even the carpet at her feet was like Christmas. It was like the wispy blanket of snow you put around the bottom of the tree, only it was pale raspberry – they named colors after different fruits now. Alicia didn't particularly like being squashed in the back next to her stupid smarty-pants sister Theresa. Theresa smelled like soap, even her hair, like Ivory soap, not even nice soap. It was the same soap her father used. A young woman should never use soap like that. Everybody else was in the car too. Only she and her mom and dad and Tommy-Tom were going to the hospital. The rest were going to be dropped off at home to stay with Mr. Ildefonso. Mr. Ildefonso had volunteered to take the bus with her older brother Teddy, because not everybody could fit in Tommy-Tom's car. Mr. Ildefonso was a nice man, nicer than her father even, and much, much nicer than Tommy-Tom, who was basically a jerk. He reminded her of a few of the guys at her high school who were destined for vocational school. They all smoked and had their girlfriends suck them off. Some even fucked their girlfriends. They were trash. But Tommy-Tom was a grown-up. He was married with a little boy. His wife wasn't much though. She always looked sickly. And she hardly left the house. Tommy-Tom obviously didn't have it so good in the love department. And this was truly dumb, because he thought of himself as a big lover. Her mom and dad didn't know it, but Alicia had almost had an affair with Tommy-Tom. This was last Christmas. Alicia wished it were Christmas again now, for all the parties. The summer was OK, but you had to get out of Hoboken if you wanted to have any real fun. Alicia hoped she could sustain her interest in this outing. It was going to be horrible to see her little brother again. She was nearly certain it was going to give her nightmares. Mikie had flown out of the sky and landed on his face, like The Road Runner.

"Mom, do you have any extra Kleenex?" Alicia asked Babs, leaning forward, her hand on her mother's shoulder.

The five Rozzo children in Diego Ildefonso's care lounged before the television watching a black and white movie. He lay on the sofa, exhausted. He had put the children in their beds, but Teddy had insisted on watching the late news. Even with the volume at a barely audible level, the television had eventually drawn all of the children into the darkened living-room with their pillows and onto the carpet. He had decided to allow them to be driven off to slumberland by the film, which featured the tedious hysterics of Katharine Hepburn and an unimaginably bland assortment of spineless young men and women in tweed suits and frothy pinafores. Hating the actress, her manner so blatantly fake in its Englishy blue-bloodedness, Diego savored the sweetness of the plain little faces hovering below him, their pale upturned cheeks illumined ultravioletly, their pillows reassuringly white. These were the faces of the 21st century, their synthesizing young minds already capable of reducing the likes of a Miss Katharine Hepburn to an animated cartoon, a daffy bird of some kind, like an ostrich with two grimacing rows of pearly white teeth.

Diego Ildefonso doubted Miss Hepburn had been among those celebrities so enamored of the politically exotic that they had risked, stupidly when one considered the cushy life-style at stake, being blackballed back in the 1940's – those square-shouldered guys and dolls the press, in their inanity, had called *Hollywood reds.* To call such impotent pseudo-intellectuals, such gutless idealists *communists* was an insult to all true Bolsheviks and especially to a fateful few, like Trotsky himself, a man so dedicated to international revolution that his untimely death, at the end of an ice-pick in Mexico of all places, had been inevitable. Miss Hepburn would have been too aloof, too cowardly really for such unflattering alliances. Money would have been her party of choice, money and the *sophistication* it can buy.

Miss Hepburn, the camera slowly dollying in to catch her in shimmering close-up, gazed over the children's heads directly at Diego. Taking a beat to add to the precariousness of the moment, she laughed at him. Laughed right in his face. Diego shuddered. Miss Hepburn's eyes overflowed with the degradation of everything he had once loved and respected about America. This was the inadvertent, the thoughtless mission of such effete *poseurs,* like the Kennedys, who waltzed through wars, marriages, Harvard, as though their ancestors had never known the taste of a raw potato. They were taking America to the cleaners with their false idealism. Now the light that darted in Miss Hepburn's eyes was captured in diffusion. Like two droplets of rain clinging exquisitely to the petals of a rose, her eyes sparkled in the depths of the dark living-room.

"Look away, children" Diego warned, then realized he'd spoken. But none of them had heard. The Rozzo kids were all asleep. Miss Hepburn and Diego Ildefonso were alone.

Miss Hepburn stopped laughing and smiled through the gloom at Diego. Again she spoke. The music swelled to envelope her lines, but he heard exactly what she said. Returning his stare, her brows steaming, she said, "What would you know about it, you fat simpleton?"

"I wish I had your slick cunt in my hand," whispered Diego, then realized with shame that Tommy-Tom Nolan had put this sort of vile remark in his head.

Gus Rozzo walked into the room and looked at the television. Apparently not registering the presence of his children sleeping on the carpet, he went out again and down the hall to the kitchen. Diego waited. Gus went to the refrigerator, took out a can of beer, and opened it.

The Rozzos' kitchen was a study in garish color. Every implement, every object, every stick of furniture had been chosen for its distinctly festive character. Many of the things surrounding Diego, where he sat in one corner by the wall phone, had faces. Some were molded sculpturally into the surface of the thing, like the cookie jar which was also the head of a clown, some stencilled onto the surface, as with the set of plates on the shelf which were adorned with the sultry smiles of veiled *conchitas,* and some applied via the slippery technique of *decaling* – cartoon mutants in pastel colors littered the refrigerator door. Gus's own face was more rubbery than usual in the fluorescent light, an unreal blue reflected up from the pumpkin-yellow Formica counters. His distracted expression, beer can glinting back and forth against his teeth, stood in vivid contrast to Babs's. Her eyes were glassy, the pupils huge, and the rims, with lashes curled back like fish-hooks, as red as the meat of a flayed tuna. Gus had opened his shirt to the waist and occasionally ran his free hand over the naked swell of his tiny melon-like tummy. Babs, whose blouse was wet where her nipples had ridden over her bra, obviously wanted Diego Ildefonso to leave so she could be alone with her husband.

"Anything else I can do before taking off?" asked Diego.

Babs only yawned.

"Something stronger might help," said Gus.

His wife glared at him. "I don't want Alicia to come in here and find us drinking."

Gus flicked nervously at the cigarette packet hanging loosely in his shirt pocket.

"I just want to go to bed," she muttered, "I just want to go and lie down with my baby," and walked from the kitchen without another word.

"I lost a brother when I was little," said Gus. "I mean, my mom and dad did. Ran out in front of a fucking delivery truck. Like bread or something. Smashed his head. With my kid you couldn't even tell who he is. At least with Vinnie you could tell him."

"I guess that would've been better," said Diego.

"After that, I got all the shit dumped on me." Gus went to the refrigerator for another beer. As he went, he threw his empty can into a cardboard box by Diego's chair. It bounced off the others brimming in the box and rolled under the chair. "Fucking leave it," he groaned.

With some difficulty, Diego picked up the empty can and carefully set it in with the others. When he glanced up, he found Gus staring down at him, eyes stricken with concentration. Gus raised the fresh can of beer to his mouth and drained it in a succession of long painful gulps. He wiped his mouth with the back of one hand while simultaneously crushing the spent can with the other. "You're the boss. What would you do about Freddie Friedrich's fucking kid?"

"I wouldn't do anything."

"He put his hand on her, on *our* Alicia. You don't do that."

"Maybe he likes her. One day he'll probably want to take her out in his car."

"Let him fucking try it." Gus moved once again toward the refrigerator, but stopped. As if he were now caught under the weight of a vast soggy net, he slowly drew up his hands. "I gotta go to bed," he said, palms pressed to his eyes. "I got work in the morning."

"What about Mikie?"

"Oh yea..." Gus gazed blearily up at the clock above the refrigerator. More faces, John Fitzgerald Kennedy and Martin Luther King Jr. *together always.* "Where's she anyways?" he wondered aloud. "It's almost quarter to one, where is she?" Suddenly Gus's face split open with an anguished sigh, and he began to weep. Diego took him out onto the back steps, so his children wouldn't hear.

Leaning over the porch's metal railing and heaving with grief, Gus drooled out the beer he'd just drunk in the kitchen. Standing there off balance holding his friend's head cupped in his hands, his huge stomach lodged painfully on a curlicue of wrought iron, Diego Ildefonso realized that nobody had bothered to offer him a cold beer.

After returning home from the fair, Dolores had lain down next to Roland. He hadn't wanted her to. He'd even turned away, to face the wall.

"But I love you," she'd said.

"You love my money," he'd replied.

This Roland had heard a man say on one of the soap operas Dolores watched around lunch-time.

Now he slept and she lay alone in her own bed.

When Diego came home, he immediately undressed and got into bed. Within moments, he was asleep. His rest, Dolores appreciated, was paramount in the scheme of things.

While Dolores dreamt of Roland, winged and noble in his determination, swooping down from the trembling gondola of the Ferris wheel to catch Mikie as he fell, Diego dreamt of the destruction of Guernica. Before him lay the foothills beyond the town, the road up to Luno segmented like a brilliant strand of mercury by the outcroppings of pine and wild oak in the moonlight. Briefly, he saw the flames rising on all sides of the Church of Santa Maria, the red stone convent with its many windows standing aglow before it. Turning back toward the town, Diego waited for the solitary cannon on the square, its golden wheels flashing under the streetlamps, to pivot round and re-create in a multitude of perspectives the conjunction of streets before the imposing Bank of Vizcaya. But where the cannon had once been there now stood a gleaming microscope, black and tall as the chimney stack of a gargantuan factory. Gus and Tommy-Tom went ambling along below it, tipsy with drink after a long evening at Bernardi's. The shadow of the microscope, as the moon raced across the night sky, kept apace with the two. Suddenly Gus and Tommy-Tom stopped, their eyes riveted to a single ray of light streaking down from somewhere beyond the moon. Needle sharp, the ray of light struck, painlessly, upon the brow of Diego Ildefonso, where it rested with the brilliance of the sun itself.

Diego sat upright in bed, transfixed, and stared into the darkness before him. He rose, very slowly, and began to move anxiously about the room, while Dolores slept. But the room's stagnant air was of no comfort and he began to perspire, his perspiration cold with fear, rivuleting over the vast roll of fat encasing his ribs.

"Diego?"

"What?"

"Come back to bed. It's still dark outside."

"I have eyes," he said, immediately regretting his anger.

Tommy-Tom Nolan would remain home only long enough to look in on Val and Billy and change his clothes for work. He found his wife asleep, the telephone on the bedside table off the hook and an empty bottle of Seagram's Seven Crown tipped over on the carpet. He found his son asleep too, with his thumb in his mouth, babyish behavior Tommy-Tom detested. He would have liked to cut the kid's thumb off with a razor and feed it to their dog Blinky, but instead he contented himself with slapping the boy across the back of the head. Tommy-Tom safety-pinned to his filthy trousers a note printed in ball-point, which read *please get out all of stain*, and put the trousers in a paper shopping bag. He would drop them off at Donelli's Dry Cleaning on his way into Manhattan.

THREE

Returning to the bedroom from showering, and feeling much better, Diego Ildefonso stood before his closet door, the beach towel he wore when shaving wrapped around his middle, and finished combing his hair.

"They're red blotches on your chest," observed Dolores, as she lingered in bed.

"I know. I'm going to try to get over there after work, to see how Gus's doing."

"I was just wondering what I could do for Babs."

"Yea." Presenting the broad expanse of his bare back to her, Diego dipped into an open drawer for his underwear. "Pink and white stripes – where did we get these?"

Dolores decided to get up. "Ruthie will be over there. She clings to Babs like *she's* the one who needs comforting. What kind of a mother is that? I know, I'm boring you." She went to her husband and, as best she could, wrapped her slender arms around him.

"It's Val you don't want to have relying on you too much," said Diego.

"I know, but I feel sorry for her. I can't help it, I just do."

"Maybe she'd be better off *not* having you to rely on. I mean, you talk to her every day, don't you?"

"Lots of people talk on the phone, it makes them feel normal, like they're doing something."

"What, rather than just sitting at home moving their mouths all day?"

"Oh, Diego..." Dolores wrenched on her bathrobe and went into the kitchen to make the orange juice.

Val had managed somehow, despite her hangover, to feed Billy and send him off to the playground – the kid's Easter holiday, it seemed, would never end. At 9:30, she lit her first cigarette and telephoned Dolores.

"I can only chat for a short while," said Dolores.

"Going shopping or something?"

"No, we're having company this morning. Chief Huff's coming over to talk to Roland. I might as well tell you."

"What? Roland do something?"

"No, it was an accident."

"I don't get it."

"We were at the fair yesterday evening with the Rozzos and there was an accident. Little Mikie fell off the Ferris-wheel."

"What, and hurt himself?"

"He fell and hit his head."

"Was it bad?"

"Yes, it was bad." Dolores wondered if perhaps Babs would want to tell her.

"Is he in the hospital or something?"

"No, he died instantly."

"Holy Mother of God." Val crossed herself. "So what's Roland got to do with it?"

"He was with Mikie."

"What, on the ride with him?"

"Yes. He saw it happen. That's why the Chief wants to talk to him."

"I'll bet."

Dolores chose to ignore Val's sarcasm. "Gus stayed home from work."

"Yea, but what's anybody doing? You know, about the kids and all."

"Diego was over there last night. He said they were fine. I guess it takes a while for these things to sink in."

"Kids are like that. It just goes right by them. At least with our Billy. I remember when Tommy-Tom's dad died, well..."

Val began moving distractedly around her kitchen, the telephone's long cord slapping over the backs of the chairs; Dolores could picture the room vividly, the sunlight pouring in in two dusty diagonal shafts through the large spattered panes on the alleyway.

"...and I told Billy at the viewing he was only sleeping and he believed me. He still thinks people go to sleep when they die."

"Maybe that's for the best. I'm sorry, Val, I've really got to go."

"Suit yourself. I gotta call Babs anyway. Don't you think?"
"That would be nice."

Val immediately telephoned Babs Rozzo. It rang for a long time, but eventually Babs answered.

"Who's that?" said Babs.

"I'm real sorry," said Val.

"Thanks." Babs took a moment to blow her nose in the balled-up Kleenex tissue she'd been carrying around with her.

"Jesus loves us all," Val assured her.

"Especially the little children."

"He loveth and he taketh away."

"He's in heaven. I mean, with Mikie." Again Babs snuffled. "Gus and Teddy went over to Klusters to pick out a coffin."

"They're expensive."

"I know."

"Is there anything for me to do, with the kids and all?"

"You can try and see what's with Alicia. In spite of everything, she didn't come home last night. And she didn't bother to call. She's not over at Patty's house either. Gus is ready to kill her."

"Maybe she was upset."

"You still *call*. Tommy-Tom was supposed to be taking her home."

"When?"

"After we all went to St. Mary's Hospital to see Mikie."

"I thought he was dead."

"To *identify* him!"

"Jeez, Babs, I'm sorry." Val could feel her friend getting angrier and angrier. "I said I was sorry."

"Well, you knew that. Didn't you?"

"But I didn't know my Tommy-Tom was with you guys. He said he was going over there, to the stadium, but he didn't say for sure. So, I guess he went."

"That's what I'm saying."

"I can always call him and ask him about Alicia."

"You should, cause we don't have that number."

"OK. Can it wait until his lunch-time?"

"It's up to you."

"Today he takes out the trash cans, I think, so I can probably call him."

"Yea, cause I have to tell Gus something when he gets back."

"When's that?"

"I don't know. Soon." Babs knew Tommy-Tom wouldn't have anything to say. She knew he had dropped Alicia off somewhere secret. He was a sucker for her. Alicia wouldn't have had to ask twice. "I need her here with me," Babs muttered.

"Sure you do, honey."

They said good-bye and Val telephoned Tommy-Tom at the Stamford Arms, but the telephone in his office only rang and rang.

Freddie Friedrich Sr. was bent over the right fender of a 1967 Chevrolet Corvair Spyder, spray gun in hand and mask on face, when Gus and Teddy Rozzo transversed the several bays of his garage to confront him. But Freddie was not about to be distracted too easily. It took Gus laying his hand on the small of Freddie's back to get him to stop working. Through the wire-mesh of his breather, Freddie shouted:

"The office is over there! Can't you see I'm busy?!"

Luckily, this was incomprehensible. Gus persisted and eventually Freddie Friedrich Sr. stood tall and straight before him. The man's red beard, imprinted with the rubber ring of the mask, stood out bushily from his pink cheeks, their roundness dappled with metallic avocado green paint. Freddie held his mouth set wide in a contented smile.

"It's for Freddie Jr.," he said. "Fuel-injected. For his sixteenth."

"We want our van," said Gus.

"I've got the primer on, but I won't be able to get around to the first coat until Thursday."

"It's been too long already."

"Hey Gus, you only brought it in on the weekend."

"Who the hell's the customer here anyways?"

Teddy moved nervously away from his father and focused his attention on a calendar over the workbench. A well-muscled girl in a gold bikini was kneeling on white backdrop paper holding a wrench up before her as if it were a prize-winning tuber.

"Yea, you need it right away – like yesterday," said Freddie, and turned to peer at the fresh paint. "Mind if I finish this up?"

"*Do I mind?* My kid just got killed and I need my fucking van!" Freddie's schlepper Ned noisily wheeled another, even more ostentatious vehicle into the echoey garage. "You know about my kid?!"

"Yea," Freddie shouted back. "I read about it in the paper this morning. I'm real sorry, Gus."

"Fuck you!"

"What?" shouted Freddie, pretending not to have heard him. He rubbed his index finger over his ear to communicate his inability to carry on the conversation.

"I'm taking the van!"

"Go ahead," said Freddie, and waved his arm dismissively over his head.

Suddenly it was quiet again.

Teddy stood by the workbench, mouth open, a swollen pimple about ready to burst on his ashen upper lip. "Dad?" he called.

Gus, distracted, shifted his attention to his eldest son.

"I wouldn't say too much about Freddie Jr.," cautioned the boy, "not if you want to press charges."

Freddie looked pained. "What's this about?"

"You'll find out," said Teddy.

"Listen Gus, why don't we discuss it now?"

"Your kid was at the fair last night," barked Gus.

"I wasn't aware of that."

"Well, he *was*."

Gus rubbed his palms over his forehead, then ran his fingers with some difficulty through his thick hair, which he'd recently dyed an unnaturally dark shade of brown. Glancing down at his hands, to see if the color, as advertised, was anything like permanent, Gus realized Friedrich felt sorry for him. But it didn't matter. It couldn't. Friedrich's son had touched his daughter on her bottom, in public, and other boys had watched with glee, their filthy minds fastened on her perfect childlike secret parts.

"And what's this about pressing charges?" asked Freddie. "I can't see what Freddie Jr. has got to do with your boy's falling off the Ferris wheel."

"It's not about falling off no Ferris wheel," volunteered Teddy.

"Be quiet," Gus groaned.

Teddy shrugged and focused his attention once again on the calendar. When he realized the two men were watching him, he shuffled on along the workbench, finally gazing curiously at a color chart on the wall.

"Just tell your kid to leave Alicia alone," warned Gus. "Tell him to keep his hands to himself. Tell him to behave himself around Alicia, who's better than him. Because she wouldn't want anything to do with him. You know what I'm saying?"

"I know what you're saying, but I'm not buying it. If Freddie Jr. did anything, and I don't believe it, I apologize. How's that?"

"Fucking kid stuck his hand. I'm telling you, your fucking kid upset her. She told me. She told me to my face, and she's not like that!"

Freddie Friedrich Sr. said nothing. He went into his office and took the keys to the Rozzos' van down from the rack, walked around behind the garage to the parking lot, got in the vehicle and drove it out onto the street. There he left it running and stood well out of the way as Gus and his boy got in. He still said nothing as Gus sat in the van and stared out at him. When they had roared off and were well out of sight, Freddie went back into the garage, in despair, knowing he would now have to re-sand and re-paint the entire front end of the car.

Roland watched as James dropped the marbles, one by one, into the toilet. Each one made a dull snap against the bowl before rolling down into the hollow at the bottom. There the marbles lay glinting, waiting to be evacuated when Roland was ready.

"Don't put so many solids in," Roland whispered.

"What about these two big ones?" James whispered back.

"They're too big."

"They'll go down."

"They will not. They're as big as Mr. Nolan's eyeballs."

"Yea, but they're cat's eyes." James dropped one of the marbles into the toilet.

"Sweetheart? What're you doing? Chief Huff and I are waiting," urged Dolores, through the door.

Roland glanced over his shoulder at the little hook resting in its golden screw-eye. "I'm wiping."

"I don't smell anything," whispered James, grinning.

"My shit doesn't smell."

"We won't be a minute," James and Roland called in unison, and laughed.

Leon Huff was sitting on the living-room sofa with his hat in his lap. An empty coffee mug sat beside him on the sports section of that morning's Hoboken Reporter. He was staring at the badge on his hat, wondering why some badges had black paint rubbed into the intaglio and some didn't. He wished his were all shiny, without the black. Apropos of nothing, he said, "Books are getting fatter and fatter. My wife's reading a book right now that's nearly as fat as the Yellow Pages."

"Oh yea, I've seen them," Dolores responded. "I think a lot of research goes into some of them."

"Like *Toboggan.* I read part of that one. The author had to know a lot about Switzerland."

Roland exited the bathroom, his pants pockets bulging and wet. He smiled at Chief Huff and walked directly over to him, his hand outstretched.

"It's good to see you again," he said.

"Likewise," said the Chief.

"Shall I sit down?" Roland asked his mother.

Dolores nodded. Roland carefully removed the mug and newspaper from the sofa, handing both to Dolores, which encouraged her to remove them to the kitchen. When she had left the room, Roland confided to the Chief, "She's still terribly upset. Don't let that calm exterior fool you."

"You're quite the clever little fellow, aren't you?" said the Chief.

"I'm not so *little,*" answered Roland, in imitation of any other stupid eight-year-old. "Not so little really."

"But you are clever," Chief Huff persisted, his lips smiling, but not his eyes.

"We won't really know until I get my final grades," the lad replied, sensibly.

"Oh? When might that be?"

"In June. Then there's summer school, if we decide I should go. It's just games and crafts. Nothing very challenging."

After first straightening the lace doily that was draped over the crown of the overstuffed chair in which she'd been sitting, Dolores once again took her place across from them.

When she appeared quite comfortably settled, Roland said, "Mom, I'm not sure you want to be present for this discussion."

"I think it's better if I stay."

Roland gazed, and continued to gaze, expectantly but calmly at the Chief.

"In fact, Mrs. Ildefonso, the law requires that you be here," said the Chief.

"You see, it'll be alright," said Roland. He then gazed so serenely at his mother that her heart began, involuntarily, to melt with pride.

"How did it happen, Roland?" asked the Chief.

"Suicide," said Roland.

"'Suicide?'"

"Yes. Mikie Rozzo jumped. I heard him praying, then he jumped."

Chief Huff stared at his badge, frowning. He glanced over at Dolores, whose eyes had glazed over.

"He must have been very depressed," Roland concluded.

"I know this sounds unfair, sweetheart," said Dolores, "but wasn't there any way you could've stopped him?"

Roland shook his head slowly from side to side. After that, he looked up at the ceiling. Then he sighed, "My concerns were elsewhere at that point in time."

"How so?" asked Chief Huff.

Roland gazed plaintively at his mother, almost as if he hadn't heard the Chief's question. "I was looking way down at a bunch of guys picking on Mikie's poor sister outside the toilets."

Diego Ildefonso's palms were damp with perspiration, and the gray troughs below his eyes had sunk deeper.

Bernardi poured more grappa. "Ramona, dig out another bottle," he called, "of the Julia Riserva Stravecchia..."

In his mind's eye, Diego hovered like a hummingbird just out of reach of Roland and Mikie, sitting side-by-side on the Ferris wheel. Their gondola rocked slowly backwards and forwards, the Ferris wheel arrested with them at its highest point. The boys hadn't as yet spied him fluttering transparently against the darkening sky. As the Ferris wheel began reversing with a violent jerk to take Roland and Mikie slowly, safely back to earth, Mikie saw Mr. Ildefonso suspended in the air like a mesmerizing cartoon character. Squealing with delight, Mikie leapt up, his tiny fingers clutching at nothing, and lunged from the gondola.

"Irish brogues," said Bernardi. It resounded nonsensically.

"Speaking of shoes," Diego managed, "I think I'd better get back to the shop."

"No more of my grappa for you then?" The restaurateur smiled.

"Don't think so," said Diego, and rose with some difficulty.

Bernardi was silent. His eyes grew moist and he stood to face his friend, then put his hand on Diego's shoulder.

"We haven't seen Dolores for these last few months," he said, his second language now mildly encumbered by the grappa.

"She's fine," said Diego, and sat himself down once more. He could feel the perspiration soaking through his shorts. Next his trousers would be wet.

"A nice woman," said Bernardi. The light drifting in from the front window settled on his slicked back hair. It shimmered iridescently. He too sat down.

"She has great democracy of spirit," said Diego.

Bernardi gazed at him curiously.

"She doesn't believe the Russians are any more threatening than we are." Diego patted his moist cheeks with his napkin. "I guess I should find that refreshing."

"I know *you* don't like communists," offered Bernardi.

"We are capitalists," stated Diego flatly.

"Through and through," Bernardi assured him.

"And you probably think things are just wonderful here," said Diego. When Bernardi didn't respond, he went on. "We're no better than pigs fed on garbage in this country, nothing but lies on the television. No one I know can even read a newspaper anymore. Oh sure, maybe the sports, but they can't be bothered with anything about the rest of the world, not even the soccer! By feeding us this garbage, this *propaganda* twenty-four hours a day, they're making us just like the *communists*. Like the workers who die without ever having read Charles Dickens, for Christ's sake."

Bernardi was silent.

"We're being manipulated, aren't we?"

Silent still, Bernardi partook of more grappa. Diego only watched, and wondered with increasing dread if Dr. Herbert might see him that evening after work.

Dolores had found Roland's encounter with Chief Huff unsettling and was eager to discuss it with her husband. She had laid Roland down to rest, like the grateful baby he'd once been, after they'd shared lunch together. He'd eaten both his hot dogs. He'd eaten them, he'd said, *with relish*. This witticism, flying in the face of such numbing events, had seemed an act of intellectual defiance on her son's part and she had committed its piquancy to the kitchen pad, just below her shopping list. Now she lay on her own bed, the drapes drawn against the harsh light slanting in from the west, anticipating the intimacy she and Diego would share on Thursday afternoon. She ruminated on what to wear, figuring up her household costs that week, hopeful there might be enough money left to buy a new slip, one she'd admired in the window of Lilette's Lingerie. She pictured the mannequin on which the beautiful pink slip was left to hang each day. She detested the mannequin. It wore such a contemptuous expression on its bland face. For Dolores, this contrived hauteur was synonymous with the emptiness in the world that threatened her happiness, and the happiness of her family. In the belly of the mannequin, death lay waiting.

Dolores gazed around the dreary room. Keeping absolutely still, loving herself and her life, she wouldn't die. But then she remembered pain. There had been excruciating pain when

Roland was born. Pain was death's companion. One day, the two would stand waiting outside on the front steps with more patience than the world, her world, had the patience to endure. Pain would return to take back each treasured notion of consolation and comfort, each sweet breath of remembrance. The dreary room in which she now lay would echo with the ashamed cries of the millions upon millions who had passed on in agony before her. Having herself suffered the ultimate despair, she would be welcomed into their fold. Her soul would be allowed to slip away, gratefully, into nothingness.

FOUR

The Stamford Arms wasn't a seriously bad place to live, but it was noisy and it was filthy. If you wanted *clean,* you had to clean it yourself. If you wanted quiet, you had to either shoot the motherfuckers or go out. Bootsy Holloway went out, although he would have preferred to shoot the scum that hung in the hallways downstairs fucking themselves up on smack and fizzy wine.

Since arriving in New York from the benighted coastal town of Belhaven, North Carolina in February, Bootsy had made only one friend. This was the janitor or *super,* as he liked to call himself, Percival Thomas Nolan, known as Tommy-Tom. This evening Tommy-Tom had invited Bootsy to go out to Hoboken for dinner. Tommy-Tom had also said they might take in the fair. He had said the fair sucked but that The Jewel, a bar nearby, had *topless* and the crowd was mixed. Anyone was allowed in as long as they didn't start any fights or, worse, piss on the floor. Bootsy was really looking forward to meeting Tommy-Tom's family too.

As Tommy-Tom, one hand on the wheel and one hand on the stick, piloted his Pontiac Bonneville expertly through the jammed-up traffic and down into the Lincoln Tunnel, Bootsy admired his new friend's lacquered do.

"Your hair always looks so nice," said Bootsy.

"I keep it that way." Tommy-Tom shook his head from side to side to demonstrate the holding power of the styling gel he used.

"My Uncle Tookus, he's got hair like that," said Bootsy, patting his own, which was electric-cut, high on the crown. "But they say he's mostly white too, like – what's that mother's name?"

"Who?"

"That big-mouth nigger up in Harlem."

"How the fuck should I know?"

"Always says 'Keep the faith, baby.'"

"Oh, that mother."

"That's the man. Pretty."

"Yea. I bet he's got some nice snatch sittin on his face."

"I could eat some right now."

Tommy-Tom, the tiles in the tunnel reflected in his highway patrolman sunglasses, stared curiously at Bootsy. To Bootsy, it looked like Tommy-Tom had a Chiclet factory inside his head.

"What's your wife's name again?" asked Bootsy.

"Val. Valerie."

"Oh yea, I remember now. It ain't none of my business, but she pretty?"

"For a white woman?"

"I ain't sayin that..." Bootsy laughed nervously.

"She's pretty as any of them. She used to have those nipples I like, until she had the kid."

"Them young black ones got the little puffy ones too."

"No shit?" Now Tommy-Tom laughed.

"No shit."

"I forgot to tell Val you're coming."

"She gonna blow?"

"I'll stop and get her a bottle."

"That's cool."

"I better call her. What the fuck – if she's in her bathrobe or something, she'll get pissed off."

"She like to look nice when y'all's got company."

"She likes to look nice when there's dick around." Tommy-Tom had to laugh at that too.

"What, even black dick?"

Tommy-Tom laughed even harder, and said, "Especially black dick." Then, "Only kidding." And rubbed his free hand over Bootsy's arm. "Nice suit."

Bootsy brightened. "I got it way downtown, near Wall Street. The label says *Cardin.*"

"Yea, I've heard of that. Maybe I'll wear a suit tonight. Fuck it, let's just stop at The Jewel. I can call her from there."

"That's cool."

Bootsy liked The Jewel. He liked it so much that it made Tommy-Tom proud. Tommy-Tom called Val and told her they'd be home after a couple drinks. Then they'd go to the fair and have something to eat. He even agreed to have little Billy come along: it would be good for him to have firsthand experience of a grown black man. Val said, *Sure, that sounds nice, Tommy-Tom.* But she knew she and Billy would be alone together in front of the television for the rest of the evening. Later, after calling to ask if it was OK, she would send Billy down to Mr. Mainwaring's for another bottle of Seagram's.

Dr. Herbert's office was very bright and Diego Ildefonso was naked. He hadn't the strength, for the moment, to put his clothes back on. Dr. Herbert had gestured for him to, although he may have only been gesturing for him to sit down.

"You have a small tumescent growth just to the south of your bladder," explained Dr. Herbert. "That's what I kept poking at. I wouldn't worry though, these things often dissipate themselves. There's really no need at this stage for a biopsy."

Christian Herbert, as far as Diego was concerned, wasn't very like a doctor. He was more like a retired airline pilot, the sort of fellow who spends his declining years, without perceptibly declining, on the sunny fairways of an expensive country club somewhere in temperate America.

"Your weight, dear boy, has it increased?" asked Dr. Herbert.

"My complaint has nothing to do, I think, with..." But Diego hadn't the inclination to communicate his own awareness of his ridiculous size.

"Mustn't eat before one sleeps," joked Dr. Herbert.

Diego's indignation miraculously provided him with the energy to drag on his clothes. Balancing on one foot and then the other, he felt sufficiently distracted to pursue with Dr. Herbert the specific attributes of his horror. Dr. Herbert communicated no impatience whatsoever from his position by the room's only window. This was due to the fact that he wasn't actually listening to Diego but watching a young boy standing at the far end of the alleyway outside his office throwing a turtle high into the air, again and again, which fell, again and again, to strike the pavement. Eventually, Dr. Herbert turned from the window.

"Don't look so grave," he said, smiling by merely showing his teeth. "How about if we do both brain and body scans? St. Mary's has the gear..."

"I only have Saturday afternoons and Sundays off."

"We can do it in the evening. I'll have Linda call tomorrow morning and see how late they keep a technician on. Come to think of it, they have a special for poor folks on Wednesday evenings."

"Tomorrow? That would be OK, I guess. Do you mind calling me at the shop, rather than at home?"

Dr. Herbert glanced over the top of his desk, then sighed. "I'll make a mental note, how's that?"

"Do I owe you anything for today?" Diego realized this was a stupid question.

"Linda's left. I'll have her write it up in the morning." Dr. Herbert turned and gazed curiously at Diego. "Are you busy? I mean, right now?"

Diego didn't know what to say.

"Want to go for a drink? If you haven't heard already, Jane and I are splitting up. We'd always intended to, when the kids were old enough. You know, when they'd gone off to college. Well, Lance is at Swarthmore now and Judy's at Bryn Mawr..."

Diego figured he'd better say yes. It might help keep the bill down. "Mind if I give my wife a call? The telephone's through there, isn't it?"

When Dolores finally answered, he asked her how it had gone between Roland and Chief Huff. She said OK but wanted to discuss Roland's frame of mind with him later at length. He said, "Barbiche wants me to stick around and have a look at the leftover stuff from Milan."

"It won't sell," was her response.

Diego knew he'd taken the right approach. "I know," he said, "but it looks smart in the window."

When Dr. Herbert suggested he and Diego take a little exercise by walking over to the Lambeth Hotel on Fourth Street, Diego asked if they couldn't take Dr. Herbert's car. He said his reluctance to walk had to do with a tendency to fatigue. Once they were in the car, he became much livelier and expressed an interest in a new drinking establishment in Weehawken, which was one place, as far as he knew, he and Dolores hadn't any friends or acquaintances. Instantly, he and Christian Herbert were headed in the direction of that useless town with its ghostly slope of dilapidated *villas* and dizzying view of the filthy mire that floats just beyond the opening to the Lincoln Tunnel.

Teddy Rozzo had taken the twins Margaret and Margery, and the bookish Theresa, to a special evening mass for their dead brother Mikie. Babs and Gus had stayed home with the baby, even though Theresa had thought this shameful and had expressed this opinion to her father. Gus had given Theresa five dollars not to go whining to her mother about it. Theresa had said she would make an offering of the five dollars to the church; it was a bribe, and therefore dirty money, which could, conceivably, be made clean by Jesus Christ. Gus had assured Theresa that this would be a commendable gesture. Theresa went away contented. Teddy had winked at his father over the girls' heads as he'd led them down the hallway and then out the front door.

"I think we'd better call Chief Huff," was the first thing Babs said when Gus entered their darkened bedroom. The baby lay sleeping against her hip.

Gus sat on the end of the bed facing their personal TV. As was usual now, due to the presence of the infant, there was picture but no sound. Groaning noisily with the effort, he pulled off his shoes without first untying them.

"I thought you said Val was going to talk to Tommy-Tom?"

"She couldn't get him."

Gus got up and went to the closet, pulling off his shirt and tossing it onto the dresser as he did. At the closet door he turned and dropped his trousers, then reached into his underpants and shifted his testicles from back to front.

"Do I *have* to wear pajamas?"

"When Dominic's in bed with us."

"Oh, for Christ's sake..." Gus kicked his trousers and his underpants into the closet and shut the door.

"Honey, what about air-conditioning?"

"What about it?"

"Is it hot enough out?"

"It's not hot enough in here."

Babs rolled onto her side and moved the baby up to her breast. She did this because she knew it would annoy Gus, who would probably want to make love as soon as he got into bed.

"Oh man, don't start with Dominic. Alright?!"

"Why're you being so mean, Gus? Our little Mikie's dead and you're acting like I don't even have any feelings." Babs began to cry. "I have feelings. I have lots of feelings, otherwise I wouldn't of had all our beautiful children. Mikie was beautiful. All our children are beautiful. Look at little Dommie, honey. He's real beautiful too." The tears streamed over Babs's cheeks, and she clutched the baby tighter.

Gus came around the bed and sat by her, his elbow pressing down into the pillow on which he would eventually lay his head. He reached out and patted her hair where she had it bunched up and pinned at the back. It felt nice.

"You have pretty hair," he whispered.

"So what?"

"It's because I love you. I want you to be happy."

"How can I be happy when you're so mean?"

"I'm not trying to be mean."

"Well then, be nice." Babs wiped her eyes.

"We scared the fucking shit out of Freddie Friedrich today." Gus hoped this would brighten her up, but instead Babs turned serious, without acting sad.

"Freddie Jr.'s already been punished."

"By who?"

"By me."

"Slapping the kid don't mean squat."

"Teddy thinks we should talk to Chief Huff about it again."

"Yea, I know, Teddy's the big expert."

"I'll bet Tommy-Tom won't know where she is. He won't know anything."

"Wait a second. Didn't you call to ask her friends?"

"I called some after school. They don't know."

"Who'd you call?"

"You know, her friends."

"Like who, Rosalie?"

"And some others. Honey, look at Dommie, he's sucking while he's asleep."

"He's dreaming. Dogs and cats do the same thing."

Now, gazing down at the baby, Babs smiled. "Who knows but maybe Freddie Jr. did something with our Alicia. That could happen."

"OK, so I call Huff."

"Just as long as he don't have to come over." Again she was frowning.

"What?"

"I don't want him staring at me."

"What're you talking *staring?*"

"At the fair, he put his arm around me."

"You sound like fucking Alicia. It must be something in the women in this family, in *your* family."

"Jesus would hate you for saying that. I know when men are looking at me wrong."

Gus eased back against the velveteen plush of the padded headboard. "I just thought of something. Kidnapping's a federal offense. Remember? In that TV movie about Lindbergh – if you go over the state line it's federal."

"What state line?"

"Like if you go into New York or Pennsylvania, even by mistake, you can get the electric chair."

"I didn't know they still had one." Babs tried to remember the film Gus was referring to but could only come up with an image of two guys, one white and one black, wearing cute hats and standing out in a field at night.

"I gotta sleep," said Gus. "There's Mikie's funeral tomorrow."

Staring at him, Babs lowered the bodice of her nightgown, so he could watch her suckle little Dominic. Eventually they both grew quiet.

Shirlee Simonaire, the topless dancer, had had polio as a child and her legs were too short. She was The Jewel's greatest attraction, aside from its dollar cocktails at *Happy Hour*. It was well past *Happy Hour* when Bootsy scored the gram of coke from another brother out in the parking-lot. He and Tommy-Tom were about to go back outside to snort some when Chief Leon Huff entered the bar. He was looking for Tommy-Tom.

"Sorry," said Huff, "but your pal Gus sent me down here to speak with you. His call was relayed to me and I was in the neighborhood."

"When aren't you?" replied Tommy-Tom, grinning up at him drunkenly. "Oh, this is my bud Bootsy Holloway, from down south."

Huff nodded at Bootsy. "You remind me a little of Hound Dog Taylor, the Chicago bluesman."

"Thank you, sir," said Bootsy.

"I believe he just died," said Huff.

"He used to be dead in my mind too," said Bootsy.

"I got to talk to your man here," said Huff.

"My man," said Bootsy, and hugged Tommy-Tom, being careful not to touch his hair. Then, gazing up at Shirlee on the little stage covered in purple shag, Bootsy commented, "That damn thang is low to the ground."

"Give it a good sniff," said Tommy-Tom and rose from his seat to take a pee.

Huff followed Tommy-Tom into the Men's Room. By the time they stood side-by-side under the lavatory's single circular fluorescent tube, Tommy-Tom was in tears.

"I feel so bad," whimpered Tommy-Tom, taking out his penis.

"So do I," said Huff, taking out his.

"That kid was my godchild."

"Good place to drown your sorrow."

"I'm sad for Mikie. He had a good little arm. Little fucker could throw. I don't know where he got it – Gus throws like a girl."

"Maybe that's why they asked you to be Mikie's godfather."

"Yea. Probably."

"I'm actually here to inquire about Alicia." Huff laid his free hand on Tommy-Tom's shoulder, to keep him from leaving the facility.

Tommy-Tom stared down at the Chief's fingers. His nails were manicured and glistening with clear polish, and he wore a high school graduation ring, a police academy ring, and a large signet ring with the letters *LHR* engraved in black onyx.

"My girl," said Tommy-Tom. He gazed wistfully into the Chief's eyes. "She gave me a real nice present last Christmas."

"What was that?"

"An ashtray." Tommy-Tom, his tears suddenly a distant memory, was now smiling with irrepressible joy.

"An ashtray?"

"A joke one. Like with a girl with her thing available to put your cigarette in."

The Chief blushed. He shook his penis, replaced himself, and carefully pulled up his fly. "This kid is, what, fourteen years old?"

"Fucking kids are premature these days," said Tommy-Tom. He too withdrew from the urinal. "She wanted to go into the city. So I took her. I stopped at the Stamford, where I work – I don't know, man – she just wasn't in the fucking car when I got back."

As they made their way back to the bar, the Chief questioned Tommy-Tom further, but only just. "Anyone see you?"

"What, at the Stamford?"

The Chief nodded.

"How should I know?"

Huff didn't know what else to ask the scumbag so he excused himself, after attempting to note any identifying marks on the black man.

"Fucking police," said Tommy-Tom to Bootsy, "in Belfast they'd blow that fucking busybody pig into the sea."

"I don't know nothin like that, man."

"You sound like me," sneered Tommy-Tom, "and I make myself fucking puke taking it up the ass from the likes of Huff."

"What's *huff?*"

"That mother that was just harassing me. You want to do some of that stuff now? We can go into the john. Nobody'll bother us in there."

"I thought *he* was just botherin you in there?"

"Man, I took *him* in there. You wanna do some or not?"

"Hey man, what's mine is yours."

When they were in the Men's Room, noses turning to ice, Tommy-Tom had another bright idea. "Shirlee's one of my girls."

"One of y'all's *whats?*"

"She shows me a good time. She'd like you."

"Hey, hey," said Bootsy, feeling positive.

"She lives off Palisades Avenue over in Union City, only about ten minutes from here. She'll do us over there."

"We gotta pay her?"

"Give her some of your toot. She'll suck the fucking thing all night long."

"I ain't got all night long. Unless y'all gives me a ride back and I don't have to worry about gettin no taxi."

"No problem, my man," said Tommy-Tom.

Back at the bar, having ordered another Schlitz for himself and a White Russian for Bootsy, Tommy-Tom pointed his finger, the one he'd been exploring his numb nose with, at Shirlee. She smiled back from her perch by the stage, then returned to slowly sipping her rum and Coke.

"He's gonna want me to service his friend too," she said to Eliot, her favorite barman, a moment or two later.

"Spades think they're God's gift to women," remarked Eliot. Then, watching Tommy-Tom and Bootsy more carefully, added, "I'd rather fuck the black stud than the other guy."

"You know Tommy-Tom, El. He's always in here," said Shirlee. But to herself, she said, *I hope he doesn't want to use that fucking car antenna on me again.*

Diego Ildefonso approached his house. The joy he knew as he gazed up at his darkened windows was nearly boundless. His wife and child lay sleeping behind those grimy panes. The grime of winter, it would vanish with the wipe of a soft cloth and a little ammonia and water, the minutiae of Dolores's life. All around him, the city begged for deliverance. As the filthy mists drew about Diego Ildefonso, like the destitute hags who had confronted so many other great men, he heard the sirens of Hoboken singing. He heard the electrifying wail of the fire, and the somber thunder of the lowering doom.

Diego mounted the steps and stood before his front door. Where had he been until such an hour, not just looking at shoes? No, he was having a drink with Lou Nasserman, the sales rep from De Palma Roma. Mystifyingly, he again heard Dr. Herbert calling from his expensive car, as he had only moments before: *Don't kid yourself, Diego, we're all animals!* Dr. Herbert had been laughing. One day, like everyone else, Christian Herbert, the mere man, would watch helplessly as his own muscle turned to mush. Diego took little satisfaction in this. There was no consolation in knowing that the arrogant bastard would perish too.

Dolores recognized Diego's weight on the bed. It was gentle. He was with her, and she was grateful.

"Roland's alright," she said.

It was nearly midnight by the time Tommy-Tom and Bootsy made it over to Shirlee's apartment in Union City. Tommy-Tom had done too much of Bootsy's coke at The Jewel and had turned very pale on the drive over. His face was rivuleting with cold sweat and he had an aching under his jaw which felt like it began somewhere in his left arm. Bootsy, on the other hand, was riding high on just the right combination of cocaine and vodka.

Shirlee had left The Jewel at eleven so she would have time to freshen up before the boys arrived. When she had company she initially pleased herself by playing the music she liked, knowing her guests would have their own ideas once things got started. She was most fond of Motown, and especially The Supremes. She figured Bootsy would appreciate the fact that a youngish white woman had such a fondness for the material that constituted the biggest success black entertainers had had in her lifetime; he did not look like the type who liked jazz. Shirlee had decided to wear a slinky sarong for the occasion. The sarong was maneuverable and looked good, even though it had been relatively inexpensive, a worthwhile consideration in case Tommy-Tom got into the rough stuff and the garment was damaged or destroyed. On top, she wore a form-fitting lycra halter that made it appear that her breasts were much larger and firmer than they were. She never let anyone near her breasts.

Well, there had been one boy, but he'd been young enough not to want to manipulate her roughly; he'd wanted only to fondle, caress, and, most touching of all, suckle her. Shirlee was tidying the kitchen when the buzzer sounded, signalling guests in the horrible over-lit cubicle her landlord referred to as *the lobby*.

"Hi Tommy-Tom," said Shirlee, opening the door without taking the usual precautions.

"He don't look so good," said Bootsy.

"Maybe I better lie down," said Tommy-Tom, "where it's quiet."

Shirlee led him into her sewing-room, rather than the bedroom. Laid in rows across what she referred to as the "baby bed" was her collection of Barbie Dolls.

"What the fuck?" said Tommy-Tom.

For an anguishing moment, Shirlee thought he was going to throw himself onto the bed, which would have meant hours and hours of checking for snapped joints and torn seams. Thankfully, he went to the mirror that hung over the dresser instead.

"I got blood in my nose hairs."

As Shirlee quickly removed the Barbie Dolls, she wondered if Tommy-Tom was going to be good for anything: she hated the idea of having to suck his limp dick for hours, while he got drunker and drunker or, worse, more and more embarrassed. It didn't matter what anyone paid her, it just wasn't any fun. Tommy-Tom lay down and Shirlee made a big fuss of seeing that he was comfortable before returning to the living-room and Bootsy.

"My man ain't used to that shit," said Bootsy. He was sitting stiffly on the sofa with one leg curled under him and the other stretched out, his foot resting on a pile of Vogue magazines.

"He'll be alright. In a little while maybe we'll fix him another drink. Sometimes that helps."

"I could use one myself."

"Me too. What would you like?"

"Anything with vodka – soda, juice, even milk's OK."

Shirlee was very much aware of Bootsy watching her through the doorway to the kitchen as she took down the bottle of vodka and went to the fridge. It felt good to have someone new checking her out. "I don't see Tommy-Tom that often."

"You'd have to be Mrs. James Bond or something to put up with that shit."

Shirlee thought she knew what he meant. "Well, Mr. Bond's on vacation now."

"The man never stops. He just works all day and parties all night."

"Oh? You want a slice of anything in with the ginger ale? I have a brand new orange – "

"Just an extra big slice of vodka."

He's cute, thought Shirlee. "That's a wonderful suit."

There was a moment of quiet before the next record landed on the turntable and the needle hopped into the groove. Shirlee heard Bootsy say to himself, "Maybe I better do some lickin of my own before the man gets up." Then, over the introduction to the song, she heard Tommy-Tom.

"I go first."

"Sure, sure, my man," Bootsy replied.

Just as Shirlee was putting the ginger ale back in the fridge, she felt Tommy-Tom standing behind her in the doorway.

"I'll bet you'd like one too," she said, without turning. She dreaded the look on Tommy-Tom's face in the harsh light of the kitchen. "You two get comfortable and I'll be right in."

"Do it," said Tommy-Tom.

When Shirlee brought the drinks in on a tray, her Mexican one with huge colorful blossoms scattered gaily over a black background, she found Tommy-Tom was now sitting on the sofa while Bootsy had been displaced to the tiny settee by the hallway door. It struck Shirlee that Bootsy was actually quite handsome, his dark head set off against the pink wallpaper, covered all over in minty green bows. Tommy-Tom had taken his dick out and laid it, like a big cold noodle, over the cloth of his trousers. Tommy-Tom wore those trousers with the tab and metal fasteners, rather than a belt. They made him look like a smart-ass hippie from the waist down. Shirlee set the tray on the carpet by Tommy-Tom's feet. She then knelt by him and offered him his drink.

"Hey, you'd make a good wife," he said. "Wouldn't she, Bootsy?"

Bootsy only stared.

"Take Bootsy his drink."

She did, on her knees.

"Thanks," said Bootsy.

"Now, you have yours," said Tommy-Tom. "But show us your ass while you drink it."

She swivelled around – somewhat shyly, it seemed to Bootsy – and raised the sarong at the back. She sipped her drink while balanced that way on one hand. Shirlee glanced over at Bootsy. She could tell he was getting excited. Her panties had ruffles joined to the elastic, now creasing the cheeks of her bottom, and she knew it looked nice.

"Stick your finger in there," said Tommy-Tom. "Not you. Bootsy."

"Please don't," Shirlee whispered to Bootsy. "I don't want you to."

"Finish your drink and shut up," said Tommy-Tom.

Shirlee could hear the unmistakable sound of Tommy-Tom playing with himself. His mouth always made a noise like he was sucking an ice-cube.

"Man, I just wanna watch. I'm enjoyin my drink," said Bootsy. But his drink only hung loosely in his hand. Shirlee worried he might spill it on the carpet.

"Don't you want me to suck Bootsy while *you* watch?" she asked Tommy-Tom, her head cocked fetchingly over her shoulder. She could feel her lips numbing with the vodka. "Don't you?"

"Put her face on the cushion, and give it to her that way," said Tommy-Tom, but Bootsy remained, slightly listing, where he sat. "What's the matter, man?"

"Maybe he doesn't like doggy-fashion," said Shirlee.

"I do," said Bootsy. "But I ain't in the mood yet."

"What a fucking bunch of babies." Tommy-Tom pushed off the sofa, down onto the carpet, taking his drink with him. He came up behind Shirlee.

Shirlee jerked to one side, but Tommy-Tom grabbed her. His glass landed somewhere between there and the kitchen, his drink soaking the carpet. Bootsy watched as Tommy-Tom yanked down Shirlee's underpants, licked his thumb and stuck it in her butt. Tommy-Tom then tried to force his dick into her pussy using his other hand, while keeping her in place with the pressure of his thumb.

"Your nail!" screeched Shirlee.

"Should I stick it in here?" demanded Tommy-Tom.

"OK, OK, just stop hurting me," begged Shirlee.

Tommy-Tom savored the moment.

"She always acts like this," Tommy-Tom told Bootsy. "It works every time...*what the fuck?!*"

Suddenly Shirlee was on her back in the middle of the room and Tommy-Tom was on top of her.

"You fucking cocksucking faggot!" he shouted, grabbing Shirlee between the legs. "Look at this shit – " he shouted at Bootsy. "Go get a fucking knife! In the kitchen!"

"You're *hurting* her," said Bootsy, standing over Tommy-Tom. "Don't be doin that, man."

But Tommy-Tom wouldn't stop. Bootsy could sense the desperation rising in Shirlee's limbs. Ramming his forehead into her throat, Tommy-Tom brought the entire weight of his body down on her. Bootsy tried pulling at his head, but Tommy-Tom was too close to the floor, his weight centered too low. Bootsy's long fingers circled Tommy-Tom's neck. He dug his nails into the flesh, trying to bring Tommy-Tom to his senses. Nothing happened. Bootsy scooped up the empty glass lying on the carpet and smashed it against the side of Tommy-Tom's head. Tommy-Tom reared back and stared at the ceiling. Down came Tommy-Tom's head again like a hammer, breaking Shirlee's nose, snapping off her two front teeth. Bootsy took the bottom of the glass, now covered in his own blood, clutched up Tommy-Tom's chin and dug into the flesh of his throat. This time Tommy-Tom's head fell with the full weight of his consciousness. Shirlee watched as he came in childlike spasms to lie beside her. His blood spread quickly into the carpet. The thick pile drank it up. Bootsy bolted, leaving the door to 3B standing open.

FIVE

"Did Nasserman pick up the tab?" Dolores asked, when her husband finally appeared in the kitchen, his hair remarkably untidy.

"De Palma Roma paid," Diego replied. "Where's Roland?"

"Putting on a sweater."

Diego stared down at the patches of perspiration soaking his fresh shirt.

Dolores put down the knife, sticky with orange, brusquely rinsed and dried her hands, and went to help Diego on with his jacket. "We have to talk about Roland. He told Chief Huff that Mikie committed suicide."

Naturally, Diego found this perplexing. "I'll ask him about it when we get to Florescu's. Huff seems like a pretty decent fellow."

"Yes, but that's not the point." Dolores returned to squeezing her oranges.

"I'll call if I get stuck after the funeral," said Diego.

"Don't let Gus keep filling your glass."

"I doubt there'll be much drinking."

Roland strode into the kitchen, hand outstretched for his juice.

As Roland and his father strolled by Lilette's Lingerie on their way to Florescu's Continental Pastries, the boy's attention was drawn to two hands fluttering high up in the front window. The pink slip his mother so coveted was being slipped in a tangle over the mannequin's shoulders. It slithered over the nippleless breasts and fell onto the dusty floor.

At Florescu's, Roland found his father uncommonly quiet. He hadn't sung in the shower either, which usually portended some dire irrelevance later in the day, like a trip over to the landlord's apartment on Washington Street to complain about some technical indignity. Basically, Roland didn't like self-important people like their landlord, who droned on about nothing. Roland guessed people like that didn't know how uninteresting they were. Or, if they did, either they didn't care or had some sick compulsion to simply make noise with their mouths. Either way, Roland could do nicely without them. His father's cannelloni arrived, one of the two flattened like a squashed sausage.

"What happened to him?" asked Diego.

"His wife must have slept on top of him," said Florescu, and went off to fetch Diego another double espresso.

Diego now turned his attention to his son. "How did it go with Chief Huff?"

"He's a nice man," said Roland, his saliva-moistened finger playing in the powdered sugar near the edge of his father's plate.

"I'm glad to hear it. What did he ask you?"

"If I killed Mikie."

"He what?"

"Well, you asked Pop."

"What did he say exactly?"

"He started out talking to Mom about books."

"No, later on, when he was – "

The espresso arrived.

"Interrogating me?" Roland thought for a moment, his finger lodged in his mouth.

Diego urged his son to have a bite of his cannelloni.

"Chief Huff knows his business," said Roland, "but he's no psychiatrist. I mean, *psycho-ologist*."

His father glanced around for a napkin. "You had it right the first time."

"On the next table," offered Roland helpfully.

"Thanks. I disagree."

"About what? Not about Chief Huff?" Roland's tone was incredulous.

"I really don't know Chief Huff. And furthermore, it doesn't really matter what we think of him – he has a job to do."

"Some job, picking on little kids."

Diego glanced at his watch, which had stopped, then up at the clock over the display counter.

"I guess it's bye for now," said Roland.

"Afraid so. I'd rather spend the day with you, my boy."

"Me too, Pop. We could really have some fun." Roland knew his father was too fat to do much of anything.

"Do you mind if I have a word with Chief Huff myself?"

"I don't know, he's pretty busy right now. The Rozzos will have him out looking for Alicia today, and then there's the Friedrich kid, who may have taken her somewhere and killed her."

"Who told you that?"

Grinning, Roland snatched up his father's cup and sucked the bitter dregs from the bottom. He then smacked his lips and pointed to his father's inside breast-pocket.

On cue, his father took out his first cigar of the day and began to dampen it with his tongue. "Don't say that sort of thing in front of your mother," he went on. "Or any of the other kids. You may think it's cute, but nobody else does."

On his way home, Roland stopped before Lilette's window.

"That lady didn't even bother to brush the dirt off Mom's slip before she put it back on that skank," he said to James.

They peered up at the mannequin. The slip had haphzardly been put back on the vapid pink figure.

"Look at her eyes," James observed, "they're like Val Nolan's. And her foot has a hole in it where the big toenail should be."

"She sucks," sneered Roland.

"So good so far," said Val. It was just shy of ten o'clock, so she was getting a late start, and Dolores didn't have time to dawdle on the telephone.

"Roland and I are going shopping in about twenty minutes," offered Dolores.

"You're not going to Mikie's funeral?"

"I don't have anyone to leave Roland with. But Diego's going."

"Nobody in the building?"

"Mrs. Finkelstein does her shopping today."

"How'd it go with him and the police?"

"Chief Huff was very nice."

"Yea, but what happened?"

"Nothing really."

"OK, so don't tell me."

Dolores wasn't in the mood. Maybe Roland's explanation wasn't so far from the truth. Certainly Val's own son was depressed, how could he not be? "It seems Mikie may have jumped rather than fallen."

"What, off a Ferris wheel?"

Dolores could hear Val pouring herself a drink. She'd always said Seagram's goes down nicely with a spoonful of frozen orange concentrate mixed in, especially when you felt like shit.

"Families are weird," said Val, apparently feeling more congenial. "You can do everything for a kid and still they turn into messes. Look at the Friedrich's kid."

"You know about that?"

"Yea, Babs told me how he was molesting Alicia or something at the fair. On Monday night when she disappeared."

"I doubt it was very serious. The Friedrich's are a nice family."

"Tell that to Gus."

"Oh, I know about Gus and his precious paint job."

"Paint job? He just don't want his kid getting felt up in public."

"Billy's at the playground, I take it?"

"He goes every day."

Dolores knew older kids hung out at the playground too. It was a dangerous place to leave your child. "Well, I guess I better sign off. You know Roland, he's somewhere in the building doing God knows what."

"Yea, at Mrs. Finklestein's probably – he likes her wiener schnitzel."

"She's out shopping, remember?"

"I guess I forgot."

"Val, I've got to go and round him up and get ready to go out myself."

Dolores had hoped Val would say *Yea sure, fine* or something equally dismissive and that would be the end of it, but instead she said nothing. Dolores sensed her struggling with some thought. Then she heard her snuffling. Val was crying. Something was more wrong than usual.

"Val?"

"I got a confession to make."

Dolores knew better than to respond.

"It's Tommy-Tom."

Dolores waited.

"He didn't come home again last night."

Dolores was sick and tired of Tommy-Tom Nolan. She thanked God her husband wasn't spending as much time with him as he used to. "He'll show up. He always does, doesn't he?"

"I couldn't get him at work yesterday. You know, he was supposed to drop Alicia off at one of her girlfriend's or somewheres. Well, he never came home after that. That was Monday night. I don't even know about last night." Dolores could feel Val sinking into a hole. "No, he did come home Monday, cause he was messing around in my sewing box. But I never saw him or nothin. I guess I was asleep. He just changed his clothes like he used to and went out again. I hate that."

"I know," whispered Dolores. "He'll be back."

"Oh, how do you know?" moaned Val. "How do you know what it's like?"

"I guess I don't. I'm sorry." Dolores was trying her best to be gentle. She knew this was what Val needed. Then she realized Roland was standing in the doorway between the kitchen and the living-room holding her purse out before him and shaking his head woefully from side to side.

On the way to Mikie's funeral, Gus went into the Police Station by himself to ask Chief Huff if he had learned any more from Tommy-Tom about Alicia's possible whereabouts. He also intended to ask him to do something about Freddie Friedrich's kid.

"How long've you and Tommy-Tom been friends?" said the Chief.

"I've known him since I was fourteen," Gus replied.

"Then you should know if you can trust him with your own daughter."

Gus couldn't believe Leon Huff was giving him a lecture.

"Tommy-Tom's a hard case," the Chief went on. "He does what he likes. And he's got a big chip on his shoulder."

"He can be a real prick. I know."

"Tommy-Tom doesn't like anybody, and I mean *anybody* to interfere in his fun."

"Yea, I know, I've partied with him. Why do you think he works in New York and not out here in Jersey with the rest of us? He always wants to get in on the big scene. Tommy-Tom knows all kinds of people I never heard of."

"Ever seen him with a black guy named Bootsy?"

"Tommy-Tom with a fucking black guy?"

Gus didn't like the sound of this. Tommy-Tom was dumber than he had thought. Gus didn't want to say anything, so he just looked around Huff's office. There was a framed photo on the top of Huff's filing cabinet: the Chief had a wife and two kids, a boy and a girl. Not much of a family when compared to Gus's.

"How often do you see them socially?" asked the Chief.

"Who?"

"The Nolans. Tommy-Tom and his wife."

"Val too?"

"Yea."

They'd just seen them. What a stupid question. Gus tried to keep a civil tongue in his head. "Whenever there's something going on."

"Like what?"

"Anything. How should I know? Sometimes we do things together, like go to the fair. That's what families do."

"Val was at the fair too?"

"I don't know. She could have went with Billy all by herself."

What was with all the questions? Gus just wanted to find out what Tommy-Tom had done with Alicia, where he'd left her on Monday night. Simple. This was a fucking waste of time.

"I get it," said Gus, "you didn't find out anything from Tommy-Tom. So, can we talk about Freddie Friedrich's kid?"

"I've been over that territory with you, I thought. Your pal took her into the city, where according to him she disappeared."

"The city?"

"That's right."

"Yea, and then Friedrich's kid took her somewheres."

"How?"

"In his car, how else?"

"He doesn't have a car. He doesn't even have a license." The Chief was looking at Gus as if he were insane.

"Yea, well, he could have taken her somewheres with some other kid, some other kid with a car, who *can* drive."

"He went home with his father."

"That's not what Friedrich told me yesterday. He told me he didn't know his kid was at the fair."

Cops could be so dumb. Freddie Friedrich Sr. was a liar. He lied about when he'd have your car ready. He even lied about what colors of paint you could get. You could get any fucking color you wanted. Anybody knew that.

"He probably didn't want to get into an altercation with you," said the Chief.

"What? Like I call him a liar?!"

"Something like that."

"I got my kid's funeral."

Nobody gave a shit, not even the fucking Chief of Police.

"I'll be over later," said the Chief, looking gravely into Gus's eyes.

"Where?"

"St. Eleanor's?"

Gus couldn't believe Huff was going to make his presence felt at Mikie's funeral. It was a publicity stunt. "I guess everybody would appreciate you being there," he said, and left.

For at least ten minutes, Diego Ildefonso had been standing at the open back door of Pretty Feet smoking his cigar and gazing at the debris in the alleyway from the Woolworth's next door. Many things had passed through his mind, not the least of which was the visit he would make that evening to St. Mary's Hospital. There really wasn't a whole lot to think about until Dr. Herbert had reviewed the results from the brain and body scans and conjured up his diagnosis. Now the back door of the Woolworth's swung open and a hand appeared, clutching a half-eaten sandwich and a crushed cardboard coffee cup, and flung them unceremoniously into the alleyway. Diego decided he had best make things ready for the day.

First, he turned on all the necessary lights, then latched open the shop's front door. He sat on the banquette before the front window, feet raised on one of the sales stools, and waited for his first customer. After a while, he got up and went into the stockroom and relit what was left of his cigar. It was stubby and damp but still tasted good. Then someone came into the shop. No, there were two: Gilbey, a wealthy old fart who appeared every so often to waste Diego's time, and a young woman supporting the old fart at the elbow.

"I don't really need any more shoes, Francis," said the young woman.

"Indulge me," Gilbey replied. "How's tricks, Ildefonso?"

The young woman, aged about thirty, went to the banquette, sat, and began undoing the straps on her shoes. Diego gazed at Gilbey expectantly.

"Bedroom slippers," he said. "Sensible ones."

Diego knew what he meant and hastened to the stockroom. There he found the item in three pastel colors. In a matter of moments, he was kneeling before the young woman. She had beautifully kept feet, and her legs were bare.

"These are so common," she sniffed. "Isn't there anything in gold?"

"How is one to cope?" said Gilbey, and lowered himself with some difficulty to sit beside her. "Why don't we see how the other two colors flatter your own?"

"My own what?"

"Color."

"I do have something in gold," said Diego.

"Actually, we're not buying them for Nina here, we're buying them for her mother."

"Oh, that's so sweet," said the young woman, brightening. "Francis, how do you remember everyone's birthday?"

"I don't know, I just do."

She gazed down at Diego's hands fiddling at her feet. "But I thought you didn't like my mother?"

"I don't." Gilbey smiled at the big man crouched on the carpet. "Ildefonso, we'll take them. All of them."

Diego thought he heard Nina laughing as he took the slippers over to the counter.

At the cash register, his voice lowered discreetly, Gilbey said, "These things can't cost very much?"

"Whatever they cost, it's too much," Diego assured him.

"Fine, cash or check?"

"Cash is always nice."

Gilbey glanced over at his companion, who was ready to leave.

"She'll just have to learn to be patient," he whispered. "I hired her as a secretary. But she can't even sit still long enough to type a letter. She says she's rather fond of me. As usual, I didn't have to do anything to deserve it."

Gilbey patted the pile of money he'd left on the counter, his hand a few old bones wrapped in blue veins. As Diego searched for a bag big enough to accommodate the three boxes of slippers, all the while keeping an eye on the front door, the young woman wandered out onto the sidewalk where she posed seductively against the passing traffic. Diego was suddenly, inexplicably jealous.

"I've left my card – there with your gratuity," said Gilbey. "Call me any time after eleven tonight. I'm serious, I have my reasons."

Diego now watched as the silly old fart left the shop, was embraced by the young woman in the street, and carried on, giggling and gesturing inanely, in the direction of Newark Street. The card had a number in Nyack on it.

The telephone at the back of the shop was ringing. It was Linda in Dr. Herbert's office. The scans were on for that evening. Diego was to be at St. Mary's Hospital just before six, so Dr. Herbert could fit him in *ahead of the needy*, as Linda put it.

Dolores was hugely disappointed to find Lilette's closed, the front window emptied of all merchandise. She knew there wouldn't be time now to purchase a similar slip elsewhere, not before her assignation with Diego the next day.

"They were open this morning," volunteered Roland.

Dolores's eyes were downcast.

"Look," said Roland, "there's a woman in there and she's getting ready to do the window!"

The woman was now backing into the display area with a big box of cuddly cloth bunny rabbits. It was Sylvia Drescher, who had recently taken over the shop's management. Dolores couldn't quite see what bunny rabbits and Easter had to do with under-garments and lingerie but she also accepted that Sylvia was very clever: she had been to art school in Manhattan. Roland went to the window and rapped on it. Sylvia ignored him. But he persisted and finally she turned, her pointed chin thrust high, to peer out over the street.

"Down here, you twat," said Roland, softly enough so that his mother wouldn't hear.

When Sylvia finally saw Dolores, an enormous smile divided her face.

"Oh, she sees us," said Dolores.

"Chirp, chirp, chirp," said Roland. "Let's go in. I'll bet the door isn't even locked." It wasn't.

"Dolores, I didn't realize it was you," called Sylvia from behind the window's backing. "I asked everybody to clear out so I could concentrate on getting things done around here without blah-blah-blah."

"Well, I hope *we're* not bothering you."

"Want some coffee?" Sylvia stepped down into the shop.

"I don't drink coffee," said Roland, glancing over a loose selection of brassieres.

Dolores laid her hand tenderly on his head. "If it's no trouble."

"I drink too much coffee," confessed Sylvia, "especially when I'm working."

Roland browsed the display cases as Dolores and Sylvia had their coffee in the office. Dolores sat quite comfortably where a potential employee or sales rep might sit for an interview, while Sylvia leaned against the wall with her foot up on the seat of the chair behind the desk.

"Do you have any idea what women are paying for sexy underwear these days?" asked Sylvia. She said this as if sexy underwear were something completely alien to Dolores.

"I have some idea. In fact, that's why I'm here, to buy some sexy underwear. My husband and I are going on a cruise and I need something for lounging around hotel suites and the like."

"Oh," said Sylvia, apparently stunned.

"Actually, I was quite interested in a rather pretty pink slip that's been in the window for several weeks now. I need that sort of thing too."

"Pink slip?" Sylvia couldn't remember any pink slip, although she must have removed the slip from the window herself only that morning.

Roland, who was now standing at the door to the office, said, "Pink. You know, the one the lady dropped on the floor and got all dirty."

"Oh, that one," said Sylvia.

Roland often astounded Dolores. He must have noted the condition of the slip on his way back from his morning stroll with his father. Now Dolores was certain she could get the slip at a better price.

"You wouldn't want that old thing," said Sylvia. "It had a smear on it from the grease they use to keep the security grate functioning. I've been using it as a dust rag."

Roland saw the pain in his mother's eyes.

"It must be wonderful to be so stupid," he said, shifting his gaze from his mother to Sylvia Drescher.

Dolores reached out and took her son's hand.

North Philadelphia was far worse than anything Bootsy Holloway had ever seen in the south, or in New York for that matter, although he'd never gone above 125th Street. Usually sunshine made things look better, happier, but the sunshine soaking the dingy surfaces of the old rowhouses, the same sunshine making the filthy train window look even filthier, only made the rundown buildings look worse. Staring down into the backyards, most littered with things no one could ever possibly use, Bootsy was sad to see a man, an older man, still living in a house where there'd been a fire, and it looked like the fire had been a long time ago. Bootsy figured the old guy didn't have anywhere else to go. He'd torn out as much of the burnt wallboard as he could and thrown it into a pile, then put some plastic over what was left of that part of the house to keep the soot from getting into his food and clothes. The old guy looked a little like his Uncle Tookus's pal Tyrone.

The gash in Bootsy's palm was throbbing. The wound was deep but clean. No stitches. His fingers were cut too, digs the glass had made along the insides, where he'd grasped its jagged edge. He'd thought of going back to the Stamford to get his things and tidy up his room, so it would look like he'd left in a civilized fashion, but then he'd decided that it would be better to just leave. Nobody kept track of anybody staying at the Stamford Arms anyway, unless they were sick and had a welfare agent stopping in. And nobody gave a shit if a young black guy disappeared. They'd figure he'd gone out on drugs. Drunks could live forever it seemed, but with smack or meth you could drop fast. Blow was different. Blow was for partying. Blow made Bootsy feel rich. Everybody'd wondered what a cool motherfucker like Bootsy was doing around there. Bootsy figured what he'd done was probably the smartest thing, although none of it was very smart.

He'd thrown his jacket, which was a bloody mess, onto the front seat of Tommy-Tom's car where it was parked around the corner from Shirlee's. Bootsy wasn't sure why he'd done this. He was passing by the car, the window was down, and in it went. He'd then gone straight to Penn Station in a taxi. The driver didn't even look at him. Somewhere around 30th Street and Ninth, maybe three blocks over from the station, he'd taken a clean jacket off a guy passed out on the sidewalk, to cover up the blood that had soaked through his shirt cuffs and splashed down his front. Bootsy had then gone back and bought a ticket for the train to Rocky Mount, which left at 9:12; it would get in around 7pm, if it didn't run late, and then he could call somebody to come get him.

If he'd saved little Shirlee's life, then it was OK to be inconvenienced so bad. Bootsy's cousin Junior was like Shirlee. He was precious as a child, and always sang the girls' parts in church. Everybody liked Junior, and nobody would've hurt him. What Tommy-Tom had done to Shirlee, even before smashing her balls, was low. But guys like Tommy-Tom were into making other people look sick. Bootsy knew that now, he seriously knew that. He never did feel right around Tommy-Tom. It was Tommy-Tom who wanted him for a friend, not the other way round. Tommy-Tom wouldn't have done anything for him anyway, only mess with him. It was a bad thing to want, but Bootsy hoped he'd killed Tommy-Tom. At least that way Tommy-Tom wouldn't come looking for him. Bootsy felt sorry for Tommy-Tom's wife and kid. He wanted to think they were better off without a guy like that. But family was family, and some people would put up with anything – *truly anything* – from the people they thought they loved.

SIX

The taxi Diego Ildefonso had called to take him to St. Eleanor's for Mikie Rozzo's funeral arrived late. As the driver jerked his way through the midday traffic, Diego thought about what Gus must be feeling at that moment. Then he thought about Gilbey. The old fart wanted something. But what? Then he thought about his appointment that evening at St. Mary's Hospital. And he thought about Dr. Herbert, who hadn't given him any idea what the required procedures would cost. He also thought about how people always just assumed these things would be taken care of in life. Years ago, being the fatalist he was, he had taken out a life insurance policy, but he'd never managed any health insurance. This was largely because Barbiche and Petit-Pont had said they were looking into a policy for *all* their employees. Naturally, nothing ever materialized. If he were mortally ill, perhaps he would be allowed to die at home. He decided to think about something else. So he thought about Cuba. For the longest time, he had wanted to take his wife and child on a holiday to some place where the people spoke Spanish, not the *Americanized* Spanish spoken on the streets of Union City, but something more like *real* Spanish. Cuba would have been ideal, if Castro hadn't overwhelmed the island, demeaning its archaic glory with the presence of his mindless uniformed drones. Cuba had always been beckoning, somewhere in the back of his mind. Now it was of no use whatsoever.

A police car went charging by, its blue light flashing. In the back seat sat Val Nolan with little Billy. She regarded Diego with an unnatural stillness, her gaze so empty one would have assumed he was a total stranger. He instantly realized Val's plight was far more important at that moment than seeing Mikie Rozzo laid to rest, and told the taxi driver to follow the flashing blue light.

Not only had the bottom of the broken glass Bootsy had used on Tommy-Tom ruptured his jugular, it had also moved diagonally deeper, tearing into his larynx, the tender vocal chords striated by the jagged edges like parmesan cheese on a grater. And, due to the violence with which Tommy-Tom had smashed his face into Shirlee Simonaire's, his eyes were surrounded by purple bruising, now verging on black.

"How much will the tooth fairy give him for that?" asked little Billy, when he saw one of his father's teeth sitting in a paper cup by his metal bed.

"Daddy's too old for the tooth fairy," his mother replied.

When Diego Ildefonso first appeared in the room, which also held seven other near-fatalities, Val ignored him, her gaze fixed on Tommy-Tom's shaved head.

"Daddy looks like an army guy," said Billy.

"Daddy *is* an army guy," said Val.

Now Chief Huff appeared in the corridor outside Intensive Care. For some reason he stared directly at Diego, perhaps because he was so big. Although he felt uncomfortable, Diego went over to ask the Chief if he knew what had happened to his friend. The Chief said everyone assumed it was Tommy-Tom's colored drinking pal Bootsy Holloway who had done the damage to both him and Shirlee, but he wasn't entirely sure about this.

"So what do *you* think Tommy-Tom was doing up on Palisade Avenue at that hour?" asked Diego.

"Making a big mistake," the Chief replied.

"Hard to believe."

"Somebody went there for oral sex, while somebody else went there for something else, and somebody else didn't know what he was getting himself in for."

Diego took this to mean that this Bootsy Holloway hadn't known that Shirlee Simonaire was a young man. Most astounding however was the notion that Tommy-Tom would have sought out the attentions of a homosexual. There had to have been some element of cruelty motivating Tommy-Tom. Some inclination to humiliate. But Diego still couldn't comprehend how Tommy-Tom had wound up in shreds. Drag queens very seldom provoked altercations between friendly fellows like Tommy-Tom and himself, although he never had anything to do with drag queens, and he wasn't black. He watched as the Chief went into the ward to stand with Val and little Billy at

Tommy-Tom's bedside. The Chief smiled down at the child, who continued to stare at his father.

Val kept trying to hold Tommy-Tom's hand, but her husband was unwilling to have her touch him, even in the distressing circumstances she now found herself. She could never forgive him for the way he had treated her over the years, so now she might as well hate him. Little Billy would miss his father only for however long it took her to find him another one. Finding another man could mean a lot of work, but Val was ready for some self-improvement anyway. The doctor, who was called Ray, had been nice to her. He had also warned her that her husband might never speak normally again. He would probably have to use one of those talking gizmos that cancer patients use after they've had the cancer removed. All Val could think of was what sweet justice it was going to be for Tommy-Tom to have to wear a diaper over the hole in his throat. Still, she felt panicky. All she really knew was that her husband was still breathing and that he was using each feeble breath to fend her off.

When Val left Intensive Care, little Billy shuttling between her hip and Chief Huff's, Diego went along. As they made their way down the corridor, he tried to catch her eye, to let her know she wasn't alone. But she didn't notice. He again confronted her in the parking-lot. The taxi was now waiting to hurry him on to the cemetery, but he offered to take her and little Billy home instead. Val didn't object: Billy was impatient to get back to the playground, and it was better than pulling up in front of her building in a cop car.

As he helped her and little Billy into the taxi, she said, "You must be crazy."

"Where was everybody?" Gus asked Babs, as he laid a slice of ham on her plate with his fingers rather than the fork provided by his mother for that purpose.

"There were people." She gestured for him to lay on a second slice.

"How can you be hungry?"

"Your mom made all this food cause she loves us." Babs glanced up to find Gus's mother on the other side of the serving table with a very large bowl of potato salad in her arms. When Mrs. Rozzo saw her, she again began to weep. "Oh grandma," said Babs, and went to comfort her.

Gus reached across the table and, with one hand, took the heavy bowl from his mother and set it down next to the punch, into which he had secretly poured a fifth of vodka shortly after their arrival. "Mama, none of our *good* friends came."

"Like who?" said Babs.

"Like your pal Val, for one."

"I don't think she's very well." Babs hugged Mrs. Rozzo a little harder. "And how could she anyways if Tommy-Tom wasn't there to bring her?"

"Tommy-Tom has a whole building to take care of. He can't come back out here when he's got work."

"So, what about Ildefonso?"

"Yea, so what about his wife?"

"Dolores has Roland."

"So?!"

Mrs. Rozzo pressed her finger to her lips for the two to be quiet. Gus hated being admonished by his mother in front of his wife. He was the youngest of her four sons – six years separated him from his next brother – and had always felt left out, while simultaneously feeling that she treated him like a little *bambola,* which was what she had really wanted. This perhaps accounted for the strange and contradictory mix of sensibilities bubbling inside Gus. He was quite capable of taking an hour to perfect his outfit for a weeknight gathering of the Hoboken Knights of Columbus. Often on such occasions he was seen in a cowboy hat, which he wore throughout the meeting, or, even more ostentatiously, his long snakeskin coat, actually a supple plastic tour de force made in South Korea, which he wore draped over his shoulders, like the diminutive *consigliere* of one of the big Mafia families.

"With Ildefonso it's different," said Gus. "Him and me, we were like brothers the other night. He loved Mikie. If he can't make it, he can't make it. End of story. What I don't get is what was Friedrich doing there?"

"Well, I didn't see him," said Babs.

"You don't even know what he looks like."

"I know what Freddie Jr. looks like."
"So?"
"He could look like him."
"He don't look like his kid. At least not as I can see. He looks like a kraut, like a big kraut. You know, like from out in Allentown or somewheres. A kraut with a big red beard." Gus waited for Babs to respond. If he knew his wife, she was picturing a pirate, a pirate with a big floppy hat and a long tendrilly red beard with tiny snails in it. "Like a kraut!"

Again Mrs. Rozzo gestured for the two to be quieter.

"Huff said he was going to be there too, and where was he at?" said Gus. He poured himself another cup of punch. "Mama, where's the glasses? Can't I get a glass for this?"

Mrs. Rozzo threw up her hands in surrender and gently dislodged herself from her daughter-in-law. The old woman, her hair softly floating over her powdery puckering scalp, went back into the kitchen, and Babs breathed easier.

"You invited him? I thought you was just going in to talk to him?" Babs began poking her finger into the slice of ham on her plate. "I want something else. I thought your mother was going to have something lighter, some cold macaroni salad or something."

"Where's Dominic?" asked Gus, sternly.

"With Dot Perosa. They're sitting on the couch in the den. He's OK with her."

"I hope so."

As he went by, on his way into the kitchen, Gus put his hand on his wife's bottom, to let her know he felt close. Standing with his mother at the sink, waiting for her to hand him a tumbler, he heard himself sob.

"Oh Guiseppe," Mrs. Rozzo whispered, *"Mi dispiace molto. Amante, permettetemi..."*

Feeling his mother's hair brush his lips as she stood on tiptoe and raised her frail arms, Gus sobbed, just once more. "We can't find Alicia neither, mama."

"She'll come home. Don't you worry too much, she'll come home. She knows who loves her." Mrs. Rozzo stared through her kitchen window at the wash she'd hung out earlier in the week. She didn't know what was happening to her. This was the second time since Christmas she'd forgotten to take the wash down. Now everything was embarrassingly dingy with the black dust that blew over from Kennedy Boulevard. Thank God, her Dominic, Guiseppe's papa, wasn't there to see it. Thank God, he wasn't there to see any of it.

By the time Diego had left Val and was back on Willow Avenue treading slowly in the direction of Pretty Feet, he was thoroughly depressed. He glanced into the front window of Lilette's Lingerie. It was empty but for one mannequin which had had its face caved in. He decided to return home briefly to tell Dolores and Roland he loved them, before going on to the shop. It would just have to stay closed a little longer.

He stood before his building in silence. He then trudged up the front steps, lowered himself onto the concrete porch, leant his throbbing temple against the cool balustrade, and closed his eyes. Perhaps he and Dolores should find another place to live. A place where his son wouldn't have to watch another little boy throw himself from the Ferris wheel. A place where a black man wouldn't turn on you and slash your throat. Now Diego dimly realized he was falling asleep, there on the front stoop of his building in the middle of the afternoon. It was Roland who found him and led him upstairs, while Dolores was sorting and folding laundry with Mrs. Finkelstein in the basement. Roland could tell by the way his father was shambling along, barely managing to climb the stairs, that he wasn't very well. He encouraged him to go into the bedroom, where he took off his shoes and closed the blinds, saying, "I'll bet Mr. Rozzo's drunk too."

Diego had less than twenty minutes rest before Gus Rozzo was standing over him, reeking of alcohol. "It's alright you didn't come," said his friend, slurrily, "but you gotta come with me now. OK?"

Roland knew his father would eventually respond and most certainly oblige Mr. Rozzo. He decided it would be best to retreat out onto the landing of the back hallway where he and James were trying to work out how to kill a rat they had trapped under a metal milk crate. Once they'd killed the rat, they planned to dissect it, probably in the bathtub.

"I have to go back to work," Diego insisted, still prostrate on the bed, as Gus wrestled his shoes on.

When Gus had finally swung the big man into a sitting position, he said, "I'll explain everything about it in the van. You know, in the van..."

But Diego didn't know *in the van,* all he knew was *I feel sick.*

The streets of Hoboken were uncommonly empty for that hour. Usually by three o'clock, or whatever time it was – the clock in Gus's van had a Woody Woodpecker decal plastered over its face – the sidewalks were picking up a little more pedestrian traffic as the wives ventured out to shop for the evening meal. Hoboken being a city of a relatively insular nature, domestic responsibilities were managed much as they are in most European cities, with food-gathering being a leisurely pursuit accompanied by much social intercourse. Diego liked this about Hoboken.

"Friedrich just stood there," said Gus, "looking at Mikie's coffin with his beard all lit up in the sun like some fucking Santa Claus or something."

Diego wasn't about to say anything. He doubted Gus knew what had happened to Tommy-Tom, but wasn't as yet sufficiently lucid to know how to tell him. This would take a moment or two of well-inflected concentration. Diego's concern was undoubtedly warranted as Gus and Tommy-Tom had been like brothers at one time, or so Diego had been told by both men individually on various occasions.

"It was a fucking insult," Gus went on. "He didn't show up at my mama's after. He just went to the cemetery to give us the finger. Babs says he was just trying to be nice. Give me a fucking break. Huff told me this morning that Friedrich was at the fair when his kid was feeling up Alicia. So the motherfucker lied."

Gus wasn't reasoning very clearly. He was drunk and he was upset. He'd just buried his son. Diego reckoned Gus should be at home with his wife and children, not driving wildly down Willow Avenue. Perhaps the best way to upend Gus's ranting was with news of Tommy-Tom's predicament. Perhaps that would put things into perspective.

"You don't really want to hurt anybody, do you," said Diego, and it wasn't a question.

Gus glared at him. "It's blood that holds this fucking country together!"

"That's one way of looking at it. There's a kid on a bike behind that delivery truck."

"I seen him!"

Diego groaned. "Look, what I've got to tell you isn't easy, but maybe it'll get your mind off Freddie Friedrich."

Eyebrows raised, jaw dropped in imitation of a simpleton, Gus waited.

Pacing his words so precisely that even in his present state of inebriation Gus couldn't mistake what he'd heard, Diego said, "Tommy-Tom's up in Union City at the Medical Center and he may die."

"He wreck his car?"

"No" – the story was obviously too long to tell in one protracted account – "his black drinking buddy from New York cut his throat." Gus was going to have a field day with this one. "And do me a favor, don't start screaming about niggers, OK? Tommy-Tom was with this guy because he liked him."

"Tommy-Tom's a dumb fuck."

"So who needs friends when they've got you, right?"

Gus slammed on the brakes and pulled the van over.

"You can't double-park here," said Diego.

"Fuck double-parking. I can't fucking believe you said that. I thought we were pals?"

"We are. That's why I'm telling you about Tommy-Tom."

"You expect me to fucking sit here and do nothing, about any of this shit?! Not about the Friedrich kid, or anything?! Not even about this fucking *Negro?!*"

Diego would remain calm. "In both cases, we don't know the whole story."

Gus gazed down at his hands on the wheel. "OK boss," he said, finally. "So you tell me."

As the van moved back into the flow of traffic, Gus plucked a cigarette from his shirt pocket and lit it. Diego watched. God, he was sick and tired of fools like Gus Rozzo. All the guy could do was pump his wife full of babies, go to work doing just about nothing, and complain about everything.

"I'll tell you what. I'll have a word with Freddie Friedrich myself," said Diego. "I'll ask the questions. If Huff isn't willing to do the research, I will. "

"Like I said, you're the boss."

After there'd been quiet for a minute or two, Diego said, "Shirlee from The Jewel had his neck broken."

Gus was silent.

"You know, *Stanley*, that short-legged kid whose mother lives way up on Washington. He was with Tommy-Tom and the black guy. They say he may be paralyzed."

"What, the one sucks cock?" Gus replied. "What's the matter with Val?"

When they arrived at Friedrich's Body Shop, it was closed. Gus said he had to take a pee and got out of the van and went behind the building, where the office stuck out making an *L*. He came running back laughing. Diego could smell the gasoline soaking Gus's trousers the moment he landed in the van.

"Look, look," panted Gus, pointing to the building's roof, "there's your fucking research!"

The office, blocked from view by the cinder-block garage itself, was billowing black smoke. Gus was so preoccupied with the glory of this accomplishment that he kept the van idling in place as the fire spread. The toxic plume unfurled in bursts, higher and higher, growing ever blacker.

Diego shifted his attention to Gus. "What do you expect me to say?"

"Nothing, and you won't."

"You're on your own with this one." Diego began getting out of the van.

"What if Babs and me prefer charges for Roland pushing Mikie off the Ferris wheel?" Gus was no longer grinning.

Diego lowered himself onto the macadam and closed the door, snapping it shut with very little pressure. As he walked off, he thought, Now I know what they mean when they say *shit for brains*.

Diego telephoned Dolores on his way back from Friedrich's Auto Body Shop to tell her he'd be late for dinner, also about Tommy-Tom, although he didn't go into the circumstances relating to his injuries, and lastly Val's desolate frame of mind. He said nothing about Gus. A short while later, Dolores telephoned Val.

"I'm getting drunk, and I'm leaving Tommy-Tom," said Val.

"Where's Billy?" asked Dolores.

"Outside."

"With who?"

"Huh?"

Dolores waited for Val to say more but she went off on one of her tangents:

"I thought I'd get a job before but now I think I just oughta get outa here. Tommy-Tom can go to his mother's house. She's alone. His father's a bastard too."

"How bad is he?"

"He won't be able to talk. What does he ever say anyway? Do this, do that, tell Billy to shut up. When was the last time anybody ever heard him say anything nice?"

"I didn't know – "

"I was always telling everybody about Tommy-Tom. Fuck him."

Dolores heard Val pouring another drink. "Do you want me to come over?"

"Why do they make these bottles square when they slip?"

"I could keep you company."

"Maybe you could take Billy. I gotta find another place. Maybe I *shouldn't* get outa here. Maybe stay. But I'd want to change it and make it nice and he always took all the money. I bet nobody ever knew that either. You say something?"

"I was just thinking about Billy, whether we could manage it, at least for a little while."

"I could go get him now."

"I think it might be best if you stay put. I can talk to Diego about it when he gets home. Or if you want some company, Roland and I could come over. He and Billy could play. It's still early."

"No, then I'm going to find somebody else to take Billy. I mean, tonight."

"You need company."

"I already called this guy I know."

"Sure that's a good idea?"

"How's Tommy-Tom gonna know?"

"I was thinking more about Billy."

"Thanks for asking Diego, OK? I gotta get fixed up now."

"Val, who's this *guy?*"

"Some guy. He's really neat."

Dolores couldn't imagine who Val might be having over, especially on such short notice. She concluded that Val was just talking, that she would be alone with Billy for the rest of the night, and it worried her.

"Why don't I give you another call later?"

"OK, but if I don't answer it'll be because we went out. This guy really likes to go out. But go ahead and call if you want." The conversation was over.

Dolores wished Diego were there. Val's life was going to pieces. Tommy-Tom may not have been a loving husband, or even a good father, but at least he gave Val something to live for. It was terrible. Then Dolores realized she was wrong. Val hadn't had anything to live for, except her son, and now it seemed that relationship was slipping away. Diego probably wouldn't mind Billy staying with them for a few days under the circumstances. No, Dolores was certain he wouldn't.

St. Mary's Hospital was a Dickensian pile of dirty red brick and crumbling slate. The x-ray equipment was in the basement, along with the boiler system. When Diego couldn't find a single door left unlocked on the ground level, he was obliged to enter the bowels of the building by way of a long concrete ramp used for wheeling the disabled in and refuse out. Once down there, he was overcome by the smell of institutional disinfectant.

"Nurse, help Mr. Ildefonso with his shoes," said Dr. Herbert from outside the waiting-room. Then, a little later, "Get his clothes off and out of here, we have to begin!"

The nurse led Diego into a room that was too tall for the basement: the floor above had had to be removed to allow the equipment into its own brilliantly lit space. He stood waiting in the usual flimsy smock, two shoe-strings at the back, his bare bottom available for all to see.

"Up you go," urged the nurse, meaning he should hoist himself onto the gurney.

This was difficult. Although his arms were exceedingly limber, they weren't very strong. Diego Ildefonso's weight was really more than his arms could bear. The nurse placed a folding chair between the subject and his vehicle to enable him to climb onto it. The actual thing into which he was about to have his head thrust most resembled a massive front-loading washing machine. Once his head had been wheeled into the hole, the inside of the scanner seamless and plastic and glossy, he had the sensation of plummeting upside down into a very large thermos bottle. Sticking out the other end, the antiseptic socks he had been provided with began to darken, or so he imagined, his feet soaking with perspiration.

"Where's Dr. Herbert?" he asked. But the nurse had left the room, bolting the door behind her.

Now, as he heard the whirring of the scanner's gears, Diego resigned himself to his anxiety just as he once had as a boy, day after day after day, sifting aimlessly through the ruins of Guernica. The whirring of the scanner's gears grew louder. It was a bleak tonality, like sand pouring down a long metal chute.

While the Ildefonsos ate their dinner – discussion at the table included Val, alcohol as a preservative, the digestive tract of the average human, little Billy, the draining off of the blood from a roast before it's cooked, Tommy-Tom, the gelatin that resides within the eye, and Bootsy Holloway, in that order – Gus and Babs were already putting their dirty dishes in the washer. As they did, they spoke in hushed voices, so their children who were straying about the house wouldn't hear them.

"The other way," said Babs. "No, not that way, with the fronts all facing the backs, facing the inside. Now, tell me again what he said..."

"He *said* Tommy-Tom was looking for trouble hanging out with this nigger from the hotel. That's fucking Ildefonso for you

– anybody knows Tommy-Tom's dumb when it comes to doing shit like that. You feel sorry for Tommy-Tom?"

"Tell me again why you think Freddie Friedrich Sr. was at the funeral?"

"No, cause you don't get it. I'm talking about what fucking Ildefonso says – "

"Gus, please try to keep it under control in the house."

"OK. I said OK!"

Babs returned to the sink and the silverware heaped over the drain-hole. If she ignored him, he would calm down.

"When I went to get him, it was like he was totally wacked. Fucking guy was passed out on his bed in the middle of the afternoon."

"Well, *you* were drunk."

"Yea, but I wasn't saying shit and punching the dashboard. He put a fucking dent in it. I'll wash those. I'm telling you, they won't fit. Christ, Babs, just look how full the rack on top is..."

"Honey, it's forks and knives. Just switch the plates around, OK?"

"Well, why didn't you say so?" Gus stared at the plates in the washer. "Anyways, I told him about how Huff wasn't doing squat and how nobody was helping us find Alicia and he acted like it was no big thing and she would just come home without anybody going out and looking for her, which really fucking pissed me off."

"I think Chief Huff will. He'll have to."

"Have to *what?*"

"Try to find her." Babs laid her apron on the counter and put her arms around her husband. "I'm tired. And Theresa can't keep playing with Dommie when she's still got homework."

"I'm getting to the best part."

Babs rested her chin on the top of Gus's head, which she thought was a cute thing to do.

"It's like he's trying to prove something. Diego, right? Like Tommy-Tom ain't the only one who don't take no shit. So when we get to Freddie Friedrich's, he tells me to wait in the van, he's gonna go talk to him all by himself. What do I care? Let him go, right? Then I notice there's nobody there. No cars, no lights on, *nothin.* So, I'm waiting, and I'm waiting, *and* I'm waiting, and I'm starting to think, *What's he doing back there, taking a fucking dump?* Then I start worrying the fat mother had a heart-attack or something. He comes back and he says *fucking drive.* He never says *fucking* anything, so I know something's up."

"What?" said Babs, not having been listening very carefully.

"Fucking Ildefonso goes and lights the fucking body shop on fire, with me sitting there. And, guess what? I'm the mother who's got the gripe with the guy who runs the place and everybody fucking knows it!"

Babs turned and looked out the kitchen window at the yard next door: Kellaway, who was old, was standing on his back steps with his shirt off, smoking a cigarette. She thanked God it was dusk and she couldn't see much of him.

"I don't get it."

"There's nothing to get," said Gus. "If anybody asks, you know what happened."

There was a standing-lamp in Diego Ildefonso's office at home which resided between his recliner and desk. It shed a dim but warm and comforting light. He felt safe in this room and always left the door just slightly ajar, so he could hear Dolores and Roland moving about.

Diego listened to the radiator softly clicking below the window. Tomorrow, or the next day, there would be a strange small voice in the house. They would keep little Billy close until Val felt better, which probably wouldn't be any time soon. Life was becoming endlessly unpredictable, and it had all begun with a perfectly mundane evening out at the fair. Hopefully, no one had seen him with Gus that afternoon. Gus would be questioned about the fire, and he would have an alibi. The horror would be if his alibi were Diego Ildefonso. Why had he ever allowed himself to trust two such incorrigible men as Gus and Tommy-Tom? Because they made him feel he belonged. And because they allowed him to feel superior.

He gazed at the telephone on his desk. It was time to call Gilbey. He eased from the recliner into his chair, straightened the stack of bills laid out on his desk, picked up the phone and dialled.

"Gilbey Residence." It was the young woman.
"Hello, it's Diego Ildefonso. Francis asked me to call."
"Oh, hi. You met me today. I'm Nina. Just a sec."
Ice cubes clinking in his glass, Gilbey came shuffling over. "Ildefonso?"
"Yea...hello."
"How's tricks?"
He hadn't thanked Gilbey for the tip: twenty crummy dollars bestowed on a poor shoe salesman. "I neglected to thank you for – "
"No need. I probably shouldn't tell you this but I abhor paying taxes. I like to experience my altruism firsthand, not imagine someone else giving my money away frivolously."
"They take it out of my salary."
"Pity."
"Here's one for you – what's socialism?"
"You tell me," Gilbey eventually replied.
"A hole in the ground to bury yourself in. Only the government provides the shovel." Diego wasn't laughing, and neither was Gilbey.
"Government," muttered Gilbey. "You know, we're just *that* close to living in a communist state. What'll be left?"
"Only the distractions provided by the higher echelons to keep us dopey. Our kids are growing up even dopier."
"Hmmm...Would you say I'm among these higher echelons?"
"How should I know?"
"Well then, if you don't mind, would you kindly name me some of these individuals?"
Diego caught himself shifting in his chair. "I don't know names. Executives. They run the big corporations. They control everything. You know the kind. Ever hear of the Bank of International Settlements? They ran the Second World War."
"Of course," said Gilbey.
"Do you know who Puhl was?"
"The Nuremberg trials. A banker."
"You've got it. And now he works for Chase Manhattan."
"How do you know these things?"
"I study."

"Good for you, Ildefonso. Now you know where to put your money."

This brought jaundiced laughter from both men. Gilbey wasn't in the least as infantile as he pretended.

"And here I am in Hoboken," said Diego.

"People don't know what they're up against, do they?"

"Basically, they don't know anything."

"Like your employers."

"They think they know about *merchandising shoes*. They'd sell anything to anybody, even if it's of an inferior quality."

"Like the bedroom slippers you sold me?"

"That's my job."

"Nina's mother hasn't any taste anyway. She'll love them, all of them. Even though she won't admit it. You're an honest man, Ildefonso. You may be somewhat deluded, but at least you feel passionately."

"Don't kid yourself. I don't feel anything."

"But you've seen things. Like in Spain, and Italy..."

"Yea, I've seen things."

"Here too?"

"Yea. A few things."

"And I guess you know that Communism is destined to fail everywhere in the world but here, because people here don't know what's happening and they don't care."

Diego felt a strange flush of contentment, as if he were listening to himself making a speech on the radio.

"They only want to know about themselves," Gilbey went on. "Like whether they're pretty, or too fat, or spending too much money for something. They couldn't care less about actually fitting into the world, or what responsibilities that might entail. And they *really* don't want to know how much everyone else in the world has to suffer to enable them to carry on with their glorious experiment. They only want to know how much *they* have to suffer, which is hardly at all. It's an ever advancing form of ignorance. Take your friends for instance, the stupider they get, the more they like it. And the more arrogantly they behave. Communism, our own form of it, is taking over this country. Nobody knows it's communism because they don't call it anything. Oh that's right, I forgot, they call it *freedom.* You know, like in the songs."

"The communists, the utopian communists, would call what you describe *capitalism.*"

"That's what they *tell* us they call it."

"So what do they really call it?"

"The plague."

Diego could hear Dolores running Roland's bathwater. She was humming loudly to herself, which meant she was anxious.

"Ildefonso?"

"Yea? I'm still here, Gilbey."

"You know, your friends are out to fuck you."

"You asked me to call you so you could tell me this?"

"I'm telling you for your own good. You should take your wife and child and leave. Go some place nice. We'd go together."

"What're you talking about?"

"I'd take care of it. You've got better things to do than get fucked over by your ignorant friends."

"Nobody's going to fuck me over."

"Not if you listen to me."

Diego could taste the dread seeping into his mouth. "Go on."

"The Rozzo girl is missing, isn't she?"

"Something like that."

"Well, she's not."

"So where is she?"

"You don't want to know, not at this stage."

"But what's it got to do with me?"

"You're the one she was supposed to be with."

"Me? You don't know what you're talking about."

"Just try to remember one thing: Pretty Feet may not need you, and Hoboken may not need you, but your friends do. Your friends need you very badly. Good timing, my glass is just about empty. Call me again tomorrow night, maybe even a little earlier. I'm serious."

"I know you are."

"Only one thing."

"What's that?"

"I wouldn't say anything about this to your wife. A very bad idea." Gilbey chuckled and hung up.

Diego walked from his office through the living-room and into the tiny bathroom next to Roland's room. There he stood in the harsh light, unable to speak, and watched his wife towelling dry their son's hair, Roland's narrow shoulders slumped forward as if he were asleep on his feet. What a sad little room it was, with its badly painted yellow plaster and faded print of Jesus blessing the poor children of the world.

SEVEN

Sunoco is a very big company, this goes without saying. It employs many thousands of people all over the world, a couple of thousand people in New Jersey alone. Several hundred work at the refinery on the Hackensack River. One of these employees in April of 1977 was a man named Don Fenton. Don Fenton was an odd-jobber, which meant he was shifted from place to place around the refinery doing various chores and wasn't paid very much for his efforts. Just after dawn on April 14th Don was assigned a pick-up truck for the day and told to take a rake and whatever else he needed and make a circuit of the storage tanks, checking to see which ones needed tidying around their bases. The tidying included picking up trash and throwing it in the pick-up truck, digging out weeds and saplings, and raking smooth the gravel laid in below the pipes that fed the tanks. This was a pretty swell job, and Don knew it. He was planning to stretch the job out to two days at least by loafing where he wouldn't be seen and smoking cigarettes. It looked like the rest of the week was going to be a piece of cake, until he found Alicia Rozzo under a black plastic tarpaulin between tanks 9 and 10. As Don said to his boss later that day after the police arrived:

"She was naked and the tarp was all slimy. I wasn't about to just leave her like that, so I put my coat over her."

To which his boss replied:

"Don't tell me. I believe you. The guys you have to convince are those *suits* over there talking to the coroner."

It was not unusual for Diego Ildefonso to have several erections as he slept, or tried to, throughout the night. Increasingly, he awoke to find his wife attending to this matter, either by gently fondling him or, with the advent of morning, by easing herself up and down on his erection with a determined cadence. But as he had come to dream more often now of unpleasant situations, he had also come to dread having to associate these entanglements with his engorged member. For this reason he had hit upon the idea of their Thursday afternoon assignation in the stockroom at Pretty Feet. Having to shift from selling footwear to making love to his wife, Diego was not easily aroused. But he always managed in the end, and often with an amplitude of grace and affection that Dolores found astonishing.

Now, as she lay with his semi-erect penis resting in the palm of her hand, unaware that he had been awake for some time, Dolores was mildly startled when Diego suddenly rolled onto his side, his mouth only inches from her ear, and said, "You don't know how bad it is between me and Gus."

"I don't have to tell you what I think of Gus," she groaned.

Diego knew she would anyway.

Dolores tucked his penis back in his pajamas and reached for the glass of water she kept on the beside table. After a sip or two, she repositioned herself then began:

"He's a little bully. He should be in the Mafia. He's the kind of guy they get to threaten people who owe money."

"A loan shark."

"Whatever they call it. And he's a braggart."

"I wouldn't deny that."

"And vain and narcissistic, and Babs not only puts up with it, she encourages it. Most likely, it's what enables him to perform sexually. Babs acting like that. I know, you should get up. There's a fresh bar of soap on the back of the toilet."

"Gus torched Friedrich's."

"He did what?"

"We went over there – I know, it was stupid, but I went. Nobody was there and he went around back and from the smell of him poured out some diesel fuel or something and lit the office on fire. I wouldn't be surprised if the whole place burned down."

"What did you do?"

"I was in the van. I didn't *see* him."

"Then what?"

"I got out of the van and walked back to the shop. That's when I called you."

"What, all the way?"

"I didn't have the money for a taxi. I'd spent all my money taking Val and little Billy home."

"Some days nothing makes any sense."

"What's that supposed to mean?" Diego nervously rubbed his face, as if to clear the crust of sleep from his eyes, and Dolores shifted to her side of the bed. She lowered her feet onto the carpet and, as he carried on talking, stared at the ceiling. "Listen, there's something else. You know, it's fine to care for people when they need you. That's what you do, you care for your friends. But does anybody do that for us? Who does Val call when she wants someone to take little Billy?"

"I called *her*, remember?" Dolores leaned over wearily on the bed.

"That's not what I'm saying."

"I know what you're saying."

Diego shifted closer. "I'll tell you something. I don't believe that black fellow broke the Fischer boy's neck. I believe Tommy-Tom did."

"And who did all that you described to Tommy-Tom?"

"The black fellow, but probably defending the Fischer boy from Tommy-Tom. You remember little Stanley, *little Stanley Fischer?* Well, he's a homosexual now, who dresses like a girl. They started out at The Jewel."

Dolores rose and anxiously began smoothing out the covers on her side of the bed. "But what was he doing? I mean, what was he doing with this boy Stanley?"

"It may be why..." Diego hadn't really thought about this before "...you know, Val and Tommy-Tom don't get along so good. They say a lot of men who don't know they're homosexual, or can't accept it, are disturbed."

"But to break somebody's neck?"

"He's violent. Val and Tommy-Tom aren't exactly the most refined people we know, are they?"

"Fine. Are you saying you don't want us to take Billy, because of that?"

"What?"

Plucking her bathrobe from the chair by the vanity and putting it on, Dolores glanced over the top of the dresser nearby for her hairbrush. "I didn't think so."

"I've already said we should take Billy."

"Thank you." She briskly set about brushing her hair.

"I don't want Roland to absorb what this place is about, what these people are about."

"What are we supposed to do?"

"I'll tell you what. *Get out of Hoboken.*"

"You're practically shouting."

"I am not. But this is one thing that really pisses me off. How these people *pride* themselves on being stupid. It would be one thing if this were Georgia or Idaho or some place where all they have is fried food and church, but we're on the steppes of Manhattan."

"I'm going to fix Roland his juice." Dolores headed for the door.

"Not so fast." Diego swung himself out of bed and strode purposefully across the room.

"Diego, don't."

"Don't what?"

"*You know.*"

"I have something to tell you."

"Why can't it wait until later?"

He looked into her eyes, which struck him yet again as being very beautiful. She turned to go into the kitchen, but he gently restrained her.

"You look so pretty, like the photograph your mother has of you in the hallway, when you played Mary in the Christmas play."

She kissed him and headed for the kitchen. Before he got into the shower Diego listened to hear if Dolores would begin humming as she sliced the oranges. But he heard only the blade lightly creasing the cutting-board.

Tommy-Tom Nolan was loaded on morphine. His thoughts thudded in his brain as one after the other they struck the firmness of the rear bumper on the Flintstones' pitted car. Sitting in the back seat waiting for Fred and Barney to return from the Rubbles' house, Tommy-Tom eventually realized what stupid thing they'd done to bring this thudding about: they'd parked too close to Godzilla – or whatever that supposedly cute spotted dinosaur was called – who was visiting one of their neighbors, and the thing was flicking its tail angrily against the back of the car. It was annoying, to say the least. Disgusted, Tommy-Tom only very dimly registered the pain deep in his throat. But something else was going on. Something almost equally annoying. Someone was relentlessly kneading his hand. This someone was a woman who had stolen unseen into Intensive Care. She was what Tommy-Tom would call *a spook*. He spied her through the crust of his lashes. Due to the woman's peculiar make-up, he apprehended Alicia Rozzo. But this person was older, and nicer.

"Bootsy killed the little faggot," said Tommy-Tom.

All the woman heard was the dried up blood and phlegm crackling on his lips. Seeing him awaken, she was thrilled with what she thought she had accomplished. Eyes brimming with tears, she softly chanted, "Know the light that breathes within your mind is the self-same light that breathes throughout the universe...breathe in, breathe out, breathe in..."

But Tommy-Tom was already back in nada-land bowling with Fred and Barney.

Again Roland found himself having breakfast with his father at Florescu's Continental Pastries.

"I'm a little confused," he said.

"About what?" Diego replied.

"About the value of having the Nolan boy stay with us under the present circumstances."

"I'm sure he won't be any trouble."

"Oh no, it's not that. It's what we have to offer him."

"How do you mean? He'll eat what the rest of us eat. We may even go to Bernardi's one night. And as far as the sleeping arrangements go, he should be perfectly comfortable in my office."

"But no one's allowed in your office."

"I'll make an exception."

"But he won't be allowed to touch anything, will he?"

"There's not much that's lying out, and we'll keep the closet locked. How's that?"

"Sounds iffy. What about your photographs of the bombing?"

"They're on hooks on the walls. I doubt he can reach them."

"I can."

"Oh?"

"Yea, sometimes I take them down and look at them."

"But you're not supposed to be in there."

"I have another confession to make too."

Florescu was lingering on the periphery, waiting for Mr. Ildefonso to cease dandling his cigar on the handle of his espresso cup so he could take it away. Realizing that Diego hadn't an ashtray, Florescu placed one before him and departed with the cup and saucer.

"Go on," said Diego, trying not to sound too stern.

"I go in there to meditate."

Diego thought this over. "Meditate on what?"

"Being in Spain. I look at the photographs of the bombing and pretend I'm there. It's supposed to be healthy to imagine what your parents were like when they were you. I mean – "

"I understand. But who told you it was healthy?"

"You know, the guy on television."

"What guy?"

"Mr. Rogers. The guy who always takes his shoes off. He has lots of good ideas. He showed us some old photographs and told us we could imagine being the people in the photographs, even though the people were dead – I mean, they must have been dead. The photographs were old, older than yours are."

"Sounds reasonable. You know that photograph I have taped on the inside of my closet door, in my office?"

"Vesuvius."

"Right. That's an important volcano I studied but never experienced firsthand. Do you remember me telling you about the other volcano, the one I saw erupting?"

"In 1950," said Roland, confounding his father.

"Right again."

"But you didn't tell me the whole story. You only told me you'd seen it on fire. You told me you'd tell me the rest later, when I was older. Well, I am older."

"Not that much older."

"How much older do I have to be?"

"About the age I was then. About 20, let's say."

"I don't think I can wait that long. And what if something happens to you in the meantime?"

"Like what?"

"You name it."

"I'd rather not."

"Pop, I'm really enjoying this, but it's getting to be about that time."

"Thanks for reminding me."

"And your cigar's gone out again."

Diego wasn't about to be rushed off to work, not this morning. He took his time relighting his cigar, all the while watching Roland watching him. "How would you like to see that volcano?"

"Vesuvius?"

"No, the one I saw."

"Do you have a photograph of that one too?"

"No, I mean the actual volcano."

"Where is it?" Roland glanced slyly at his father. "Pop, don't tell me Wildwood Amusement Park, OK?"

Diego had to laugh.

"Is that funny?" Roland seemed genuinely surprised.

"You're always one step ahead of the game."

"I am? I guess that's good, isn't it?"

"Roland, I've made up my mind." The lad stared at him, his wide and empty face gradually contracting inward, as if something bitter had emerged in his mouth. "What's the matter?"

"We're not going to adopt Billy, are we?"

"I should hope not. No, I've made up my mind. We're going to Sicily – for a nice long vacation."

"What? Where the volcano is? Is that wise?"

Roland's questions came all in a rush, as he was becoming more and more excited, the soles of his shoes tapping wildly against the tiled floor.

"Go home now," said Diego. "This is our secret, alright? And stay on the side-walk. And don't forget to look both ways before you cross the street, those idiots are heading into New York now."

Roland came around the table and put his arms around his father. He felt like an enormous squishy animal bound up in a tent made of some fragrant material.

"I love you, Pop," he said.

Before ringing the Rozzos' bell, Chief Leon Huff tried to remember Alicia from the evening he'd encountered her at the fair and later observed her behavior at St. Mary's Hospital, but all he could remember was Tommy-Tom Nolan flirting with her as Mikie Rozzo's broken body lay at their feet.

"Oh Christ," groaned Gus, when he opened the door.

Huff waited to be asked in, but wasn't. Gus only walked ahead of him down the hallway and into the kitchen, where he and Babs were drinking coffee.

"You want coffee?" said Gus.

"Thanks. Sorry I couldn't make it yesterday," Huff apologized, "but I had to look after your buddy Tommy-Tom."

"Yea, I gotta go up to U.C. and see him myself. You wanna sit down?" Gus was again seated at the kitchen table, Babs sighing over an insufficiency of caffeine in the background.

"All I've got's decaf," she said, glancing over her shoulder. "You want mine? I hardly touched it."

"No, that's OK," said Huff. "Could we go into the livingroom where it's not so bright?"

"Whatever suits you," said Gus. He shrugged at Babs before leading the Chief deeper into the house.

"She should join us," said Huff.

When they were all comfortably seated in the living-room, Huff began: "I guess you know about the fire at Friedrich's Auto Body – well, we can talk about that later, on another day, when we all have more time. I guess you're not working today, huh?"

"No," answered Gus, "I've got a head about the size of my asshole. We were over at my mama's yesterday and everybody got into the punch. It was sad and everything but we all pulled together. Well, except for Tommy-Tom and Ildefonso and them."

"Ildefonso strikes me as a pretty dedicated guy," said Huff. "I mean, to his friends, like Tommy-Tom and his wife. He took her and her kid home from the hospital in a taxi."

"I bet that wasn't cheap," said Babs. "We heard all about Tommy-Tom."

"He's been looking out for me too," offered Gus.

"How's that?" asked Huff.

"He went over to Freddie's with me yesterday – to try and straighten out the mess between Freddie's kid and Alicia."

"I didn't know there was a mess," said Huff.

"I told you'se, his kid's fucking nuts for her." Gus laughed to communicate his contempt for the boy.

"For Alicia," said Huff. He wondered where the baby was. This woman, Babs, she looked to be about thirty, although he knew she was older. She had a nice fat face and her tits were big. She was sassy and she didn't care who knew it. She was staring as him, as if to say *Don't feel bad, every guy wants to fuck me sooner or later.*

"You probably don't want to know who set that fire, do you?" barked Gus, again laughing.

"That's not why I'm here."

"Tell him," said Gus, and reached over and squeezed his wife's knee. They were sitting on the sofa together, a plastic tricycle with a Woody Woodpecker head on the front fender lying on its side between them. "Babs, tell the Chief."

"Whose bike is that?" asked Huff, not wanting Babs to lie to him so early in the game, and most decidedly not before he had told them about their daughter's death.

"It was Mikie's," said Gus.

"You don't have to tell me anything if you don't want to," cautioned Huff.

"It's OK," said Babs. There was no shutting her up. Glancing at Gus, she became more emphatic. "Yea, I do. It was Diego Ildefonso. Gus told me he got real upset and started throwing matches at the place, or whatever."

"He threw some gasoline around. Remember?" said Gus.

Huff saw the color rise in Babs Rozzo's cheeks. She glared angrily at her husband, as if to say *So why tell me to do the talking, you fucker?*

"How did it go...?" asked Huff.

"He didn't mean to burn anything down. He just wanted to let Friedrich know we're serious," said Gus.

"About what?"

"About his kid keeping his hands off Alicia. Go ask Ildefonso, if you don't believe me."

Huff guessed he'd seen this sort of rank insolence before, but he couldn't quite remember where, perhaps on television, but he wasn't even so sure about that. Then it came to him: his kids acted like this when they were bickering between themselves or talking to their friends on the telephone. Gus smiled at his wife, who didn't smile back.

"Detective Sergeant Molloy can take down your statement later," Huff informed them.

"I think I hear Dommie," said Babs, and left the room.

Huff was playing with his rings. Gus hated all these gold rings Huff wore like they were war medals or something. One was only a high school ring. The Chief came over, set the tricycle on the carpet, and sat down next to him. It gave Gus the creeps to have Leon Huff, another guy who wasn't his friend, sitting so close. Maybe the Chief was a fairy. That would be a laugh. Some Marines were fairies, Tommy-Tom said so. Gus got the feeling the Chief was going to hold his hand or something.

"I came here to talk to you about Alicia," said Huff, softly.

"You know where she is?"

The Chief nodded. But he didn't say anything. It was then that he reached out and took Gus's hand.

In all of the photographs Alicia's fine long fingers pointed out at impossible angles, the joints snapped. Her naked body lay on a bed of gravel, her arms making a diamond shape, her broken wrists pressed to the top of her head. Gus was sickened by this detail, by the brutality with which his daughter's hands had been twisted into the pose of an oriental dancer. His eyes trailed down her body, taking in the blackened bruises on her breasts, belly, and thighs. When the teeth marks around her pudenda had fully registered Gus began to vomit. Chief Huff set his hat in Gus's lap to catch the contents of his stomach. He didn't expect Gus to be grateful for this, but Gus was, taking the

Chief's hat into the back yard to wash it out with the garden hose. Huff was relieved he didn't have to witness Babs Rozzo's reaction to her daughter's death. Gus said he wanted to tell his wife himself, without anyone else present.

The Chief left and Gus stood staring down at Babs, who had fallen asleep with little Dominic fastened to her nipple. He remembered Alicia as a baby fastened to that very same nipple fourteen years before. Two of their children were dead. This was impossible. No one lost two children in one week. What had they done to deserve having two of their kids killed? God was a fucker. Gus had always known this, but could never admit it, not even to himself. Babs believed everybody had a score card, that God was keeping track of what you did that was good and what you did that was bad. It was stupid. All you had to remember was to do more good things than bad – if you wanted to wind up in heaven. Everybody knew about the score card. It was a joke. The best way to score plus points with God was to have as many kids as possible and hand them over. Gus had gotten beyond his problem with fucking for the sake of having kids by always concentrating on how much he liked to make Babs say and do bad things. Gus wished you could make love at a time like this rather than have to say anything. They should be allowed to make another baby exactly like Alicia, but it didn't work that way. Alicia would never squirm around again. Never. If she did something naughty – well, she was just too slippery to catch. She was a squirmer. It was like she had some kind of amazing oil on her, like an eel. Babs was better off asleep. He would leave a note telling her to call him at his mother's house. He would tell his mother about Alicia first and then, with his mother there to help, wait for Babs to call. Maybe his mother would even do it for him.

Dolores Ildefonso had discovered that her prettiest panties were dirty. She'd returned home from being with Diego the previous Thursday and had dropped them back in the drawer without examining them first. The light in the kitchen was the best for hand-washing things and she was confident the panties would dry if she hung them in the back window, which faced the sun in the east. When the telephone rang, Dolores noted that it was now approaching eleven.

"There was some *woman* sitting with him this morning when the nurse comes in," Val began.

"'Some woman?'"

"Yea. Nobody knows who."

"Did you see her?"

"No, the doctor called Ray told me. He's the only one I know. He called to ask me. How should I know? I told him I don't know who Tommy-Tom knows, he could know anybody."

"I wonder."

"What? I can't hear you. Are you doing something?"

Val was drunk again, or she was still drunk.

"Did you get some sleep last night?" asked Dolores.

"I was asleep when Doctor Ray called. He woke me up."

"Where's Billy?"

"I don't know. At the playground, I guess. Remember me telling you about Ralph? We had a real fun time. I'm meeting him again this afternoon. He likes me."

"Where?"

"The Ramada Inn. I'm in Atlantic City already. Look – "

"All the way down there? Atlantic City's out from Philly."

Now Dolores heard Val giggling, then lighting a cigarette, then slushing her drink in her mouth, then giggling again. After blowing more smoke, Val said, "Dolores, you're so dumb. I'm not in Atlantic City or anything, I'm here in my place. How could I get down there so fast? I *just said* I was asleep. Ralph's coming over. And then we're going out somewheres."

"What about Billy?"

"You thought I'd go all the way down to Atlantic City just for a date?! What else would I call you for when I'm getting myself ready? I called to get you to take Billy. I got Ralph coming over."

"That's fine. How about if Billy and I call you later?"

"I got your number written down, but I always remember everybody's number. It's in my purse, along with a lot of other junk I didn't think I'd ever need. But I need it now, even the eye-liner!" Val's laughter was teary.

"I'd like to meet Ralph sometime."

"Oh, you will. He's great. I'll call you."

That winter, Dolores had begun entrusting Roland to Mrs. Finkelstein on Thursday afternoons after school. Mrs. Finkelstein liked the company, but Roland seldom stayed very long before asking to be allowed out into her garden. Mrs. Finkelstein was the longest surviving tenant in the building – her lease dated from 1926 – and it was in that year that she and her husband had built the shed that still stood against the brick wall that separated her garden from the alleyway behind the apartment building. The shed had a work plank along the back wall which was lowered into position and secured with two lengths of chain. There were also two stools in the shed and a deck chair with a rotten canvas seat. The deck chair remained folded up and partially hidden behind the shed's door, which swung inwards and was invariably fastened open with a long metal hook. It gave the impression, due to the encumbrance of Mr. Finkelstein's cotton gardening jacket, its pockets still bearing various rusty implements, of a small crouching figure. Mrs. Finkelstein had draped the jacket over the chair's wooden frame the day her husband had dropped to the earthen floor with a massive coronary and died. It had remained there ever since. For Roland, Mr. Finkelstein's gardening jacket served as a manifestation of the unacceptably willful James.

His head silhouetted dramatically against the paint-spattered panes of the shed's only window, Roland rocked precariously back and forth on the stool at the far end of the workplank.

"Don't scrape!" he ordered.

"I'm not," said James, who cowered in the dust, his obsequious gaze fixed on the door's lower hinge.

"And don't talk back."

James was mute.

"That's it, stare at nothing. Maybe you'll listen better that way. Now, when Mrs. Nolan said Mom could bring Billy over this afternoon, it wasn't just a figure of speech. Billy is definitely coming over. That means it will be our job to entertain him. And you know what that means. It means playing with him without hurting him. Billy Nolan cries at anything. He cries and he wets his bed and he chews with his mouth open."

"Yuck," said James.

"He'll even be using our toilet. Come to think of it, he'll probably pee in Pop's office. James, do you understand?!"

"Yes, I understand."

"Well, you better, because I don't need Chief Huff coming over here anymore on account of you."

"That's not fair," James argued, in a whisper. "I didn't do anything."

"Of course you didn't *do anything*. Ha, ha, ha. Just remember one thing, dickhead, if you want to come along to Sicily with us you better not get finger-printed for anything before we leave or they'll throw you in jail over there. Chief Huff knows all the police everywhere, even in Sicily. You can bet your fucking fat bippy on that."

"I could join the Mafia," said James. "Couldn't I?"

"You can only join if you've killed somebody, and you're saying you didn't. You go to the Mafia and tell them you want to join and not kill somebody first and they'll get a plastic bag and put it over your head until your eyes pop out. I *said...*"

"I'm looking at the wall!" whined James.

"Good. Now, when Billy Nolan gets here, first we ask him if he ever had sex. And I don't mean by spitting on a picture of a naked girl in a magazine and rubbing his finger around in it. I mean by at least using one of his mother's things to make blood in a glass or some other see-through container. He won't know anything. His mother is made out of wax, with an egg-beater for a brain, and his father is going to have to buy batteries to make himself talk. So you can bet they're not going to tell him what he should expect. Our job is to sex-educate him. Do you understand?!"

"Fully," said James.

"Good. Now, get up and go out and get the rat. I want to work on it in here." Roland gazed out the door of the shed at Mrs. Finkelstein, who was mixing something liquid and blue in a yellow plastic bucket. "Forget it, I'm going myself."

Roland ventured out into the daylight.

"Do you want me to stir?" he asked Mrs. Finkelstein, as he shuffled noisily up behind her, so as not to frighten her in her deafness.

Now Dolores, who had her own key to Pretty Feet, stood at the shop's very center, listening. It was just seconds past three o'clock. Diego entered unceremoniously through the door at the rear of the premises. She seated herself and waited to be served. He advanced slowly from the stockroom, knelt silently before her, and set about removing her shoes, which were far more elegant than anything the shop had to offer. As he slipped her shoes from her feet, noting that her stockings were of the sheerest and finest quality, his eyes lingered on her legs. Her dress, which was intended to be buttoned from neck to hem, had been allowed to fall open in two folds which lay parted over her knees. Regardless of whatever surreptitious encouragement this casualness might suggest, Diego Ildefonso's manner was courtly, until he came to touch her feet.

At first, his hand rested only for the merest fraction of a second too long on her instep, which he knew to be unnaturally sensitive. Seconds later, her foot held delicately on point, his other hand gripped the shivering tendons just above the taut calf. Now Dolores grew more seductive. This she accomplished in several ways: by the almost imperceptible shifting of her weight upon her hips, by the slow movement of her hands upon the rolled edge of the banquette, and by the arching of her back. At last Diego's hand, now beneath her slip, closed down gently on the swell of her thigh. She sighed with the mildness of his touch as his thumb brushed a wisp or two of hair along the elasticized inner edge of her panties.

"I would prefer the doors were bolted," she whispered, and he rose to do her bidding, and to pull the shades.

Behind the shelves in the stockroom was a recliner – it had been brought in several months before when Diego had been suffering with a bad back – and it was upon this squarish mass of rubber and steel that he now lay, watching his wife disrobe. It wasn't long before he had eased his erection out into the dim light, where it lay for her delectation. Dolores removed all her clothes. Standing over him, her breasts so seldom appreciated from this angle, her thighs more inviting too, she reached down to touch him. Diego rose from the recliner and took her in his arms. "Don't close your eyes," he said. And she pulled him down, onto the floor. In fits and starts, he too was eventually naked.

As he moved over her, his huge pale back was, in its roundness, like the dome of the earth as it drifts in the utter darkness of the universe. But Diego Ildefonso was wholly there, and Dolores drank in his mouth, and he filled the emptiness inside her, effortlessly.

EIGHT

Bootsy and his Uncle Tookus had driven out to Lake Mattamuskeet to see if the swans had flown off yet. Thousands of the ungainly creatures converged on the vast body of water each winter, its shallows guarded by countless dead cypresses rising up out of the stillness like gigantic fish skeletons. As they drove down the stretch of road that bisected the gloomy expanse, the sky was overcast and the lake the color of dead leaves. Bootsy worried the butt of the cigarette he had taken from the pack his uncle kept on the front seat. He was embarrassed because Uncle Tookus had told him not to go to New York, that New York was a trap for men like Bootsy and himself, men who wanted what they couldn't have, and shouldn't. Bootsy wanted to say something to let his uncle know that his time in New York had been worthwhile, and that he had returned of his own volition, that the city hadn't got the better of him.

"What it is is, nobody knows how nobody else sees it," said Bootsy.

Uncle Tookus waited, his jaw pitched high, his few remaining upper teeth gently grinding down on the empty gums below. He had known Bootsy all his life, and he knew when Bootsy turned philosophical he was usually in some kind of trouble.

"Bootsy, you ain't tellin me nothin. Who's this mother goes around messin with some weaker man? You talkin about *you?* Y'all knows why Goldie got a pistol stuck in his mouth and you ain't got no father no more."

"He was bein hit on for money he owed. Mama told me that. He lost his job and he borrowed some money."

"Your mama don't know. He was messin in smack. You messin in blow. I know what you do. You bringin that shit down here. They don't tolerate no drugs around here. Sure as dogs eat shit, them white-assed motherfuckers is gonna bring the law on you. It's them white kids gonna fuck you up."

"Fuck me up? I don't even know no white kids around here do blow. I don't know nobody."

"What about from high school?"
"I been long gone. Shit man, you don't know."
"So what's it?"
"I'm takin another one of these, OK?"
"Smoke away."

Bootsy looked out at the lake. It lay on either side of them and went on forever. Bootsy knew he was destined to drift on that lake after he died, he knew he was destined to drift over the featureless silvery surface of infinity, making that slow loop-de-loop like a slug on a ribbon of cold steel. If he was going to die with the long end of the white man's cross shoved up his ass, he would do it where nobody could see him. He would roam the fields surrounding this lake like a scavenging dog, staying clear of those people who'd just as soon smile at you as gas you. When he got tired of that he would find a lonely tree, wait for the birds to start singing before dawn, and put the noose around his neck. On the other hand, if nobody ever found out about any of it, he might just be left to think about what he did or didn't do for as long as he lived. Bootsy figured that even if he did get lucky, he might still like wandering around that lake until he fell down dead.

"Uncle Tookus, I don't know what I did. I got this white man does all the cleanin in the hotel where I been stayin. He wants to be my main man and shit. You know. I give him some cocaine from time to time. I wasn't dealin no cocaine, I just got some from a guy in the hotel who was crippled up and asked me to bring girls in for him. He give me the blow for doin that. I'll cut it short. We go out to New Jersey this night to meet the man's wife and get it on. I gave him some toot and he got sick on it, but he kept to his plan."

"Y'all didn't do nothin with his wife?"

"No, *I did not do nothin with his wife.* Man, what kind of a dumb ass you think I am?"

"Bootsy, you don't know nothin bout how they can behave. Married people, white married people, can take you straight motherfuckin down."

"I didn't do that. I went out with him and the girl-boy from the bar. Check it out – this fuckin honkie didn't know the girl-boy was a girl-boy. He's a big macho man and gets real tired of gettin his dick sucked all the time, so he wants to be the big pitcher, only this bitch don't catch, and he comes up with her balls. Wants me to go into the kitchen and get a knife."

"Slow down. He wants you to get a knife?"

"Dead straight. He wants me to cut her, man."

"A mother like that *knows* it's a girl-boy. He's just out to cut her."

"Well, that there might be what it was, but he was workin the thing. You never seen a man go after anythin so harmless as this poor little stumpy girl, and this mother is strong, and he's fuckin loaded."

"Where were you at?"

"Sittin across the room. Until I see what he's doin. He's smashin her face in with his head, and he's punchin her *balls* and shit. I went after him. I took his glass and broke it and I cut his head and then, cause there was no stoppin the mother, I cut his neck. And he was still goin. Then he stop. It must of been when he seen so much of his blood. I got out of there, man, and come back to New York, but I didn't go in, I just got on the train." Bootsy had just lit the wrong end of another cigarette. "Did I do the right thing? Man, I don't know what I did was right."

Uncle Tookus pulled the old Chevy over onto one of the patches that served as fishing ramps down to the lake. There was a white boy, about twelve years old, with a line in the water, his bicycle lying in the long grass. He looked up for a brief moment, saw that the men in the car were black, and instantly feigned disinterest. Now Uncle Tookus took a cigarette and lit it. Bootsy tore the scorched filter off his and relit it. They sat in silence for a while, watching the boy and searching the horizon for migrating swans.

"You never saw nobody die?" asked Uncle Tookus.

"Never did," answered Bootsy.

"It was the macho man you cut, while he was beatin on the other one."

"He beat her bad," said Bootsy. Then he mumbled, "Now his wife and kid know," and started to cry.

Uncle Tookus gazed up at the sun visor over the windshield. There was a playing card shoved under the clear plastic that made a pocket along one side. It had a kneeling model on it, her nipples covered with two bright red pasties, her g-string a vivid blue, her hair a mane of white, reminding Uncle Tookus of Hopalong Cassidy's horse. Her smile was like a tiny silver airplane shining out to reassure all men of the certitude of their determination to live life to the fullest.

"If one or the other dies," he finally said, "somebody is gonna put the blame on you. You know the white man is gonna put the blame on you. And your fairy..."

"Shirlee," volunteered Bootsy, eyes staring blindly down at the cigarette he held in his lap.

Uncle Tookus rested his hand on the back of Bootsy's neck. "Your fairy gonna be too afraid not to say anythin."

"*And* a fuckin police chief saw me with Tommy-Tom, at the bar," admitted Bootsy.

"Man, that says it all," sighed Uncle Tookus. "I don't think you can be around here. Not if you said anythin to anybody at that hotel about being from here or anythin."

"Where can I go?"

"Someplace where they don't cooperate with the law. Someplace where they have the black man's law all by itself."

Bootsy, his face a welter of frowns, stared at his Uncle Tookus: as far as he knew, no such place existed.

"What about Haiti?" said Uncle Tookus. "You can get on a boat from here. There's boats don't have anythin to do now but cruise. I know the Moore brothers don't fish all the time, and Henry's boy is out at Caswell for stealin a hi-fi. I think we should go over there. We don't have to tell Henry nothin, just talk to him."

"Where do I get any money to get set up?"

"From me. You take the money I got for sellin my gas station. I'll meet you in Haiti next year or some time. Every since my Dottie passed on I been wantin to travel. Now I got a place to go. I didn't ever have no place in mind. Except Paris again, and I don't have enough for that."

Uncle Tookus flung his cigarette out the window and backed the Chevy up onto the road. They carried on heading east in the direction of Engelhard, on the marshy fringes of which the Moore brothers had situated their wholesale fish business in 1951. When Bootsy glanced back he saw the white kid who'd been fishing pick up Uncle Tookus's cigarette from the macadam and casually put it in his mouth.

Having to confront Diego Ildefonso with Gus Rozzo's bullshit upset Chief Leon Huff. The guy was meant to be the fat man's friend. There was a case to be made for tragedy having deranged Rozzo's typically uneventful frame of mind, but Huff had the distressing feeling that Gus Rozzo hadn't been feeling anything. If he had, it wasn't enough. Vomiting was one thing – Huff gagged when he smelled Brussels sprouts cooking – and solemnly enduring such pain was another. There was no solemnity to Gus Rozzo's grieving. Babs Rozzo was another matter altogether. It seemed that as long as she had a new baby to suckle she could more or less contentedly endure anything. But there was something even worse, something unhealthy gluing these men together – Rozzo and Ildefonso and Tommy-Tom Nolan – and it wasn't the usual gunk one found in so-called criminal minds. By the time Huff reached Pretty Feet, or so he imagined, Ildefonso would have returned home, or perhaps stopped off somewhere for a drink. Now he pictured Mrs. Ildefonso, whom he had instantly liked, and who, he assured himself, would never have committed herself to a man capable of such stupidity. He parked in front of Pretty Feet. The shop was dark, shades drawn.

It had been a mistake to have his mother tell Babs about Alicia's death on the telephone. So Gus asked his mother to go over to his house to try to quiet Babs down and make amends, if she could, for his insensitive behavior.

Mama Rozzo had always known her youngest son to be a coward, but she forgave him because, basically, it was her fault for having coddled and pampered him all his life. If he had been born a girl, as she had hoped and prayed, no one would ever have thought a thing about it. His fragility would have been granted by God.

Gus became anxious moments after his mother had boarded the bus that would take her across town. He picked up a bottle of Suntory at the liquor store, drawn to the whisky by its exotic label, and set off driving aimlessly in his van, the bottle on the seat beside him. After twenty minutes or so, he decided he needed company and guided the vehicle down Willow toward The Jewel. As he passed the shop where Diego worked, he saw Val Nolan. She was weaving along from window to window. Gus stopped and called to her.

"I'm going to meet someone!" she called back.

Gus coasted the van along beside her. "Who? Who're you meeting?"

"A friend, you don't know him, neither does Tommy-Tom."

"What time?"

"When he gets here, he's on his way up from Atlantic City."

This didn't sound right. Gus figured she was just wandering around drunk. She had good reason to. He pulled over and got out. At first, when he tried to take her arm, she pulled away, but then fell into him, nuzzling his hair: she stood nearly a foot taller than Gus, but at that moment her disdain for men shorter than herself didn't surface.

"Val, I gotta tell you something, but I need a drink. You wanna get in the van? I got some whiskey, some expensive stuff."

"I'm going out," she insisted.

"You *are* out. Let's go over to The Jewel..."

"Why?" She was trying to appear pert.

"Because I don't want to have to get you in and out of that thing, it's too high up." Gus now guided her along, one arm circling her narrow back.

"Oh," she said. "OK."

In the parking-lot in front of The Jewel, Gus said, "You're not meeting some guy. You're just fucked up, Val."

"Ask Dolores," blurted Val. "She knows about Ralph!"

"Ralph who?"

"Ralph *Discoverer*."

"Come on, let's go in and sit down."

Once they'd gotten themselves situated in a booth in the back room, Val slumped in the corner, Gus said, "Our little girl's dead. Son of a bitch raped her. He hurt her. I seen pictures of what he did to her."

"*Wha?*" came slurring from Val.

"Some motherfucker killed my baby girl."

"I wanna drink."

"You gotta drink. It's looking right at you."

"Oh. That's OK. It looks nice." Val took a long slurping sip, then ran her fingers through her thinning hair, the fine strands stiff with spray. "I'm waiting for someone."

"Didn't you hear what I said?"

Eyes wide, Val whispered, "Didn't she ever come home?"

"Oh Val," Gus managed, beaten by frustration, and began kissing her hand. He then began sucking her fingers, not individually, but four at once.

"Your mouth feels good cold," she said.

"Where's little Billy?"

"When?"

"Right now."

"Dolores and Diego came and got him."

"Can we go to your place and drink what I've got instead of sitting in this fucking hole?" Gus knew he could do just about anything he wanted with her. "We can tell the guy at the bar about your boyfriend coming."

"He's not a boyfriend," argued Val, "he knows about money and is real professional at what he does. I was with him at the racetrack this winter. He gave me a tip and it really paid off."

"Good," said Gus, and got her up and out, and into the van.

Later, after Gus had made love to Val's mouth, which he imagined he was doing with considerable feeling, he telephoned Babs. Thanks to Val, he had finally found the confidence.

"You won't believe how sorry I am," he said, "I should of told you myself. Do you know how much I love you and the kids?"

"Why can't you come home?" Babs replied.

"Cause I promised to take Val up to see Tommy-Tom, and visiting hours are just about over. I called her from my mom's to volunteer."

Val, who was listening to their conversation while lying on her bed next to Gus, said, "No you didn't. And you can forget about me seeing Tommy-Tom."

Gus had no intention of going home any time soon. His only intention was to have real sex with Val, which he'd wanted to do for a very long time.

"Do you and Billy like your supper?" Dolores asked Roland.

"I can only speak for myself."

"And?" said his father.

"I like the bone-ring in the ham."

"How do you like yours?" Diego now asked little Billy.

"There's no bread for a sandwich."

"This is supper," Dolores gently explained. "Sandwiches are usually for lunch-time."

"I like the Jell-O."

"So do I," said Roland, and smiled broadly at their guest.

Dolores's heart went out to Val's little boy. He seemed so helpless, so forlorn. And he was one of the homeliest children she'd ever seen. He hadn't much of a nose, so that his nostrils were constantly dilated and wet, his eyes were too far apart, giving the impression of wandering disconnectedly, and, for long periods of what appeared to be almost total distraction, his upper teeth clung to his lower lip. Also, consistent with her own apathetic attitude toward life, Val had allowed little Billy's hair to grow too long for the style in which he wore it, which was a lamentable imitation of Tommy-Tom's quiff. Saddest of all, there was absolutely no flush to his skin. His coloring was like skim milk.

There was a knock at the living-room door onto the front stairs. Diego Ildefonso instantly excused himself. Chief Leon Huff stood, hat in hand, silhouetted against the shiny coral pink enamel paint covering everything, every balustrade, every brass knob, every single nailhead.

"I hope I'm not interrupting anything...like your dinner. It smells delicious," said the Chief.

"I'd offer you a place," said Diego, "but we already have one guest."

"Not Gus Rozzo?"

Diego found this allusion mystifying. "No, not Gus. Can I offer you a coffee? Like to come in and sit down?"

"No, I'd rather speak with you out here, if you don't mind."

Diego stepped into the hallway and pulled the door partially closed behind him. He waited, arms crossed over his napkin, one corner of which he'd tucked into his loosened collar.

"I think I know what this is about," he offered.

"It's not about Mikie Rozzo. This is awkward, because it involves you and Gus Rozzo. Any idea what's awkward about it?"

"No." Diego didn't appreciate the Chief's tone.

"Gus and Babs Rozzo have both given me their account of what transpired yesterday afternoon." Now he would be interrupted.

"I don't see what Babs has got to say about it."

"He had her speak for him, at first. Then he gave his own account. He says he feels sorry for you."

"I haven't anything to feel sorry about." As he uttered these words, Diego realized they didn't make any sense.

"You will when I tell you about their daughter Alicia." The Chief watched as Diego Ildefonso unfolded his arms, untucked the napkin, and crossed the hallway to lean with his back to him, hands on the banister. "Do you want me to go on?"

"She's dead, isn't she?"

This the Chief hadn't expected. Now he was doing the job of the Newark Detective Bureau and he wished he weren't. "Is that just a good guess?"

"I've had a bad feeling ever since Monday night," said Diego, turning to confront the Chief, "ever since I was sitting with those kids in their living-room while the rest of them were with Mikie's body. I thought Alicia should have been with me, with the rest of the kids. I don't know why they took her down there."

"She was murdered," said the Chief, "raped and murdered, out at the Sunoco plant, the big one on the Hackensack."

Diego saw Alicia in Tommy-Tom's car. She was pressed up against the gear-shift lever, her arm thrown across Tommy-Tom's back, her fingers playing in the inky curls at the back of his neck. "How did she get out there?"

"We don't know. We thought you might."

"I'm sorry, I don't." Diego wondered where Gus was now, and he remembered how his friend had suffered with Alicia's absence the night Mikie had fallen from the Ferris wheel – it seemed like such a long time ago.

"The Rozzos never did say anything about your boy." The Chief needed some help, he hadn't any idea where to go with this. Hopefully, Ildefonso would show him the way.

"I don't want to contradict anything Gus said. You can tell me whatever you want, but I'm not going to say anything that might create even more problems for them."

Huff admired the fat man. He had will power and he had integrity. Diego Ildefonso was now gazing hopelessly down the hallway, listening to his son and Billy Nolan leaving the kitchen and going out onto the back landing. "It's too dark for them to be going outside now," he said.

As they both listened, they heard Dolores ask the boys to come back inside. Then they heard the television go on.

"You know what he said, don't you?" said the Chief.

"He said I set the fire."

"At this point, it's your word against his."

"I don't want that."

"Nobody does."

"What happens now?"

"What do you want to happen?"

"Nothing. I just want to be left in peace. I want me and my family to be allowed to go about our business without having to worry about Gus Rozzo or anybody else."

"Let's try it like that for a while, until I can get some men out to look for witnesses. This happened in broad daylight, I presume?"

Diego nodded.

"I won't keep you any longer," said the Chief.

"Thanks."

Gilbey had asked Diego to call earlier that evening. Again the young woman called Nina answered the phone. As he waited for Gilbey to come on the line, Diego glanced around his office. Dolores had borrowed a cot from one of their neighbors for little Billy and had plumped it up with a mattress pad and two pillows. It looked so inviting that he was tempted to carry on his conversation with Gilbey while reclining on it, but it undoubtedly would have snapped into several pieces under his weight.

"Ildefonso," said Gilbey. "How's tricks?"

"I hope I'm not calling too early."

"Not at all. Now, where were we?"

"Something about my friends fucking me over."

"Oh yes. Yes, indeed."

"Well?"

"Has your life become somewhat more complicated since we last spoke?"

"You could say that."

"How complicated?"

"You tell me, seeing as you seem to know more about what's going on than I do."

"No, you tell me."

"I've just had some very bad news."

Gilbey waited.

"Let me put it this way, there's been terrible sadness in two of the families we know best this week. We've had to take in a little boy whose father was very badly injured and whose mother isn't coping very well."

"Will the father be alright?"

"No, not really. And the police are involved. It's what *you* might call a sordid matter." Diego told himself not to sound so indignant. "The kind of thing that happens every so often in Hoboken."

"I see. And the other family?"

"There's already been one funeral, and another coming up."

"You don't sound quite like yourself. You sound – what? – too formal or something. Christ, listen to me!"

Gilbey laughed, and Diego laughed too, but it wasn't easy.

"Let's cut the bullshit," said Gilbey.

"What bullshit?" Diego's tongue had begun to thicken.

"I told you I was serious. How do you expect me to help you if you won't tell me the truth?"

"All I know is that a friend of mine is accusing me of burning down some guy's auto body shop – "

"That will be Gus Rozzo."

"You know Gus?"

"Everybody knows Gus."

"Right. Then you probably know that their daughter Alicia has been murdered."

"Let's not forget the bit about her being raped too."

"That's supposed to be funny?"

"No one said it was funny."

"So what's going on?"

"Nothing we can't remedy, I hope."

Previously, Diego hadn't thought of the necessity of hiring a lawyer to protect him from Gus. Asking Gilbey for the money to retain one was suddenly a very real possibility. Obviously, once Chief Huff had organized his case – Jesus, what was he thinking? – *two* cases, arson and murder, he would be very much in demand. Diego pictured himself sitting in the holding room in the courthouse waiting to testify, waiting to be proven a liar, waiting to be sentenced for something he hadn't done. Then he pictured himself staring up at the ceiling of a prison cell, with the dreaded light searing his brain.

Gilbey cleared his throat. "Listen, why don't you drive up here tomorrow evening. We'll spend the weekend together. Nina loves to entertain, at least she says she does. I'll probably be out when you arrive, but she'll be here."

"Only one problem – "

"I know, your wife will wonder what you're up to. So bring her along. Bring your boy along too."

"And we have a house guest. Did I mention our friends' little boy?"

"You did. Bring him along too. The two lads can roam all over the place. You know, woods and streams and the like. And you and I can have a nice long talk."

Diego could hear a certain joy coming into Gilbey's voice, which usually sounded so tired and brittle.

"Watch for 9W off the parkway," Gilbey went on, "then carry on, all the way through town, until you see an open field on your right. You can't miss it. There's a brick chimney standing right in the middle, nothing else – that's what's left of Lee Tires. Take that right, Lescher Road. About a mile on, there'll be a lane off to the left. No sign. Take that lane. Eventually, you'll see the gates. The lane goes on for a long time, through grazing pastures and whatnot. Don't let it fool you. When you see the gates, you'll know you're on target. You'll still have to carry on another five hundred yards before you see the house. The house is quite large. You can't miss it. That's all there is. Just the house, and the lake beyond. Oh, I forgot. Watch out for the peacocks. If you hit one of them, Ildefonso, it'll cost you five points."

NINE

Now Gus Rozzo knew, in his own particular way, what it was like to be Tommy-Tom Nolan, at least what it was like to lie in the same bed with Val and stare through the open bedroom door through the living-room and into the kitchen. Gus guessed this was why Tommy-Tom hadn't been coming home much anymore: the place was a mess. But Gus hadn't come there to judge Val's housekeeping, he had come there to make love to the girl he had wanted ever since the ninth grade.

Babs desired Gus. She would always desire him, and he intended to keep it that way. Simple. She had everything an indiscriminate man could possibly want, but she was lacking the one element Gus found most exciting in a woman: character. Val Nolan, née Jacobowski, was an interesting person. Tommy-Tom was too egotistical to recognize this, but Gus had been captivated by Val's unruliness, and recklessness, for the entirety of his adult life. He just hadn't quite realized it, not until one evening when, all of them out on the town drinking, Val had slapped Tommy-Tom. This had surprised everyone but Gus. Initially, he didn't know why, but then his memory had kicked in and there stood Val in all her adolescent glory.

Fourteen-year-old Gus had been sulking. He had gone to Elysian Park to be miserably alone, humiliated by another boy on the junior varsity basketball team. The boy had said that when Gus wore his basketball jersey, the sleeveless kind that swooped low over the back and chest, you could see his cleavage. This had given rise to a barrage of jokes from the other boys about Gus's little tits, big clit, etc. Now, as Gus lay nursing the last of the Suntory Whiskey, Val passed out by his side, he vividly remembered what he'd witnessed, his adolescent heart pounding in his throat and his adolescent penis rising to distress and enrage him.

Gus had been sitting on the far side of a gentle rise covered in daffodils – it had been spring as it was now – watching a multitude of ants swarming over a sheet of saran wrap, its sticky square smeared in what even from a distance of three feet smelled distinctly like sweet and sour sauce, when he heard voices. Shifting lower behind the daffodils, his diminutive legs folding easily under him, he observed Val and Tommy-Tom cavorting around a broken drinking fountain, its bowl sprouting weeds. She was taunting him, her blouse opened to the waist, her bra and bare tummy available for anyone passing to see. But Elysian Park was empty. Only an oblivious boy on a bicycle darted by beyond the gates. Frustrated in his pursuit, Tommy-Tom sauntered off to recline invitingly in the shadow of the spotty hedge that surrounded the swings and sliding-board. But Val had been the superior one that afternoon. She had danced over the ground, holding herself aloof, and poor Tommy-Tom hadn't known what to do. Alicia had had that same slipperiness. Gus knew that many of his friends had found his daughter sexually exciting, and Tommy-Tom had been one of them. But this wasn't the time to think about Alicia. Gus couldn't save his crazy daughter now, but he could begin living her life for her. And he wasn't going to waste any more time. Tommy-Tom, the lout, had lain by the hedge in Elysian Park stroking his erection through his trousers, while Val had stood over him laughing. Now she lay beside Gus waiting for him, not Tommy-Tom, to make love to her.

Gus took the pillow from behind Val's head and slid it under her hips, which weighed nothing. Rolling her onto her stomach, he unzipped her dress. Then, as gently as he could, he rolled her over again and pulled the dress down from her shoulders, shimmying her strapless bra down along with it, over her ribs.

"My money's in my purse," mumbled Val, her tiny breasts melting.

"Your money's in your pussy," laughed Gus, and felt to see if he were getting hard.

In the dim light from the street, Val's breasts were a pale, pale blue, the veins a waxen purple. They reminded Gus of two little blue parakeets lying dead at the bottom of their cage. Gus wanted to play with them but he was too pent up and concentrated instead on removing her pantyhose. Having got the pantyhose down as far as her knees, he tucked her dress up under itself at the waist. The pulpy swell of her belly shone a bluish white, while the naked cleft below hid itself in furry darkness. Gus leaned forward and sniffed. He sniffed again, wanting to remember forever. Then he shuddered. There was something sad about this very special woman, Valerie Nolan, walking around drunk without any panties. For Gus, it was as if the stale air of the streets had invaded her private parts. But it was only alcohol he smelled. The pillow he'd shoved under her was damp with it. She must have spilled it on the carpet too. Gus leaned forward and sniffed again, remembering how the sunlight had fallen on her thighs as she'd stood over Tommy-Tom in the park and exposed herself. And he grew larger and harder. Now he would touch her. But the feeling of her pubic hair, moist with the Japanese whiskey, was too much for him and Gus suddenly reared over her. Insinuating himself between her legs, his knees sank into the mattress, pressing the taut web of her pantyhose into a gully. This drew Val's legs more tightly around him. Finding himself entrapped and unable to perform, Gus was furious. He lifted his foot and thrust it down, so that the sheer stuff binding her knees was raked along her shin by his shoe.

"I'm not much help," he heard Val say, her voice weakening as if she were drifting off to sleep.

"I can do it. That's what I'm here for," panted Gus. "I'm here to make love to you."

"You should of had enough practice with Babs."

Val's words were mostly lost in Gus's sweet-smelling hair, but he got the gist.

"I can do it just as good with you. Better even."

"Sure," said Val.

Then he came.

Diego Ildefonso awoke desperately wanting a sip of his wife's water. As he reached blindly over her, brushing her bare shoulder, she lifted the glass herself and pressed it into his fumbling hand. Tongue wetted, he was grateful, and sank back into the quagmire of his incoherent dreaming.

Having replaced the glass on the bedside table, Dolores stared for a while at the grayish smears Diego's mouth had left on the glass's rim. She wanted to get up and bring a clean one from the kitchen – the smears as they glinted haphazardly in the light from the street bothered her that much – but the room's darkness held her fast, and she shifted her determination once again to sleep. Now there was something else. Thoroughly annoyed, she dragged herself out of bed and went to answer the telephone in Diego's office.

For a few seconds, Dolores stood over little Billy, telephone in hand, unable to tell if the shrillness of the bell had awakened him. The room smelled mildly of urine. She was glad they'd borrowed the cot, rather than put the two boys in the same bed. She reckoned it would be Val, but it was Babs, and she was sobbing.

"What's the matter?"

"Diego didn't tell you?"

"I'm sorry, Babs, I have to whisper. Little Billy's sleeping in this room. Now, what did Diego tell me?"

"About Alicia?"

"Did she come back?"

"He didn't *tell* you...?"

Dolores thought she heard Babs say, "She's dead."

"Honey, please...what did you say?"

"Somebody killed her. They took her out to the marshes and killed her. And where's Gus? Where is he? I don't even know where he is."

"You haven't heard from him? Babs?"

"Yea, hours ago. He said he was taking Val up to see Tommy-Tom. I don't believe him. He was getting drunk. He doesn't even want to see me. He had his mother call me about Alicia. Can you believe that, that he would have his mother call me?"

"Have you called Val, to see if she's home?"

Babs didn't answer.

"Would you like me to come over? Diego would have to stay here with the boys, but I could."

"I didn't call Val's, cause she shouldn't of been with him. She should of told him to come and *be with me!* I guess if somebody came over here I wouldn't have to be so upset in front of the kids. They don't even know yet. I guess I'll call my mom. She always knows what to do."

"How about if I call Val?" offered Dolores, not liking the coldness coming into her voice. "How's that...I'll call Val."

"You're gonna start thinkin we're a real mess, and we're not." Babs was sobbing again.

Dolores said good-bye as gently as she could. She was enraged. Gus had behaved loathsomely. She didn't believe for a second he had been out doing Val a favor. What was the matter with these people? She decided to telephone Val. If she were there, fine. If she weren't, then she was probably out with the ubiquitous Ralph. Either way, Dolores would feel better not having to ask Diego to look in on her on his way to work. She would let Val's phone ring twelve times before giving up. It did ring twelve times, and then twelve times more. After that, Dolores went into the kitchen and took the piece of stale wedding cake she'd been saving from her cousin Roxanne's wedding out of the fridge and sat on the floor in the darkness and ate it.

Gus lay on top of Val, somewhat still inside her, asleep. Val lay staring at the clock, remembering her childhood – the railroad tracks, her family's house below the watertower, walks with her brother by the reservoir, her father's new car, the names of all the cats they'd had – as the hour passed from 1:18 to 2:18 to 3:18, when she finally pushed him off and went into the bathroom. There, she quietly gagged down all the sleeping pills she'd been saving for the past two years, and went back to bed, Billy's cold wet washcloth pressed to her mouth. She only wished she could be there when Gus woke up and found her dead. Later, when she no longer had the strength to move, her nerves motorless, around 4:18, she came to regret she would never have the joy of seeing her son grown. But she quieted herself, deep down inside, with the image of a fine young man wearing a nicely pressed suit and conservative tie, standing with his arm around a pretty young woman she didn't recognize.

As Gus slept, he recovered without any concentration whatsoever the rest of the memory he had abandoned upon becoming aroused. Again Tommy-Tom Nolan lay in the shadow of the spotty hedge. Fourteen-year-old Val came to stand over him, her coltish legs spread wide. Gus, who had been unable initially to see everything she was doing from his hiding place behind the daffodils, could now see perfectly. Onto Tommy-Tom's face fell a stream of urine, golden and straight. There it was, exactly as it had been that spring afternoon in Elysian Park, as shocking in its haughtiness as any disgraceful act Gus had committed in later life, except perhaps the act he had just committed there on Tommy-Tom's bed. The telephone, left on the floor by a dresser nearby, began ringing and wouldn't stop. Gus rolled onto his side. He promised himself he would ask Val to demonstrate this feat of peeing – with such fantastic precision – when the two went in to shower, after he had made love to her again, and this time with considerably greater longevity. To this end, he lay his hand on her thigh, its coolness and firmness a delight to the touch, as the stench of Val's vomit dilated his nostrils. In an instant, Gus had risen from the bed, the telephone ringing, ringing, ringing. Val's face was partially covered with what appeared to be a damp washcloth, but her eyes were plainly visible. They were fixed. Gus snatched up the bottle from the carpet and left the apartment. His jacket however remained slung over the back of one of the kitchen chairs. He would have to get home as quickly as possible now. Why not shoot up Park, which was one-way and wide, and then cut over to Clinton? Gus figured it would be best not to have any idea what time it was when Babs, hopefully groggy with sleep, asked. It would also be best to still be drunk.

"Babs thought you knew," Diego dimly heard Dolores say as he stood gazing through the blinds at the street below. She was crying. Alicia was dead. Chief Huff had told him. And somehow Gilbey knew. So why hadn't he told his own wife? He didn't know. The windshields of the parked cars were wet with morning dew.

Dolores went to the window and laid her head on his shoulder, crying. He held her for a very long time, waiting for Roland to appear and ask what the matter was.

Eventually, with one hand, Diego began unbuttoning his pajama top. "Why don't you see to renting the car this morning?" She was doing a little better. "A big one, like a Buick or something."

"How should I pay for it?"

"Like we usually do."

"You want me to use cash, *the* cash?" Dolores moved unsteadily to her right. Diego realized she was after a tissue and went into the bathroom for her. "Thanks," she said. "And what about driving?"

"You know the answer to that."

"But I only drive my parents' car."

"Then rent a car like your parents' – an automatic – even if it costs more."

"I'm sorry," said Dolores. "I'm having a hard time imagining any of this."

"He's just a nice old fart who wants to give us a little holiday. And we could use one. It'll be fun for the boys. Honey, I'm sorry, I've got to get going here."

Before he stepped into the shower, Diego looked deeply into his eyes in the mirror. There was nothing there. Alicia's death, it seemed, didn't mean a thing to him.

The shadows of the streetlamps went hurtling over the windshield of Gus's van as he drove past his house. Just as he'd turned down his street, he'd realized he'd better keep to his original story – of having promised Val he'd take her up to the Medical Center in Union City to visit Tommy-Tom. He could say he'd gone to her apartment and she wouldn't open the door, or said she was too sick or something, and he'd been obliged to go alone. There wasn't anything he could do for Val now anyway. And why give everybody the chance to blame him? He hadn't done anything awful to her, had he? Nothing criminal. Furthermore, it wasn't his job to tell Tommy-Tom about Val, not when it would just mess things up even worse. Tommy-Tom would find out soon enough. If he showed up to visit Tommy-Tom now, he could say he'd been in the parking-lot sleeping all night. Poor Val. Gus remembered a bar in Union City he'd been to once with her and Tommy-Tom. Maybe after visiting Tommy-Tom he'd go over there for a drink, for old times' sake. He figured he was going to need one.

There weren't visiting hours as such when you were in Intensive Care, at least this was Gus's impression as he walked straight into the ward, plastic tents and oxygen tanks everywhere. Tommy-Tom was asleep with his mouth hanging open. He had bandages around the top of his head – really short hair was sticking out at the very top – and around his throat. The ones around his throat looked gooey. Tommy-Tom was a great-looking guy. Even all cut up he looked liked a movie star. Gus was envious. Then he remembered that Tommy-Tom probably wouldn't be able to talk and he felt better, although he also felt worse. It was a shame Val wouldn't be there to help Tommy-Tom make the adjustment. She would've been his voice for him, like that girl with the droopy-eyed sock-puppet. Val would've loved that. Eventually Tommy-Tom would've shot her or something. Gus could see it. Tommy-Tom would've gotten fed up being treated like a baby and done something fucked-up to Val. She wouldn't have deserved that. She hadn't deserved any of the shit Tommy-Tom gave her. Maybe Gus would've taken her out of there and set her up someplace nice. Yea, but what about little Billy? He would've had to come too. There was always some fucking hitch. OK, so let's try to talk to him, Gus told himself.

Pulling a loose chair up to the side of Tommy-Tom's bed, Gus said, "Tommy-Tom you're looking good. No shit, really fucking good." Then, when Tommy-Tom didn't respond, he said, "Hey bro, whada'ya do for laughs around here?" Gus realized that maybe he sounded like the spade who'd sliced Tommy-Tom up, so he took another approach, a less cheerful one. "You think you got it bad, wait till you hear what's been happening with me and Babs."

Tommy-Tom turned and stared at Gus.

"Jesus Christ," said Gus.

There was a look in his friend's eyes like he wanted him dead. But then Gus noticed Tommy-Tom was pressing his finger into something, a slip of paper or something that was lying on the bed next to him. Tommy-Tom reached out and took Gus's hand, and Gus saw that it was a photograph of Tommy-Tom and his father, taken when Tommy-Tom was a kid, maybe seven or eight. There were tears in Tommy-Tom's eyes.

"You loved your dad?" guessed Gus.

Tommy-Tom shook his head furiously from side to side, then screeched with pain, like the high-pitched wail little girls make when they're playing together and get too excited.

"You *didn't* love your dad?"

Watching Tommy-Tom's mouth, as if he actually expected something to come out, Gus was amazed to see Tommy-Tom's lips, teeth, tongue, nose, all conspire grotesquely to say, without any sound whatsoever:

"He fucked me up. He fucked my mother up."

Gus had heard all this before, when Tommy-Tom was drunk. He'd also heard, when Tommy-Tom was drunk, how much he loved his father. So who could say for sure what Tommy-Tom ever meant? Now, obviously, for some reason, he hated his ole man.

"Tommy-Tom, we gotta talk. I mean, I gotta tell you something, for your benefit as well as mine. You comfortable? Want some water?"

Tommy-Tom nodded.

Gus could smell the liquor on his own breath – maybe he should have tried to bring a drink in for his pal. He picked up the plastic cup from the tray nearby. It was empty. Gus took hold of the plastic pitcher and poured. The pitcher still had some ice in it, which was a nice surprise. Tommy-Tom had a few sips. Gus offered to return the cup to the tray, but Tommy-Tom held on to it.

Eyes fixed on the tube going into Tommy-Tom's arm, Gus said, "Who can believe it, Tommy-Tom, Alicia's dead. Our little play pal is dead. She disappeared after we all were identifying Mikie at the hospital, and now she's dead."

Again, Tommy-Tom was staring at Gus. Unable to hold his friend's gaze, Gus looked down at their hands. They lay lifelessly on the bed, only inches apart. Gus intertwined his fingers with Tommy-Tom's.

"Everybody was asking where you took her. Nobody could find you. We're all like, where the fuck is Tommy-Tom? And where the fuck is Alicia? You know, to find out where you dropped her off or whatever. I figured you left her where she wanted, like at her friend Linda's house, or Patty's, or even in New York, if she talked you into it?"

Gus glanced up, but Tommy-Tom only continued to stare at him.

"OK, now here's the other part. I gotta problem with Ildefonso, a serious fucking problem. This is no bullshit. Me and him went over to Freddie Friedrich's and burned the fucking place down, only Diego's gonna see to it that my ass gets hauled in. Everybody knows I was pissed off with the guy. It figures, don't it?"

Now Tommy-Tom nodded his head, much to Gus's relief.

"Good boy, you're doing fine." Gus patted Tommy-Tom's hand. Suddenly there was activity in the corridor. Another body was wheeled in. One of the interns pointed at Gus, like he wasn't supposed to be there. Gus drew even closer to Tommy-Tom. "If anybody asks you – this is the important part, Tommy-Tom – you gotta let me know you get what I'm saying. You tell whoever, it was Diego who was with Alicia. Just say you dropped her back at our house – you left her with him, with Diego. Say the black guy who cut you up was a friend of his or something. Alicia's dead. I don't care who fucking killed her. I mean, I *care* but I gotta look after my family, and I don't need Ildefonso or anybody else fucking me over. If you say he knew Bootsy – and who's gonna say otherwise – they might figure *he* killed her. Bootsy, I mean. And then anything Ildefonso says about me won't count. You do this for me – it's the only thing I'm ever gonna ask you again – and we'll take care of Billy. I promise. Me and Babs, we'll take care of Billy for as long as you say. We'll even send him to college if you want."

In response, Tommy-Tom made only one word with his face.

"You say what?" whispered Gus.

The bandages around Tommy-Tom's neck made a soft sucking sound as he again formed the word. But Gus already knew what Tommy-Tom had said, he'd said *Val*. He wanted his wife.

It was late by the time Diego hit the street. Chief Leon Huff's broad immutable face had loomed up before him as he'd showered. The Chief's visit the night before had only confirmed what he had dreaded ever since leaving Gus in his van, Friedrich's Auto Body Shop billowing smoke: he was now the traitor.

When he had walked away, he had become the weakling, the one who fears confrontation. It was often this sort of petty misadventure that ruined men like Diego Ildefonso, men who had bigger fish to fry. As the colors about him grew warmer, the sun steadily penetrating the mists of Manhattan to bathe Hoboken in the shimmering light of a new day, he worried on, stride for stride. What an ugly mess. And what did that old fart Gilbey know that he didn't?

Having fretted over Val's silence long enough, Dolores finally telephoned Chief Huff to express her concern. Eager for some excuse to get into the Nolans' apartment, he told her his visit could have "wider implications," to which she responded, "I just hope Val's alright."

In repose, Valerie Nolan looked very like her idealized self. Throughout her childhood she had been unaware of a tendency to make faces when she spoke. This may have been due to having had a French mother who pursed her lips and raised her eyebrows with the intensity of many of her people. Val had communicated as much with the muscles of her face as she had with the muscle of her tongue. By the time she realized how much this distracted from her innate beauty she was eighteen. Stopping herself from screwing up her face had been a tremendous feat of self-discipline. By nineteen, she had achieved the facial serenity of Nefertiti's sarcophagus.

For Tommy-Tom, who hadn't been keeping track of this extraordinary transformation, Val suddenly seemed almost unapproachable. He was enthralled. Compulsively, he broke down her air of invincibility by humiliating her during the act of lovemaking. Insidiously playful at first, his behavior grew more violent until he took to slapping her breasts and buttocks with a cruelty that terrified and depressed her. Then, after she'd had little Billy, he'd taken to remarking unkindly on the distressed state of her body. Laughing, he'd say she'd turned into a piece of fruit, a piece of fruit that should have been eaten a long time ago.

This was the kind of thing the Chief could only guess at as he gazed down at Val Nolan, and watched Detective Sergeant

Molloy wipe the vomit from her mouth with little Billy's damp washcloth.

After a quick shower, Dolores set about getting Roland and little Billy organized to go pick up the car from the Hertz franchise on River Street. It would be a longish walk, but she was looking forward to chatting with the boys and enjoying their reaction to anything of interest they might encounter along the way.

The first thing they encountered was a smell.

"What's that?" said Roland, as they approached Washington Street.

"It smells like candy!" shouted little Billy, who was lagging behind.

"Or hair spray," offered Dolores, her eyes fixed on the traffic ahead.

"It's that blue building!" little Billy again shouted. "Look, it has a candy bar on top!"

Roland stopped to stare at the building. "It's electronic," was his interpretation.

His mother glanced up at the sign in the distance. "It says Lancelot Switches."

Little Billy carried on ahead of them. "I'm hungry," he said, distracted by the hot-dog vendor's cart stationed at the end of the block.

"It's a socket cover, like the ones we have, the brown ones," said Roland. "I mean, a switch cover."

"But that's not electronic," Dolores gently corrected him, "that's just electrical."

Roland puzzled over this, then noticed that little Billy, who was now several yards ahead of them, had taken out his penis and was urinating in the gutter.

"Mom, look what Billy's doing."

"Billy?" Dolores called.

The boy lifted his head to grin at her. It was the first time Dolores had seen little Billy smile.

"He must like doing that," said Roland.

"That's not so terrible," Dolores assured him.

"Come on, hit me!" shouted Billy, now grimacing. "I'll pee on your shoes. Come on, try and hit me!"

"Some fun." Roland frowned up at his mother.

Dolores promised the boys they'd stop and buy hot dogs on the way back – it was too soon after breakfast for a snack – but little Billy didn't believe her.

"What's the matter," Roland asked him, "you think my mom's lying?"

"She's just saying that so I'll shut up," little Billy whispered.

In the yard by the car rental office, Roland and Billy spent a long time admiring a huge Cadillac convertible, its wheels graced with what appeared to Roland to be spiralling universes of chrome soda straws. Eventually, he drew his mother over.

"Mom, let's get this one," he said. "It's big enough for Pop and all the rest of us too."

On the ride home, Dolores driving with the care usually demonstrated by the elderly, Roland and little Billy sat like visiting dignitaries in the back seat basking in the morning sun.

"I don't need a hot dog now," said Billy.

"Think about all the starving kids in India," said Roland.

"Huh?" said Billy.

Dolores, her eyes fastening on little Billy's in the rear-view mirror, said "Sometimes we have to sacrifice, for those who are less fortunate."

Roland pondered this, then whispered to Billy, "Kids in India don't eat hot dogs anyway."

Gus stared at the glass of beer he'd set on top of the pay telephone. It was his second and he felt somewhat better.

"You can come back whenever you want," said Babs. "I'm taking Dommie over to my mom's. I can call Dolores to sit the girls."

"That's a dumb idea. What're we doing being friendly to them?" Gus wanted a cigarette.

"It's the other way around. Anyways, I'm not gonna lie for you no more. I decided. If you can go off like you did last night, you can lie for yourself."

"I wasn't lying. I was up at the hospital with Tommy-Tom, like I told you. Only Val wasn't home when I went over there, after I talked to her on the telephone, and I just went up there anyways, cause you didn't sound like you wanted me to come home."

A long silence followed. Gus had to say something.

"If you go over to your mother's, I'm gonna come over and pick you up."

"For what?"

"So we can be by ourself."

"And where're we gonna be by ourself, a hotel?"

"Forget Dolores. Teddy can sit the girls after his music lesson."

"He didn't go. He went in to the city, to the Museum of Natural History. He said he wanted to be with the animals."

"If Dolores calls, tell her *thanks* but we don't need her. Say it nice. OK? If we have to, we'll call Mrs. Claverie or somebody."

"When're you getting back?"

"I told you: after I look in on Val. I don't like it she wasn't there after making such a fuss about going up to see Tommy-Tom."

"She told *me* his mother could take care of him. She was *sick* of him."

"Beats the fuck out of me. All I know is what she told me. I'm still in Union City. I stopped for some breakfast. I guess I could be home by eleven. Call your mother and tell her you're not coming, OK?"

"I might and I might not, I haven't made up my mind yet."

Gus put the rest of his change into the telephone: thirty-five cents.

"What was that?" said Babs.

"What'd you think it was? Listen, we should go somewhere, even for tonight. I'll be home around eleven, after I stop in and see what's with Val."

"If she's drinking, don't *you*. OK?"

"Why would I drink anything?"

"Promise me."

"For Christ's sake..." groaned Gus and, without thinking, hung up. He instantly grabbed at the receiver, hoping he hadn't lost her. The line was dead.

"You have to put the money in first," called the guy behind the bar.

Standing by the telephone in the corner, sunlight crowding in through the dirty window high up on the wall, Gus thought about Val, and then Alicia, and began to cry.

"What're you looking at?!" he shouted at the barman.

Ivy covered the brick front of Dr. Herbert's office. The ivy gave the building the look of a fraternity house in one of the smaller New England cities, or so Diego Ildefonso imagined. He stood watching the furious activity of hundreds of little birds. They were swarming over the ivy, which he assumed must be infested with caterpillars or insects of some kind. Approaching the door was difficult, as the birds were easily startled, scattering white fecal matter into the air. Once inside the building, Diego had to retire to Dr. Herbert's lavatory to sponge away the numerous splotches of white that decorated his suit, each oozing a small amount of clear oily fluid and dotted with an even smaller amount of black, like a tiny ashen worm. This took some time. Unexpectedly, Dr. Herbert entered the tiny room, went directly over to the toilet, and proceeded to empty his bladder.

"No appointment? – I don't mind," he said, over his shoulder. "I see the starlings got you."

"What's out there?"

"Someone said they're gypsy moths, but they look more like hairy little butterflies to me."

"An infestation." Diego unstoppered the sink. "They're gorging themselves silly."

"Where were you?"

"When?"

"Yesterday evening," blustered Dr. Herbert. "Remember? I called several times. Then it got late and I got into a big scene on the telephone with Charlene."

Diego didn't want to discuss Christian Herbert's extra-marital affair again, or the resultant illegitimate embryo. He decided to refill the sink. "Dolores and I were out shopping for an hour or so. I'm sorry."

"No need to be sorry." Dr. Herbert squeezed by. "Meet me in my office, not the examining-room – uh, your sleeve's in the water."

When he entered Dr. Herbert's office, Diego was surprised and somewhat relieved to find that no report had been laid out on his desk. Only an empty coffee cup stood off to one side with a smoldering cigarette butt at its bottom.

"Anxiety," said Dr. Herbert, by way of an apology for the smoke still hanging in the air. "I don't have anyone coming in until this afternoon. It just worked out that way. I was supposed to be visiting with old Johnny Strano at St. Mary's this morning, but he passed away last night in his sleep. God must have been his best buddy. The bastard is rumored to have eliminated more than half a dozen men, and I mean personally. Not that any of them are missed."

"You know what they say?" muttered Diego.

Dr. Herbert stared at him, obviously uninterested. His hands were trembling. Not much, but they were trembling. He placed one over the other as he caught Diego's inquiring glance.

"It's getting worse for me," he confessed.

"Me too," said Diego, hoping this would move him on to the subject of his scans.

"I know now I could never love Charlene. All she ever talks about, other than herself, is other women – who I don't even know? I don't go around talking about my patients all the time, do I? What could be more boring?"

"So what do you talk about?" Diego knew Dr. Herbert would have to work his way through this. "I mean, when you're with her?"

"I don't know. Lots of things. Take painting and sculpture. I've been thinking I'd like to get involved with one of the museums. I don't know anything about it, but plenty of wealthy people get involved in that sort of thing."

"Without knowing anything about it?"

"Absolutely. But I'd like to know something about it, before I get involved. Take some of the courses they have on offer. You know. Charlene says she wants to get involved too, accumulate some power. She likes to buy things. She could get herself on the acquisitions committee, if she played her cards right.

Obviously, it helps to contribute." He reached for his cup, then remembered it was now an ashtray. "But all she ever *really* wants to talk about is how well her girlfriends are doing, who they're marrying, are *they* pregnant yet? Blah, blah, blah. And then, you know, she wants to go someplace nice for dinner, and then to the St. Regis for a fuck. If you see what I mean?"

"I hope this doesn't sound insensitive, but couldn't you just pay her off?"

"How do you mean?"

"To get rid of the baby, and for her to leave you alone."

"I don't think I've got that kind of money. At least not that I could take out of trust and still leave enough for the kids. I want our kids to have something to remember us by. I'd be settling with two women."

"I don't see the difference."

"You would if you were me." Dr. Herbert lit another cigarette. "There's something in there." This was it. "And I'm afraid at present we don't have the means to get it out, not surgically." Diego felt sick. "They're working on other procedures, to get into the brain, but they're a long way off. If this were twenty years from now, we could burn it out."

Diego saw himself gazing for the last time at a parrot in the zoo. How many beautiful creatures had he seen only in books, creatures who stoically awaited death, denying the indulgence of sentimentality? What majestic resolve there was everywhere amongst them. This inclination toward sentimentality, he would ignore it.

"I'm not a specialist in this area," said Dr. Herbert, "but my buddy Jim Heinemann is. We went to pre-med school together. I asked Jim how this thing would go – you know, what you should expect – and he said it's usually quite slow. Nothing much happens at all, for a while."

"But what about the symptoms?"

"Obviously, if we can't get at it, there's no way to know if it's malignant. You don't have to take my word for it, Jim would be happy to see you. He can explain it all much, much better than I can. That's what he does."

"What?"

"He treats and removes them, when he can." Dr. Herbert attempted to smile at Diego with all the pitying affection he felt for him.

"Will I lose my ability to think?" Diego suddenly dreaded this more than any amount of pain.

"Look at it this way – if you do, it won't be much of an issue, will it?"

"And my other faculties?"

"Which ones, specifically?"

"Walking, for instance."

"I'm sorry, I really don't know. I do know that quite often the presence, as it develops, can be debilitating. But this may never happen. If the tumor isn't malignant, it most likely won't have the same impact on your ability to function normally, although various things may go awry."

"Would I have seen this light, which I saw again last night, either way?"

"Some people never see anything, not like you've described. Sometimes they just have a headache or, conversely, a numbing somewhere in their body, usually in the limbs."

"Are you certain I haven't had a stroke, or two strokes?" Diego couldn't actually remember how many times he'd seen the light.

"No, it's in there," said Dr. Herbert.

"How big? How big is it?"

"About the size of a robin's egg."

"But that's not very big."

"It's big enough."

When Diego left Dr. Herbert's office, the ivy was empty of the confusion and upheaval that had confronted him upon his arrival. The starlings were gone.

TEN

Why Tommy-Tom Nolan, eyes closed, should have been smiling so broadly when Chief Huff entered the intensive care ward to inform him of his wife's suicide was anyone's guess. This man, as far as Huff was concerned, had nothing to be smiling about. Firstly, he was present when Stanley Fischer, aka Shirlee Simonaire, had been so badly beaten. Secondly, he had piloted Alicia Rozzo away from St. Mary's Hospital the night she was raped and murdered. And thirdly, Valerie Nolan had just that previous night died of a massive overdose of barbiturates, which didn't say much for his marriage. Maybe Tommy-Tom was just a happy-go-lucky guy.

As Huff approached Tommy-Tom's bed, he realized why Tommy-Tom was in such a good mood: someone had given him a miniature radio with an ear-plug. If he listened closely, concentrating on the sizzling emanating from Tommy-Tom's ear, Huff could hear K.C.'s chorus of happily laboring insects, known as the Sunshine Band if Huff remembered correctly, singing something about *boogie nights*. Apparently, this recent hit was one of Tommy-Tom's favorites. Huff glanced around the ward. There'd been eight litters present during his last visit, whereas now there were only three. His prejudice against Tommy-Tom Nolan was so great that he immediately wondered if Tommy-Tom were in some way responsible for their removal. Of the two remaining, one patient lay face down, his or her back and limbs swathed in diaphanous dressings loaded down with burn gel, while the other, a Puerto Rican teenager with a wispy goatee, lay truncated from the waist down, tubes eddying out from under a very thin plastic sheet. Not much there now, in either case, for Tommy-Tom to mess with. But then Huff wondered how ingenious Tommy-Tom actually was at finding things to do when bored. Although Detective Sergeant Molloy hadn't found anything of real interest in the Nolan apartment, no one had as yet explored Tommy-Tom's so-called workshop in the basement. The Chief would see to that himself.

"Tommy-Tom?" he heralded the smiling mute. "Tommy-Tom, please try to concentrate on what I'm saying."

The patient turned to stare at the Chief. Now the smile sank and the broad jaws opened in a stagnant yawn. Huff grabbed the same chair Gus Rozzo had inhabited less than three hours before and pulled it up to Tommy-Tom's plateau of chrome and stiff white cotton.

"I'm afraid I have some very bad news," said Huff. "Your wife has died."

Nothing. The eyes kept staring, lips and teeth ajar.

"From what we found in your apartment – I hope you don't mind – I assume you and your family are Catholic. It appears Valerie took her own life and we have to advise the family and they have to advise the church. The only relevant address or telephone number we could find was your mother's. We know Valerie's name was Jakabowski, but the only other Jakabowski living around here is Emil, a retired mason, about seventy, and he claims he doesn't know her, or you. So, should I go to your mother with all this, or do you feel capable of dealing with it yourself?"

Tommy-Tom nodded his head *yes*.

"Which one? You or your mother?"

Up went two fingers.

"Cremation or burial?"

Up went one finger.

"The church won't deal with this."

Tommy-Tom shook his head *no*. Then he did something which struck Huff as rather odd. He began poking at his mattress. As the Chief went on outlining what would need to be done and what he would tell Tommy-Tom's mother, the poking continued until it was obvious that Tommy-Tom had more on his mind than his mother's ability to cope with the ordeal ahead.

"What is it?" asked Huff.

Folding his lips inward, so that absolutely no pink showed, then splaying them outward, twice, Tommy-Tom silently spoke the word *paper*.

Without hesitation, Huff went out to the nurse's station in the corridor and plucked up a note pad and ballpoint pen. Having set them down next to Tommy-Tom's agitated finger, he waited. What Tommy-Tom wrote on the note-pad, to Huff's immediate dismay, was as enthralling – Huff had himself formulated a similar configuration only the day before – as it was perverse:

> *Alisa I left her with Daygo he know*
> *Bootsy who try to kill Shirly Daygo*
> *tell you he don't know or I did it*

Tommy-Tom looked away. He knew he'd written more than enough to confuse the Chief, like Gus had said.

"What if Diego says he last saw her there, at the house, with Gus?" argued Huff.

Tommy-Tom continued to stare out over the ward, the air a dead watery blue. Again he picked up the ballpoint.

Daygo lies

Huff's first thought was that Gus Rozzo had gotten to Tommy-Tom before he had. Gus had been pretty busy on Thursday night, Huff was now certain: he'd been to visit Val Nolan, had intercourse with her, and left his jacket there like he was coming back, plowed up to Union City in his dented van for a one-sided chat with Tommy-Tom, then scooted off somewhere on foot – his van was still outside in the parking lot. Huff decided to interrupt the flow of Gus's day by confronting him with the fact of Val's death, whenever he returned to climb back in the van and head off to God knows where.

Unfortunately, Chief Huff didn't say good-bye to Tommy-Tom quickly enough and Gus's van was gone by the time he returned to the parking-lot. Maybe it was time to speak with Stanley Fischer, if the boy were able. Huff went back into the Medical Center and up to the fifth floor, where the Fischer family had secured Stanley a private room. When the Chief glanced into Stanley's room, he found Mrs. Fischer sitting holding her son's hand. Stanley, whose face had been mummified, was apparently asleep.

"How's he doing?" asked the Chief.

"He'll never be beautiful again," whispered Mrs. Fischer. She obviously knew all about Shirlee Simonaire.

Huff quietly pulled a chair up to the bed. "Has he said anything?"

"His teeth are broken, and he can't breathe right." There was the oxygen line entering the hole in his throat.

"I take it the Union City police – probably Seiffert or Langley – have been in to see you?"

"One of them was talking to Stanley's doctor yesterday."

"But they didn't speak to him?"

Mrs. Fischer looked away.

On the way back to Hoboken, Huff struggled with the prospect of informing both Tommy-Tom's mother and his son of his wife's death. He reckoned Detective Sergeant Molloy was the man for the job. Huff knew Molloy would find Billy Nolan with Dolores Ildefonso, but it was pointless to send him out until that evening to find Mrs. Nolan. This was because each and every day, as if she were still searching for something precious she'd lost years before, Mrs. Nolan attempted to sell Avon cosmetics, door to door. In the end, rather than entrust two such delicate chores to Molloy – Huff liked Mrs. Ildefonso that much – he decided to go over to Willow Avenue himself.

Diego Ildefonso stared down at the tips of his shoes pointing over the curbing on Bloomfield Street. A preponderance of woolly blue lint had gathered, mysteriously, in the cuffs of his trousers, giving them the appearance of two scuttled boats in miniature. Then he realized from whence the blue lint in his cuffs had come. It had come from Roland's baby blanket, with which his son still slept. Roland had asked for it to be taken away and washed (coincidentally with his father's trousers) before Billy Nolan arrived. Diego was overcome with love for his son. Next there would be Bernardi's. Diego wondered how be would behave once he'd sunk into the restaurant's familiar atmosphere, what emotion might wrench him from his determined dignity.

At home, Dolores sat chatting with Roland and little Billy. They had had their lunch and were settled on the sofa in the living-room, the boys stationed on either side of her. They were playing a game that she and Roland often played.

Dolores said, "In the autumn the temperature grows colder and...?"

Roland answered, "The days get shorter."

She then said, directing her attention to little Billy, "And the leaves on the trees turn yellow and then brown and...?"

"The guy across the street burns them."

"Not right away," Dolores said. "First they have to fall to the ground."

"Oh yea,"said Billy. He gazed dejectedly at her, his pale head with its soggy mane of dark hair slowly nodding. His tiny plastic comb waited in his pocket for his next visit to the bathroom. There he would stand in front of the mirror compulsively wetting and styling his hair, trying to make it look like his father's. Dolores had noted this behavior and wondered how she'd ever get him to stop. It was like having a miniature Tommy-Tom around the house.

Dolores excused herself, assuring the boys she'd be right back after conferring with Mrs. Finkelstein about shortening one of her skirts for the weekend. Within seconds, there was a knock at the door onto the front hallway. When Roland opened it, he found Chief Huff smiling down at him.

"Your hat," said Roland, meaning the Chief should remove it when entering the apartment.

"Gladly," replied the Chief. "It's stuffy in here."

"You can open a window," said Roland.

"Your mother wouldn't mind?"

"He said it was OK," intoned little Billy, taking what he assumed to be Roland's belligerent lead.

"No need for that," Roland scolded him.

Chief Huff lifted a window on the alleyway, mindful not to tip over the large urn-like lamp on the inadequate side-table before it.

"Ugh," he grunted.

"I know," agreed Roland, "they shouldn't put their garbage out there, not even temporarily."

"It's your mother and father I need to speak with, if they're home."

"Pop's at work. And Mom's downstairs with Mrs. Finkelstein. You should check her out."

"I figured as much, about your dad, but I suppose it's really your mom I need to speak with anyway." The Chief was staring at Billy Nolan.

"I didn't do nothin," said the child.

When the Chief reached over to pat his head, little Billy ran out of the room.

"Hmmm," came dolefully from the Chief. He sat on the sofa where the boys had been sitting with Dolores.

"Still warm," said Roland, going over to the open window.

The Chief didn't comprehend.

"From my mother's bottom."

The Chief peered through the open door into Diego Ildefonso's office, taking in the corner of the cot on which Billy Nolan was now curled.

"Like to see me fly?" asked Roland, hands outstretched, the large urn-like lamp blocking his path to daylight.

"Why don't you come over here and tell me what you and Billy've been up to?" the Chief said to Roland.

"Want to see Billy cry? He cries at anything."

"Crying's for babies!" shouted Billy.

Roland was already concentrating on something else. "Sir, is pissing in public worse than spitting? I mean, can you go to jail?"

"Very rude behavior," answered the Chief, "often punishable by a fine, unless there is intent to offend or shock, especially when a minor is present, then it gets a whole lot worse."

"I told you!" Roland called to Billy.

Billy ignored him.

Roland came away from the open window, to stand a yard or so from the Chief.

"How about a tour?"

"A *tour?*"

"Of our house."

"I doubt your mother would approve."

"I learned from her. Come see our actual belongings. Come and stare," insisted Roland, reaching out his hand. His long fine fingers were like those of a little girl gifted at playing the piano, or perhaps the flute. "Mrs. Finkelstein does, and she sniffs, like this..." Roland tipped his head back, smiled sadly, like a heartbroken clown, breathed deeply through hugely dilated nostrils, then sighed, "Not so abnormal after all. You know, Chief Huff, we're really quite ordinary."

"But you're no ordinary young man."

Taken aback, Roland sought to decipher the meaning behind the man's opaque staring eyes. As he stood with his mouth gawping open, which was very unlike Roland, his mother re-entered the apartment.

"Where's Billy?" she asked. Roland responded by pointing to his father's office. "Why don't you and Billy have a look at the scrapbooks."

"What, of Spain? Pop wouldn't mind?" Roland couldn't believe his good fortune.

"No, he wouldn't mind. Just be careful with them."

He dashed off, then returned to shake the Chief's dangling hand. "I hope I've been of some assistance."

"Invaluable," muttered the Chief, then cleared his throat.

"Shall we sit?" said Dolores.

"Thanks. Would you mind shutting the door?" He nodded in the direction of Roland and Billy, now to be heard scrambling noisily under Diego's desk. While she did, the Chief returned to the sofa.

Dolores eased back into the stuffed chair nearby. "I don't know what to say about Alicia Rozzo. Especially after what happened to Mikie. I spoke with Babs this morning. She wasn't doing very well."

The Chief was silent.

"Is this about the fire?" Dolores was feeling very uneasy. "You know why Diego was there, don't you? He was concerned about Gus."

"No one has brought charges yet."

"Mr. Friedrich knows Diego didn't have anything to do with it."

"Tell me, does Tommy Nolan know his son's here?"

"I don't know."

"You obviously don't know about Valerie Nolan."

"I know she isn't capable of looking after Billy right now."

"She's one of your best friends, isn't she?"

"I guess." For some reason, Dolores thought, *I shan't have another child.*

"I'm afraid she died yesterday evening," said the Chief. "I'm sorry."

"Billy's safe. He's here," was all Dolores could say. She wouldn't allow herself to cry, not with the boys there. "How did she die? Not in a car accident, not while driving drunk?"

"No, she took her own life. She consumed a large quantity of sedatives. God knows where she got them all."

"She'd been saving them, for when she got cancer. Val was convinced she was going to die of cancer, and she didn't want it to be unpleasant for anyone, including herself. I'm sorry she wouldn't talk to me. I mean, really talk to me. She had her problems, like any of us, only different."

Mrs. Ildefonso stared down at her hands. The Chief hadn't recalled her fingernails being red. The polish, as if wet with anticipation, sparkled so hard in the dreary room that he heard music playing.

"Will you look after Billy until we can get ahold of Mrs. Nolan?"

"She lives over in Jersey City, I think."

"I know." The Chief got up and walked over to Dolores and reached down and took her hand. "Just tell your husband he has a kind and caring wife."

"I don't have to." She smiled up at him, tears in her eyes.

When the Chief had left, Dolores went in and held both boys pressed to her hip. Roland would have her explanation about Val later, maybe in a month or two, while little Billy, his eyes now fixed abstractly on the marble pen-holder on Diego's desk, would have to be steeped in happiness for a very, very long time before she would tell him anything even vaguely resembling the truth.

Bernardi had wisely gone home to rest before the evening's onslaught, and so it was Ramona who woke Diego and led him from the restaurant out into the street.

"I was an optimist once," were the first words he uttered, in a daze, as he took her arm. "Don't tell me it's dark already?"

"Only a very big cloud," Ramona assured him, happy to have Diego Ildefonso all to herself at last. But then he turned to her, pain in his eyes, and the emotion poured from him. But what he said meant nothing to her.

"It wasn't Franco who killed my mama and papa. It was Rufino Unceta. Him and the workers of Astra-Unceta. They sold their hardware to the Republicans – to *the Communists.* You can't blame Von Richtofen for doing his job."

What had he dreamt, his head nestled in his arms on table No.7? Diego Ildefonso had dreamt his parents' death, and their resurrection. They had slipped effortlessly one into the other, joined forever, their ashen faces magically lightening into sunny smiles, their crushed and dusty limbs recovering their lusty volume, like balloons blown full to bursting. They had died crossing the Market Place, scurrying out from beneath the proscenium of the Bank of Vizcaya, Uncle Isidro's restaurant their point of desperation. Into the street they had run. And the debris had fallen on them, bombs screaming down everywhere, heavy as black bulls. Falling, an avalanche of shattered masonry, and meat torn from the bone. Diego, the child, had felt the slick flesh sliding through his hair, the droplets of warm blood sprinkled over his brow. And he had run ahead, hearing them fall behind him, their knees breaking open like eggs on the pavement. It seemed this was to be the last memory he would have of them, shadows falling behind him, dull as lead. But then up had come their smiling faces again.

"I think maybe we'd better sit for a minute," he said, and Ramona guided Diego to the front steps of someone's house.

Two police cars sat parked alongside Val and Tommy-Tom's building. What was the point of being interrogated by Huff's dummies when all Gus wanted was to pick up his fucking jacket? So he drove on, intending to arrive home in time to catch the local news. But then he had a better idea. He stopped at the drugstore, bought a box of ribbed condoms, and went on to The Jewel for one last drink. He figured it would help him think more deeply about his daughter and Val. After that, he would go home and convince Babs they should go to a motel he knew in Lido, out near Point Lookout Park, for the night, without the kids. He knew the owner of a place called Sweetie's Clam House where they could drink all night and try to forget their heartache, although Gus guessed there'd be plenty of crying at some juncture in the evening, probably around Babs's fourth cocktail.

"Teddy's OK with watching the kids," Gus said later. Babs was refusing to pack her bag until she'd spoken with her mother about coming over.

"I'm trying her number one more time," she said.

"Give me a kiss," said Gus. He wanted to put his finger inside her too – she had only her underwear on and he could plainly see the cleft in her pussy.

"If we're going, I'm wearing black," she said.

Gus knew it would put a damper on the scene at the bar, at least at first, until everybody got used to it. "That's a slip, not a dress."

"Nobody'll know if I wear this scarf around the waist."

"Suit yourself." He was supposedly dialling her mother's number for her. "See, no answer."

Babs grabbed the telephone. He had dialled the number of his office at work, knowing no one would be there. Gus really didn't need Babs's mother telling them they were sinful to go off and leave the kids right after Alicia had been found dead.

"We can drop Dommie over there on our way out of town," he said.

"How can we drop him if she's not there?"

Teddy knocked on their open bedroom door.

"There's a cop in a suit here," he said.

Babs looked at Gus as if to say, *This time, you can deal with it all by yourself, smart guy.*

"Might as well let him in," Gus told his son.

"You got it." But Teddy didn't leave, he kept hanging in the doorway. "Oh Dad, I forgot to tell you. Mr. Friedrich had a heart attack."

"So, I'll send flowers."

Gus's jacket now lay in Babs's lap. Detective Sergeant Molloy had left and Gus stood over her cursing him.

"I don't care what the motherfucker said, I was just over there on my way home. If she was in there, I sure as fuck didn't know it. I figured she left the fucking door open drunk. I wasn't gonna go into hers and Tommy-Tom's fucking bedroom, was I? Teddy, I thought I told you to go into the kitchen! Who would go into Tommy-Tom's fucking bedroom? What the fuck's this Molloy know? If somebody's that fucking drunk, what're you gonna do anyways? You heard what he said, she drowned on her vomit. How was I supposed to know, I don't go around looking for stuff like that!"

"Aren't you even sorry?" said Babs. "Val was like our little fucked-up pal. I can't take much more of this."

"Me neither." Gus took the jacket from her. "I wonder why Molloy didn't keep the fucking thing for evidence. That's the kind of crap real detectives do."

"Oh God," groaned Babs. She got up, straightened her slip, already masquerading as a dress, and said, "Let's go. I'll get Dommie. You get his bottle."

"Suits me fine," said Gus.

Ramona was standing at the bottom of the stairs. Behind her, on the floor of the apartment building's foyer, sat Diego Ildefonso. His wife, who was taking their bags down to the car for the trip to Gilbey's, regarded the waitress.

"Do I know you?" she asked, even though she did.

"He isn't drunk," Ramona replied.

"Pop must have been with Mr. Rozzo!" shouted Roland, as he and Billy Nolan came tumbling down the steps.

"I'm just tired," said Diego. He struggled to his feet and gave the waitress's hand a little squeeze.

"Your husband's a dear man," Ramona murmured to Dolores.

"I can't wait to tell him what the Chief of Police thinks of me," she replied, and laughed, much to everyone's surprise.

"Thank you," came weakly from Diego. "Dolores, tell her, *thank you.*"

She realized she should, but Ramona was already halfway down the front steps onto the street.

"I'll call her Monday," said Dolores.

Later, as the Cadillac sped onto Route 19, Diego leaned into Dolores, whose concentration was fixed on the emerging traffic, and said, "I'm hungry. Why don't we stop in Palisades Park for sandwiches?"

Outside the sandwich shop on Broad Avenue, Dolores delayed him in the parking lot as the boys went skipping into the restaurant to use the toilet. He assumed she was going to quiz him on his non-existent relationship with Ramona, but the gravity of her stare convinced him otherwise.

"You've spoken to Dr. Herbert, haven't you?" he said.

"What for?" She didn't look right. Her eyes had a preoccupied cast to them. "It's about Val."

He waited for her to go on. But she only stared, not at him but at something far off in the distance, a cloud or an airplane.

"Val took an overdose last night," she said, finally.

"I don't believe this."

"She never had anything, only that poor little boy."

Diego put his arms around her, but she only shrugged and walked across the parking lot. He could hear her sobbing. By the time she was again standing beside him, she had quieted herself. "I don't want the boys to see me like this."

He kissed her cheek. "Don't worry about Tommy-Tom. He may say he wants Billy but...well, you know."

Stamping her foot on the macadam, Dolores chanted, "Never, never, never..."

Nothing, it occurred to Tommy-Tom Nolan, connected him to Hoboken anymore except his son, and his mother would gladly look after him. She had wanted to get Billy away from Val anyway. It was time Tommy-Tom vacated the Medical Center. It didn't matter that he still took his nutrition intravenously and that he hadn't walked since fully regaining consciousness only two days before, he had to go. His mother would somehow see to the arrangements for Val's funeral. It was a shame Val's folks had both died so young, they could have taken care of a lot of this mess. But they'd always made her feel bad, saying they'd never done enough for her, which obviously they hadn't, otherwise she wouldn't have been so fucked up. Tommy-Tom guessed Val just wasn't cut out to be a mother. His mom would do a better job, if only she'd stay home and give up her career selling cosmetics door-to-door. The worst thing would be for Tommy-Tom to stick around and make things even more complicated for her. No, Tommy-Tom would go and get his money out of the bank and head south for Mexico. Later, when he'd gotten himself situated, he'd send something back to Jersey City to help with Billy, maybe even send something back every month. Billy would always have this idea of his dad in some far-off place making a go of it among strange and frightening people. Tommy-Tom would always be an inspiration for his son. One other thing he would have to do before leaving was clean out his workshop.

Unfortunately for Tommy-Tom, Detective Sergeant Molloy had already gotten a search warrant, due to the suspicious nature of Valerie Nolan's death. But it was Chief Huff who had drifted over there first and now found himself studying a scene totally unexpected in its orderliness and invention: fluorescent lights hovered over spotless Formica counters and cabinets, each apparently crafted by the gifted Tommy-Tom. Huff had expected a filthy den replete with bulbous sofas covered in dull black plastic, a kidney-shaped bar, its curves armored in bamboo, an avocado-green refrigerator stocked with beer and moldy mixers, pornographic magazines, and perhaps some dried blood on the chartreuse shag carpet – that sort of thing. The sanitized character of Tommy-Tom's workshop, surfaces immaculate, new paint making the poured concrete floor glimmer, initially caused Huff to wonder if he were investigating the right person. But Huff had seen this before: the seemingly crudest among the group was in reality, in his own secret way, the most meticulous. He lowered himself into a swivel chair that stood on a rubber mat before an empty expanse of pristine gray wall. Leaning back, the Chief's cap cushioned his head nicely against the cool foundation.

The Chief now examined the room with even greater care. Over the workbench at the far end of the room hung an array of tools. Under the workbench resided a black navy footlocker and a gray metal ammo can. Tommy-Tom had welded two new fastenings to the ammo can which were secured by two combination locks. The footlocker however, which was large enough to hold the usual assortment of prized electric tools, was unprotected. The ammo can wasn't large enough for anything but bits of hardware, which couldn't have been worth very much. On impulse, Huff leapt from the chair, took down the crowbar, and pried off the locks, prying off the two new fasteners in the process. Inside the ammo can were piled a number of opaque plastic sandwich boxes. He laid the boxes out on the red Formica counter. When he opened the first, he reeled backward into the room: the contents were infested with maggots. When he gingerly opened the second, he found, much to his surprise and relief, the pudenda inside freshly powdered with Johnson's baby talc and smelling of Chanel No.5.

Engelhard wasn't the only town in Hyde County where three black men wouldn't easily find a bar in which to have a drink on a Friday evening, so Bootsy and his Uncle Tookus and Henry Moore didn't bother looking. They went back to Henry's trailer-park on the long road to Fairfield. The Mexicans who rented from him – they'd come north to help with the tobacco and stayed – were partial to his company, and he'd kept one trailer for himself. He called it his *hideaway.*

No sooner had the black men left their vehicle then Henry's Mexican pals, who were in a jovial but boisterous mood, sought to inveigle the three round to the back for a lamp-lit card game fuelled on tequila and beer. Behind the trailers, along with a couple of flimsy tables and chairs, were the wives of two of the men and several children. Uncle Tookus didn't like the look of this scene, but Bootsy was game.

"They'll take your money," laughed Henry, his white hair shocking to behold in the moonlight, especially for the Mexican children.

"I ain't bothered," Bootsy replied.

"What money?" said Uncle Tookus. "Y'all just told me there won't none."

"Music's good," commented Bootsy, ignoring him. He hopped jubilantly from one foot to the other and shook out his long tired limbs. His wide stubbled jaw went slack with pleasure as he breathed in the intoxicating redolence of tobacco emanating from a rusty shed nearby. Above his head was the yellow lozenge-shape of an open window, the air filled with the wild strumming of taped guitars and the freakishly high-pitched voices of urban troubadours singing *lino, lino-lino-lino...*

"Congoleum," was Uncle Tookus's riposte.

It was within this haphazard atmosphere of international fellowship that Bootsy Holloway met his undoing, not mortally so, but romantically so, as he fell deeply in love with one Esther Estrada. As the teenager wafted around the tables of card players, whistling sweetly to the children whenever they wandered off toward the deep irrigation ditches bordering the vast flat fields, Bootsy found himself absorbed increasingly by her presence. At last, as she passed over his shoulder, perspiration dampening her blouse, she whispered, "Take me with you. You won't be sorry."

And he did, much to Uncle Tookus's chagrin, and Henry Moore's delight, for she would be accompanying them on his fishing boat all the way to the West Indian Islands. But it was Esther's father Emilio who expressed the greatest joy, as he felt a deep and unselfish sense of relief: from the moment her big round baby eyes had looked up in innocence and beheld man, his daughter had been an enchantress.

Lido was a glamorous name for a dirty little seaside town full of deplorable people, or so it occurred to Babs Rozzo as she sat sipping her second rum and coke while staring at her husband in the mirror over the bar at Sweetie's.

"I like this place," said Gus, "it's got class."

"When're you going back to Avco? They gonna be able to use that other guy...uh..."

"Tony."

"Yea, if he doesn't even really know how to put the casings on or whatever."

"Problem is if he learns too quick. But he don't." Pushing his pile of cash along the bar, Gus hailed the barman. "Hey Jimmy, want to set us up again here?"

"I'm not ready," said Babs.

"You will be," snapped Gus, his attention focused on Jimmy, who gave the impression of not having heard him.

"Hey," said Gus again, and pushed a quarter across the bar and onto the floor. "That'll get him."

"Oh, for Christ's sake," moaned Babs, irritated and embarrassed.

"I guess you know a better way, huh?".

"Pretty black get-up," said Jimmy to Babs, as he sidled over, registering the contents of their glasses.

"We lost two of our kids," she said.

Jimmy frowned at her.

"Yea," said Gus, "the second one was murdered. Mikie fell off a Ferris wheel."

The barman said nothing, knowing better.

"This is my wife Barbara," said Gus, "and I'm Gus Rozzo. You'll probably read about us in the New York papers."

"Honey, tell him what they call me," insisted Babs.

"They call her – or used to call her – *Cheeks*."

Babs blushed deeply, as Jimmy stared. "I meant Babs," she mumbled.

"Oh, yea," said Gus. "You wanta make mine a double?"

"Sure," said Jimmy. "Well, I like your dress."

"I made it up myself," said Babs.

Gus poked her leg under the bar.

"I'm not ashamed," she declared, seemingly to the room at large. "All of the best fashion is made up and some of it on the spot."

A *combatant relationship* was the way Jimmy would have described these two in clinical barman's terms. He didn't like it. Trying to remain civil himself and intending to recover his aloofness, he said, "I'm real sorry to hear about your losses."

"I could tell you more, but it might be upsetting," said Gus.

Jimmy was opening a fresh bottle of rum.

"She was raped too," Gus went on.

"Honey, don't say anything," Babs implored him.

"It's OK," Gus assured her, "everybody and his brother is gonna know anyway."

Again the barman frowned.

"Somebody took her out to the Sunoco plant on the Hackensack, out where they have those big storage tanks. They tied her up and stripped her and left her like that. Her arms were broken.

They did everything to her. They even bit her. You could see it in the photographs. "

"My husband doesn't know what's right," said Babs.

"About what?" demanded Gus.

Babs was silent.

"I think she means, you didn't have to tell me all that," Jimmy explained.

Gus stared at the barman. "I just told you all that about my daughter who I love and you fucking insult me?"

"No offense intended." Jimmy smiled sadly at Babs before moving on along the bar, or attempting to, as Gus grabbed his sleeve.

"You fucking apologize."

"Gus, he's OK..." Babs's face was flushed with embarrassment. "Come on honey, we're having a good time and all."

"He better shut his fucking mouth."

Jimmy cocked his finger at Gus, meaning he wanted him to follow him somewhere. Gus got off his elevated bar-chair and followed him into the office at the back of Sweetie's.

Taking off his shirt to reveal a long ugly scar running diagonally across his abdomen, Jimmy said, "See this? I got it right out there. The guy who did it got his face punched in anyway and his head smashed open. You know why I smashed his head open? I wanted to see what the guy had for brains. Only, I'd never seen brains like that. They were the sickest fucking – "

"You don't have to say that."

"Say *what?*"

"You don't know what it's like."

"Like you telling me how some sick fuck tore your daughter apart out in New Jersey somewhere? Why does your wife need to hear that? – you telling that to somebody you don't even know like you're proud of it or something."

"Yea, well, you're wrong. If you can't listen with any feelings, then that's your problem."

"No, pal," said Jimmy, "that's *your* problem. I'd say, you finish your drinks and go off to wherever you're going, but I don't want to see you ask to eat in here. It's not going to happen, and she's been through enough already. Just leave the money on the bar. I don't even care how much. I'll come back out when you're gone. And tell your wife good-bye for me. How many kids you say you have?"

"Seven," said Gus, "but only five now."

"She must be some woman."

As Gus returned to the bar, he tried to work out why the guy had said that – *she must be some woman* – like the father of all those kids, himself, was just there to stick his dick in and then go on paying for it the rest of his miserable fucking life, like he was *nothing*. He approached Babs, her cheeks glowing prettily.

"The fucking guy was asking to hook up with us later. Who can fucking believe it? Come on, let's go. I know an even better place in Lido."

But then Babs wanted to find a church. And this was even before they'd had dinner, which meant Gus could forget finding another bar as good as Sweetie's. Because after dinner, she'd just want to go to the motel and go to bed and watch television.

The Ildefonsos and Billy Nolan had stopped in the shadow of Tallman Mountain on what was known locally as Rockland Road to lower the Cadillac's convertible top. The night had turned radiantly clear, stars scooting across the heavens. A cold piney wind bathed Diego's face as he stood gazing down into the darkness beyond the guard rail. Dolores and the boys, who had insisted on helping, did the work of lowering the gently flapping canvas.

"The Nazis lie in wait," whispered Roland.

"Where?" Billy whispered back.

"Down there," announced Roland, and from the height of the car's back seat pointed his tiny white finger down, as he'd seen God do, into the forbidding chasm beyond his father.

"Oh my," said Diego, rapt and wanting for nothing, "how wonderful."

Later, nearing the gates of Francis Gilbey's estate, Dolores said the same.

ELEVEN

Huddled in the darkness in a bed sufficiently large to double for the *Raft of the Medusa,* Roland's favorite painting by the histrionic Gericault, he and Billy Nolan silently prayed for the soul of Mikie Rozzo. This had of course been Roland's idea.

"Mikie didn't cry when he jumped off the Ferris wheel. I wouldn't let him. I did that," whispered Roland, eyes slit and staring, now only inches from little Billy's. He would do his best to frighten little Billy, to get him to whimper and wet the bed, as he'd heard Billy so often did, from Billy's own mother.

"You didn't do nothing."

"I did," Roland insisted, lazily. "I stopped him from crying."

"How? You didn't even know how he jumped. My mom told me, you didn't even know!"

"How foolish. How *very* foolish. And your mom doesn't even know about Tommy-Tom."

"About what?"

"Don't worry, I know your dad can't talk anymore. It's good he can't. Otherwise, he'd have to tell what I already know. He'd have to agree with *me.*"

Roland was enjoying watching Billy squirm, unaware that by frustrating his little friend he was simultaneously opening the wound opened countless times before by Tommy-Tom. Having once proudly identified Billy's anxiousness as of his own making, Tommy-Tom had proceeded on with the fun, just as Roland was doing. Billy would hate Roland for it, but never ever, consciously, his father, who had impressed him unforgettably with the magnificence of his freewheeling presence on the earth.

"Tommy-Tom showed me the hair," said Roland, teeth gleaming. "He said it came from the floor of the barber's shop, but I know where it came from. It came from the mannequins, like Lilette's. I smashed hers in – not for my mom, like everybody thought – I smashed hers in because its thing didn't have any hair on it. Your dad takes the hair off them. He saves it and hides it. I'll show you – in your basement. Nobody knows but me and Tommy-Tom." He sighed, wanting some response, then smugly conceded, "Only, you know now too."

"You can't scare me," said Billy. "My dad has his tools in the basement. He made my mom a cheeseboard."

"You can think what you want, but I'll show you when we get back," Roland assured him, and punched his pillow to soften it up for the long night ahead. "I'll show you the sandwiches your dad makes with the mannequins' fuzz. We saw stuff like that when my mom and me and Mrs. Norquist went to that museum that's shaped like a toilet. They had stuff like that lying on the floor. Some of it had nails in it."

"That's different," said Billy. "My dad works in the city but he doesn't do stuff like that."

"Your dad's involved in a crime. All of you are going to need a mental doctor. I mean, your mom and Tommy-Tom are. They probably won't bother with you."

"If you don't shut up, I'll kill you."

"How?" Now Roland would taunt him, good-naturedly, as he once had James.

"I will," Billy replied, solemnly.

"Maybe you better go and sleep on the floor then," urged Roland, his hands firmly on Billy's shoulders. "Only kidding, Billy. You know I like you. Give me a hug."

Billy lay stiffly in his arms, like a dead cat.

"Oh, honey, you fuck so nice," grunted Babs, her knees and hands pressing ever harder into the wide firm mattress.

Gus had asked for No.11, which had a Jacuzzi as advertised in a brochure he had picked up at the restaurant, but it had already been occupied for four days by a black pimp who'd come up from New Orleans to recruit what the night attendant had called *white trash pussy*. Naturally, Gus hadn't told Babs any of this, and she'd been quite pleased with their accommodation. I like Marylou's Seaside Motel, she'd said.

"It feels so big," muttered Babs, "I can really feel it..."

For about fifteen minutes, Gus had been standing, one foot on each telephone book, white pages and yellow, thrashing his scrawny hips against his wife's opulent buttocks.

"It's getting a little sore," she said, but whenever she said this, and she had several times already, Gus would thrash harder and she would grab up more of the quilted rayon coverlet between her fingers. "Can you come, honey? Can you?" she wished aloud for him, her hair parted over the nape of her neck. "Let's make a little pal for Dommie, let's fucking do it," she said, and reared up, the spring connecting her shoulders to her hips making a valley deep enough for an infant to lie in.

But Babs didn't know what she was talking about. The ribbed condom Gus had secretly slipped onto his member was fulfilling two important roles. Firstly, it was giving Babs the time of her life and, secondly, it was guarding against the creation of more life, as its design intended. Gus was grateful for the wisdom of the blank-faced men at their drawing boards. Into their receptacle tip now gushed the very essence of Gus Rozzo's disenchantment, and with it came a terrible realization: Gus was always so pissed off because he always felt so trapped. Presto-bingo, there it was, way up inside his wife with no place to go. It was nice they'd had this night out together because, Gus promised himself, it would never happen again.

"Did you come, honey?" inquired Babs, her pretty pink cheek glaring with perspiration. "Did you?"

"Oh man," sighed Gus, "did I..." and kicked the telephone books under the bed.

"My titties hurt hanging down like this," said Babs, and flopped onto her back. "Want some milk?"

As Gus suckled at Babs's gorgeous breasts, he felt a weight lift from his brain, and then a quickening of thought, as he imagined himself in the Merchant Marine. He could still be a good daddy that way – sending crates of oranges home and the like – while roughhousing with other men, real men, and occasionally having a prostitute while docked at a foreign port. Life was going to be fun for a change, and he wasn't going to have to fake it. Sure, there'd be lots of hard work, but the kind Gus would relish: shovelling coke into a hot furnace, hefting sacks of ore, that sort of thing. When he opened the locket he kept around his neck for his buddies to see inside, there would be Mikie and Alicia, his tragic legend secure in his stoical masculinity, like The Duke. Gus was destined to have wide appeal.

He was destined to be admired by everyone he met, including his children, when he returned to Hoboken every seven years, like clockwork.

"Could we order some champagne?" Babs cooed, nuzzling.

"It's after one o'clock," Gus managed, half-asleep.

"Oh, come on, honey, this is fun." She picked up the phone. "And I better call Mom too, and see how she and Dommie are doing."

"Yea, fine," said Gus, rolling over to face the air-conditioner, thinking *she might as well be twelve.*

"Wouldn't it be best if he didn't know he were about to be arrested?" said the intern to Seiffert and Langley of the Union City Police.

"Yea, he's right, Chief," said Detective Sergeant Molloy to his boss.

"You know, they may have already moved him," added the intern. "I'd better check."

"We won't venture further," the Chief assured him flippantly.

At last Tommy-Tom Nolan was about to be arraigned for the battering of Stanley Fischer. Unfortunately, Huff hadn't any evidence to offer Newark with regard to Tommy-Tom's possible involvement in the rape and murder of Alicia Rozzo. Thankfully, due to the suspicious circumstances of Valerie Nolan's death, the Chief did however have a plethora of damning items from Tommy-Tom's basement (although *forensic* still hadn't sorted through the human matter) that could very well link him to a series of killings, all involving mutilation of the female sexual organ, that had gone unsolved in the Hudson County area for several years. The lack of an arraignment in that case – there had been six suspects in all – had not been an embarrassment for the Chief because all but one of the crimes had occurred in other townships. Now, windfall of windfalls, the Chief could very well have a shoo-in on his hands.

"He's gone," said the intern upon his return. "No one seems to know where he is."

Seiffert and Langley stared at Huff.

"The scumbag's your problem," said the Chief. "I'm only here because of the Rozzo girl."

"I thought you said he was in there," insisted Seiffert.

At that moment, the Chief wished he were his wife. He imagined himself taking a nice hot shower and shaving his legs in preparation for himself coming home for dinner.

"What was he wearing?" asked Molloy. "I mean, where were his clothes? Could he get at his clothes?"

"He had a locker, but I don't think he would have known where it was," the intern replied. "He never left his bed, as far as I know."

"Can we check that?" asked Seiffert.

Ignoring them, the Chief left the building. When he laid his hands on the steering wheel of his car, he barely noticed the bits of broken slatting from the flimsy storm fence surrounding the Medical Center parking lot that had been tossed, obviously by some creep, onto the seat beside him. He was depressed. His fingers had turned yellow, the blood drained off by his reeling mind. His fingers *and* his toes were exceedingly cold, and had begun to ache.

"I need a drink," said Leon Huff to the Chief.

"So, get one," said the Chief.

Very few bars opened much before eleven in Union City and so at that unlikely hour Leon Huff, his Chief's hat tucked under his arm, would not be on display no matter which door he chose to walk through. He could easily have a quiet couple of shots before going on his way, his faith in God restored. Occasionally it was essential that the Chief turn to Him for deliverance. What God said to the Chief, whom He'd always liked, gazing down upon him where he sat nursing his second whiskey and looking miserable, was:

"Leon, the motherfucker's gonna get his, regardless."

The Chief knew the truth when he heard it. It wasn't that he felt absolved of his failure to act in a timely and responsible fashion, it was just that he knew God wouldn't let Tommy-Tom Nolan slip through His fingers, even though the Chief, through no fault of his own, had let him slip through his. The Chief could do better. The Chief would do better. God would be proud of him once more. Now, the Chief felt better. His circulation was back to normal. His hands were pink. He glanced up, as if the roof of the bar had magically flown away, and said, "Give me the wisdom to do what I can, and the strength to accept what I can't."

But later that night, as the Chief slept snuggled in his wife's fragrant arms, he would dream of Tommy-Tom and Gus Rozzo sailing off together into the sunset, a sunset that could not possibly have been of God's making, and he would grow sadder and sadder, knowing that life could be horribly unfair, despite one's belief in heavenly retribution. He would awaken and walk through his dark house and into the kitchen, where he knew he'd find a cold drink of some kind in the refrigerator. Thankfully, there were some things you could rely on in life, especialy when you had a good wife like Lois. The Chief would accept that he had become profoundly confused. He would also accept that he was congenitally unable, not to mention philosophically unwilling, to accept that such an evil paradox should even be possible: that Tommy-Tom should walk off unobstructed into the sunset and that his little buddy Gus, who it seemed always sailed along on a lurid cardboard sea, should be allowed to go on thinking his crappy little life was something special. There had to be some way to communicate to Gus that it had most probably been Tommy-Tom who had sexually brutalized his daughter and then, casually and coldly, strangled her. At this point, the Chief's sadness would turn to indignation. He would feel it welling up in himself as the sadness shifted on, like sand on a windy highway.

Icy Coca-Cola fizzling under his tongue, Chief Huff would savor the anticipation of bringing one metallic verity to bear emphatically on the lives of Gus and Babs Rozzo, in spite of the pitiful tragedies that had so recently befallen them: life was unfair because people like themselves insisted on it. God could find Tommy-Tom Nolan and punish him if He liked, but Leon Huff would find Babs and Gus Rozzo – what was their address? – and punish them for cultivating such ugliness in the world. Their children would be taken from them and turned over to the nuns to be raised as *proper* Catholics, the kind who know what fear is for.

The haze rising over Freeport this morning was unnaturally silvery and bright. Although Babs had wanted to return home immediately after breakfast, Gus had it in mind to go fishing: they didn't get out to the ocean very often and the manager of Marylou's Seaside Motel, who obviously knew about these things, said the blues were running. And so, Gus and Babs, along with about a dozen other paying fishermen, watched from the upper deck of the retired trawler, recently renamed *Neptune's Slipper*, as Point Lookout Park slowly became little more than a patch of astro-turf glinting at the foot of an aluminum door.

Gus, who had been drinking beer ever since boarding, said, "I wish Val and Tommy-Tom were here."

"What, so you could flirt with Val and let Tommy-Tom boss you around?"

Why Babs said such things, Gus could only guess. He shifted on his feet and leaned more heavily on the railing that circumscribed the deck. Their rods jangled between them. Maybe she said such things because she didn't know what it was like to *truly* love somebody, somebody other than herself. That had to be it: Babs couldn't imagine what it was like to be somebody else, to be him for instance. She'd never love beyond her own skin. It wasn't in her repertoire.

"Maybe you need some time to yourself," he said.

"What're you saying?"

Gus glimpsed the consternation creasing his wife's babyish features. "I'm saying maybe you'd be better off without me for a while, seeing as I always say the wrong thing and do the wrong thing."

"Like what?"

What Gus wanted to say was *like finally making love to Val after all these years,* but instead he said, "Like trying to get even with Freddie Friedrich for his kid insulting our Alicia."

The gulls had begun to follow the boat, waiting for the paying fishermen to begin casting their bait ineptly out upon the water.

"I don't get what you're saying?!" Babs was desperate.

People were staring.

"Go on and fish," Gus whispered. He would ignore her.

"We're not even out there yet!" Babs shouted. "Take a look around – nobody's fishing, they're just staring!"

"Come on, honey, let's just forget it and fish."

"I told you, nobody's fishing!" Babs leaned out violently over the railing and addressed the man standing on the other side of Gus. "Are you fishing?! See, he's not fishing!"

"I'm going below," said Gus, and set down his rod. "Maybe I'll get another beer. Want one?"

"You don't say that to me!" She began pushing him along, toward the metal stairs.

A few more uncertain steps, Babs pushing him all the while from behind, and Gus turned on her.

"Don't push me one more time," he said. "Don't."

But she did. She couldn't help herself. She pushed him on, singing, "Gus wants a beer, Gus wants a beer..."

"Don't. I said *don't*, Babs!"

When he turned again, and stepped back, cocking his arm to strike, she said, calmly, "Look out, there's a guy behind you who wants to get by," but there wasn't, and Gus pivoted on his slippery leather soles and fell, head striking step after step after step, all the way down to the lower deck.

As Gus lay unconscious at the bottom of the steps, the man at the railing Babs had just spoken to came forward, put his big hairy arms around her, and steadied her.

"I saw it," he said. "He fell all by himself."

Diego and Dolores Ildefonso stood beneath the ancient oak that dominated the garden that swooped gently down to the lake. The enormous pink house, known as Lakeview, loomed behind them. They watched as the butler and maid unloaded a long table and a dozen chairs from the back of a horse van that had been borrowed from the stables. Gilbey and Nina had purposefully not as yet arrived on the scene so that the Ildefonsos could acclimate themselves to their surroundings without feeling self-conscious. Roland and little Billy had immediately gone to investigate the rowboats. They lay tipped over in a row of six by the edge of the lake, their hulls recently painted a smart robin's egg blue. The lake was vast. Mature trees towered over its placid surface, while a swarm of rushes, lathered softly by the breeze, eddied in under a stone bridge in the distance. Beyond the lake rose deeper woodland, which one imagined carried on thickening right to the very edge of the cliffs overhanging the Hudson River. And there were the swans too, in a grouping of perhaps twenty, gliding brilliantly along in the sunlight. Dolores moved closer to Diego. His arm went around her waist and held her firmly to the extravagant curve of his own. Their son came scampering up to them, while Billy lingered by the boats.

"He wants to feed the swans," Roland panted, "he wants to go out in one of the boats, but we don't have anything to feed them with."

"Those aren't real swans," said Dolores, "they're only made of rubber."

"Mom! You can't fool me!" Roland danced around on his spindly legs, his shorts, which were large enough to grow into, splayed out like a sail.

"Tell Billy that anyway," said his father.

"No swans for Mr. Gilbey, no swans that I can see," sang Roland, "only a bunch of rubber ducks for Billy, Billy, Billy..."

"That's enough," said Dolores, reaching out to quiet him. "Billy looks upset."

Billy was now perched on the hull of one of the boats, head in hands.

"Oh," said Roland, and scampered back to the edge of the lake. "Come on, Billy, let's explore!" he called as he darted by, arms flailing at the bridge in the distance.

Billy climbed down from the boat and took off after him, his feet gone wild. "Not so fast!" he shouted.

"Our boys," said Diego.

"It's nice." Dolores waved to little Billy.

"You are too."

They walked on, taking the path the boys had just found, as the horse van slithered up the grassy knoll behind them. On the bridge, they stood breathing lightly, and gazed out, eyes finding the far shore, above which sat the magnificent Greco-Italianate pile.

"How's tricks?" called Gilbey from the bottom of the bridge. Rummaging in the shrubbery behind him for a spring blossom or two was the young woman.

Dolores and Diego watched as Gilbey gestured briefly to the landscape, his hand nearly as vibrant a blue in its translucence as the sky. The two couples met on the bridge and made their way back along the path, picking up Roland and Billy as they went. When they arrived at the great oak, the table was set, loaded with food and drink, and gleaming. The butler, who was now introduced as Clive, uncorked the champagne and poured. Roland and Billy happily sipped their sodas through peppermint-stick straws provided by the maid.

When Gus Rozzo lifted his head from the lower deck of *Neptune's Slipper* and glanced heavenward, up the glinting metal steps he'd just come down, he saw two Babs's in black descending, like dispossessed angels, to lift him to his feet and carry him, bleeding, into the vessel's lounge.

"I never thought you'd fall," she said, blotting at his brow with her scarf.

"I crushed my sight," he moaned. "There's two of everything." Gazing down, Gus saw that he did indeed have four red feet. "I'm getting blood on the fucking carpet."

"They say nothing bleeds like your head. Here, sit here."

While Gus twitched with pain, Babs carried on blotting and wringing out his blood into a Styrofoam cup someone had left on the bench.

"Maybe we should find some towels or something, or a doctor for Christ's sake," said Gus. "It's not stopping."

"I think it is, a little," said Babs.

"How do you know?" He plucked petulantly at his trousers, the fabric torn at the knee. "There wasn't even anybody there. You *wanted* me to fall. What if I have a fucking concussion? I'm telling you, everything's double."

"Don't you ever see double when you drink so much?"

"I never drink like that. You're thinking of Tommy-Tom." Gus was trying his best to be incisive. "Glasses won't cure this."

"Probably not."

"You don't care!" he raged, fending off her hand, and got up.

"What?"

"'What?'! You aren't even listening..." Gus stumbled forward, then fell back onto the bench. "You just do what you think I want, you don't even care how I *really* feel!"

Babs looked at her husband. It was true. She did do almost anything he wanted. If she didn't he would sulk or, worse, go out and buy something they couldn't afford, just to make himself feel big and important. That's why they were there on that stupid fishing boat, and why they'd gone to Sweetie's the night before. That's why he'd embarrassed her, talking about Alicia as if she were just some dead girl written up in the National Enquirer. *To show off.* She was always going some place stupid with him, all dressed up in his new clothes, having to act like she couldn't wait to get home and fuck her big tough guy. She did it for him, not for her. All she ever asked was that their kids should grow up nice, not spoiled, just nice. The sad thing was she did love Gus. She didn't know why, and she'd been over it like a million times before, but she did.

Babs was tired of thinking about him. He could do whatever he wanted. She would get a job. Her mother could look after Dommie and the twins while she was at work. She would be a receptionist. That's what she studied at vo-tech. She was still attractive, and able. Maybe she would go work for Dr. Herbert, who was looking to replace Linda. Everybody knew Linda couldn't keep anything straight. Whenever you went into his office, he complained about her. Things would be different, if she got a job like that. Then she could get dressed up every day, and go out to lunch, and have people to talk to, not just the kids.

"I don't want you to come home," she said. "You can go to the doctor's when we get off and then you can go over to your mother's or somewheres. I don't want you around there tonight. I've been nice to you, Gus, but I'm tired of it. You think this is having a good time? Look at us."

"How can I go anywhere when I'm seeing two? I mean, double."

"That's why I think you should go over to your mother's. When you're safe to work, one of your brothers can drive you."

"You can't run those machines when you're seeing two of everything, for Christ's sake!"

Without responding, Babs went out into the bracing sea air, then back up onto the higher deck, where she stood next to the man who had steadied her after Gus's fall. She waited, staring out over the water, for Gus to rejoin her. Ten minutes or so passed.

"What's your name?" asked the man and his voice was kind.
"Barbara."
"Mine's Bill."

Tommy-Tom Nolan blotted the pinkish lymph oozing from his neck wound onto the velveteen upholstery covering the altar railing. Intent upon not having the Lord working against him too, he had stopped in at St. Pat's to take mid-morning communion. He left the cathedral feeling somewhat better and took a taxi downtown to arrange a date, via sign language, with his favorite prostitute Frosty June for that afternoon. He wanted to score some cocaine and Frosty June was to be his procurer. What Tommy-Tom had in mind was a cocktail of sorts. He intended to mix the cocaine into a glass of ice cold vodka, at the appropriate evening hour, as a kind of sick tribute to Bootsy. He also desperately hoped this concoction would make the massive wound in his throat, which really, really hurt, go numb. The whole thing would have pissed Chief Leon Huff off like nobody's business. Tommy-Tom got a laugh out of that, thinking about the look on the Chief's face. But then he started choking, which opened up the wound, which began bleeding all down into his shirt and onto the white plastic attaché case he had found in the taxi.

After returning uptown and having lunch in the cavernous quiet of the China House Bar & Restaurant, moo shoo pork falling through the hole in his neck onto the table – well, it wasn't, but it felt that way – Tommy-Tom strolled along Broadway to just above the Lowe's Theatre where he would wait for the downtown bus. The bus would take him very near the point of his assignation.

Tommy-Tom sat at the very rear of the bus, on the wide blue plastic berth traditionally preferred by dozing drunks. He looked out the window and was grateful to be back in the world, and especially back in Manhattan. The big city suited Tommy-Tom. This comforting feeling led him to think on about where he might eventually settle, having once left America. Tommy-Tom found himself, via memory initially and then via pure imagination, thumbing through his fifth-grade geography book. Many exotic cities were thusly superimposed upon the familiar scenes flowing by the bus's window: Rio, Buenos Aires, Rotterdam, Warsaw, Athens, Rome, Damascus, Bombay, Singapore, Hankow, Peking, Hong Kong, Cairo, and Mombasa, although Tommy-Tom couldn't remember the name of this African port, only a jostling sea of black faces.

It was very unlikely that Tommy-Tom, due to his mute condition, would be allowed to work his way to any one of these faraway places on board a ship. Furthermore, he didn't know anyone in the maritime trade. It was most likely that he, like any other world traveller, would have to pay his way, no matter how crummy the vessel. Logically, if Tommy-Tom were to choose a retreat on a southerly route from New York harbor, in Central America for instance, rather than halfway round the world, it would cost his benefactor – because that's exactly what he needed – less.

Tommy-Tom wondered if Frosty June might know some rich john they could invite along. That could be fun, taking the sucker's money and charge cards, then dumping his body in a fetid alleyway behind a gambling den in – pick a city south of the border – so that it appeared he'd stupidly crossed a man more powerful than himself and got what was coming to him. After that, scoot off to some high-flying European capital and spend. But then what to do with Frosty June, who was a hopeless drug addict? The answer was quite simple: keep her working, as she was now, to support her habit. Tommy-Tom could then have sex with her whenever he pleased. He had always liked it best with Frosty June when she was completely zonked-out. She was prettiest that way, with her big hollow face like a rubber mask.

Frosty June was waiting for Tommy-Tom in the pizza shop around the corner on 41st. They'd agreed this location earlier that morning, Tommy-Tom gesturing emphatically from the open window of his taxi. But he'd roared off, back into the traffic, before she'd convinced him she hadn't the money to front him for the cocaine. So, when Tommy-Tom got off the bus, Frosty June was drugless.

"You ain't got no color, except for that fucking stain," she said.

Tommy-Tom didn't understand.

"Your neck."

He reached up to feel the moisture dampening his scarf, then tried to say, *It's not an expensive one.*

"When you've got style, you don't need money," Frosty June assured him.

Tommy-Tom's condition was appalling. Frosty June had never seen anything like it, and she'd seen many of her friends lying in hospital beds. He had wrapped a rayon scarf, one with giraffes on it, a fake Hermes or something, twice around his neck. The scarf was glued to the wound's nylon stitches with seeping viscid matter, like maple syrup. The two smaller superficial wounds, one running across his forehead and the other down through the stubble above his right ear, were filling in nicely with soft orangish scabs. Frosty June couldn't possibly present Tommy-Tom to Neal Blaine, who always had plenty of blow, in this revolting state. She would have to take him over to the welfare hotel where Tommy-Tom worked, get some of the cash he kept in his locker, and try to convince him he should stay put until she got back. It might even be best if he let himself into one of the empty rooms and stretched out for the duration. A slice of pizza cooling in her purse, she managed to get them pointed in the direction of the Stamford Arms.

Today, Frosty June was especially pleased with her appearance. Because Tommy-Tom's own pal Bootsy had fucked him up she'd decided as a special treat to do something extra nice with her hair. She'd had the highlights that were her trademark freshened up and her tresses sang. Her bouffant, very like Marie Antionette's coiffeur but in miniature, shone like spun aluminum. Her dress was cool too. It had ridges at the bosom, made out of what looked like sparkly wrapping paper, and two slits, like Suzy Wong's purple one.

"You can hold my hand," she said, and shifted her purse over to the other side.

When Tommy-Tom finally allowed Frosty June to take his hand, she coyly rubbed the big knuckles against her pubic bone. His nerves still heavy with liquid acetaminophen, Tommy-Tom could only barely feel himself becoming erect, but he didn't like it, not there on the street with people walking right by them.

"Think you can do it?" she whispered, having remembered that he found a little annoyance exciting.

"I can fuck," he insisted, although it came out *agfa,* a word Frosty June associated with photography.

Poised before the buffet, Diego watched as the butler laid the perfect cuts of cold salmon on his and Gilbey's plates. It was he who resumed their conversation:

"Gilbey – "

"You really must learn to call me Francis. It's much nicer, don't you think? Just the parslied potatoes, thank you, Clive."

"Francis," Diego continued, "before I worked at Pretty Feet I – "

"No, no asparagus."

"None for me either, thanks."

"It doesn't look overcooked," observed Gilbey.

"I shouldn't have any more hollandaise."

"Have the vinaigrette."

"I think I will. Please, about a half-dozen."

Smiling serenely, Clive responded to Diego's request with great care: his white gloves would remain immaculate throughout the serving of lunch.

"You said any *more* hollandaise," commented Gilbey. "I don't see any on your plate."

"Did I?"

"Oh, that's right, Clive took you up Eggs Benedict this morning, didn't he?"

But Diego couldn't recall having had Eggs Benedict.

When he didn't respond, Gilbey rambled on:

"I remember a time when my life was one lavish meal after another. It may be hard to believe, but I was nearly as large as you. Look at me now, I'm just a slip of a thing. My wife was very big on entertaining, and of course we had our little boat. As anyone knows, there're only three things to do on the sea: eat, drink, and – ?"

"Play cards?" offered Diego.

Gilbey found this very amusing. Taking up a napkin and silverware, he said, "The worst thing in the world for the prostate: playing cards. You're better off doing the other. They say doing it regularly is the best preventative for that particular strain of cancer."

They seated themselves with Dolores and Nina around the wide linen-covered table. The two boys elected, with everyone's blessing, to take their picnic down by the rowboats. As he tended to the bounty on his plate, Gilbey watched the lads having fun with their asparagus by the water's edge.

"I assume Billy is the son of your friend involved in the aforementioned sordid matter," he inquired of Diego.

"Billy Nolan," Diego replied, uncertain as to what to say.

"Billy's father got caught up in a predicament in a bar," explained Dolores. "He was attacked and very badly injured. Diego visited him in the hospital on Wednesday."

"Someone cut him around the head and neck with a broken glass, didn't they?" said Gilbey, without inflection. "And he may be permanently disabled, mightn't he?"

"His vocal chords were severed. Excuse me, I am sorry to be saying all this during lunch," Dolores apologized to Nina, whom she'd just seen stare off, apparently repulsed.

"Francis started it," was her response.

It was true, he had, and Diego couldn't see to what end. The details Gilbey was bringing to the table were particularly unsavory and, it seemed, calculated to throw himself and Dolores off balance. More disconcerting however was Gilbey's exacting knowledge of Tommy-Tom's condition.

"Billy just lost his mother too," Dolores went on. "She suffered from depression. She took her own life."

"You haven't told him, have you," said Gilbey.

"We thought we'd wait until we know more about his father. I mean, how things are going to go for him," Dolores explained further. "Anyway, we feel we should keep Billy with us for the time being."

Gilbey again focused on the boys. "Look at them," he said, "they're having a grand time. I'd say Billy Nolan's lucky his parents have friends like you."

Dolores glanced doubtfully at Diego, who shrugged to communicate his own lack of enthusiasm for Gilbey's transparent flattery.

"Now, what about the others?" asked Gilbey. "Didn't you mention a second funeral, or is that it? I mean, Billy's mother's?"

"Diego must have been referring to the Rozzos," answered Dolores.

"There's nothing else we can do for them," mumbled Diego.

"You mean, it's all too overwhelming, where the Rozzos are concerned. They're very difficult people," Gilbey concluded.

Dolores couldn't help but wonder why her husband would choose this man, obviously an indolent and spoiled snob, to talk to. She pictured them sitting idly in the shop going over the same anguishing facts she and Diego had raked through only hours before. This wasn't like Diego at all.

"Nina wants to open a flower shop," said Gilbey, "a floral decorating service in Manhattan. I think it's a bad idea, committing so much time to such a terrible place."

"People think New York is the *living end*," offered Dolores.

She gazed at Diego. He was nervously arranging the capers garnishing his cut of salmon in a long row with his fork.

"It is, except for Calcutta perhaps," laughed Gilbey. "Even Hong Kong is more hospitable. I worked in Manhattan nearly all my life, I know. So where's a good place to go? And don't say Paris."

"How about Palermo?" offered Diego.

"Sicily? Why Sicily?" sneered Nina.

"It's too long to go into." Diego had found he really detested her. "Trust me, Palermo is very grand."

Gilbey smiled contentedly round the table. "I could live out the rest of my life on the sea, which is what I've always wanted to do, while Nina runs around delivering flowers."

"Watch out for the food – it's too good," said Diego, wondering when Gilbey was going to make his move. There had to be something here, something he could turn to his advantage.

Gilbey had already said as much on the telephone, with the usual obliquity employed by the very rich. Diego only hoped Dolores wouldn't be made to feel any more awkward than she already had.

"Listen Ildefonso," Gilbey began, "I've been thinking, why not hire someone like yourself to run the business? Then Nina can concentrate on what she does best."

"What's that?" asked Dolores. The sarcastic tone in her voice was unmistakable, and Diego gave her a look.

"I don't see how I'm any better suited than anyone else," ventured Diego.

"You speak Italian, don't you?" laughed Gilbey.

"How do you know?"

"Your accent."

"I'm Spanish."

"We're all something. Listen, you'll run the shop. Imagine how beautiful we could make it with all my money. That would be my gift to you and Nina. And the money to get over there and relocate. That would be my gift to you and your family. After getting set up, you and Nina would be on your own. You'd have to find a way to get on together. But, look, if I can get along with Nina, surely you can."

Gilbey reached out and patted Nina's hand.

"Please, oh please," Nina sighed, "don't fucking condescend to me."

"One question..." said Diego.

Gilbey glanced up.

"What kind of money are we talking about?"

Dolores was astounded.

Gilbey now appeared to want to concentrate on his meal. "You and Nina can work it out."

"Look how the swans have all gathered under the bridge," observed Dolores, hoping to change the subject.

"Yea, what kind of money are we talking about?" demanded Nina. "I mean, compared to what I'm getting?" Gilbey laid a withered hand on her knee. "That thing's like ice," she hissed, and fixed the hand firmly in her lap.

"Oh, that's better," sighed Gilbey, "my circulation *improves*." He then addressed them all. "It's funny," he said, "but my father ordered hundreds of people around every day. I used to watch him, and I never understood what purpose he saw in it, other than producing a product. Fortunately for him, this was something everyone needed. Our family manufactured those clever bits of metal and rubber that allow toilets to flush. We didn't even do the porcelain work, which was the part that interested me, like sculpture really. My grandfather took another man's idea and patented it under his own name. The man used to cut our lawn. My grandfather was an avid golfer. That's all he did: play golf, smoke cigarettes, and drink scotch. He already had money he'd inherited from an uncle in London but, naturally, he wanted more. He also wanted power, obviously over the man who cut his lawn. I remember this man. He lisped. My people were the least interesting people on earth. Fine, fine people, which of course only means lots of money, but extremely boring."

Gilbey now leaned back in his chair and allowed his head to loll back on his neck, the skin on the underside of his chin as taut and fragile as a dead bat's wing.

TWELVE

After Frosty June had left the Stamford Arms with one hundred and eighty of his hard-earned dollars, Tommy-Tom Nolan lay on Bootsy Holloway's old bed and thought about the night they'd gone to visit Shirlee:

It could of been OK, me and Bootsy and Val going out together. I would of showed him she was worth me having for a wife. Val was better than OK. She just had inferiority. Nobody knows that but me and I should keep it to myself now that she's dead. I hope Billy's smarter. I hope he's got more of what it takes. You only go around once, like the man says. Gus always thought she was so special, but how would anybody know when she never opened her mouth. He was always impressed with how she was like that. Like she'd just sit there and look at you. Gus must of thought she was thinking about what it would of been like with him. He was always wanting to do it with her. I registered that shit. He don't know it, but I did. Him and Val? Give me a fucking break. She talked plenty when she was plastered, but who wants to hear it? All that crap about me being an absentee whatever, even a prick towards her, especially when she don't mean it. She never means nothing but come over here and kiss me and fuck me nice, Tommy-Tom. Maybe she wouldn't of got so drunk with Bootsy there. Maybe having a black dick around would of stopped her. She probably would of been afraid of him. Good thing she didn't know what a faggot he turned out. Where's he now anyways? I don't see him here cleaning up his fucking room. Probably went back to his fucking sugar shack in stinksville, North Carolina.

Tommy-Tom laughed a little, but it hurt. He didn't know what he was going to do without Val, but then he remembered:

How about the way she spoiled Blinky? That fucking dog could piss anywheres and she wouldn't even say nothing, just clean it up so I wouldn't notice. I bet my mom's gonna spoil the little shit too. And Billy. Billy's gonna have it great, a lot better than he did with Val. She was turning him into a fucking sissy. Always crying about anything. Always, always, always. Who can shut a kid like that up? Not me. That Roland's a little fucker. I wish I had a kid like that. What a great kid. He's gonna know what to do with anybody who talks back, especially cunt. Jesus Christ, I forgot all about my collection. I gotta find some way to get them snatches and whatnot out of there, and pretty fucking fast. Yea, Diego's kid. He's the perfect choice.

Again, Tommy-Tom laughed, but this time he was better able to control the pain.

Kid would of licked one. Couldn't take his eyes off them things. Anybody can make a snatch out of your own pubic hair dyed different colors and some pieces of pork skin and salami. But who could make it look so real you could fuck it? Me, that's who. The ones I made never looked like Val's. Mine were fat. Hers was real skinny, like a lady's. She always made it smell nice too. It was probably tighter than Frosty June's, or Samantha's, but I could never figure out which way any of them was tighter, only Alicia's, because she wasn't even wet. I shouldn't be thinking this stuff, not when Val's dead. How can I make it up to Gus? I guess I did part of the way already by doing like he told me about Chief Huff. That dumb fuck. He thinks Alicia would let Ildefonso take her someplace to screw?

Tommy-Tom was about to laugh again when he heard footsteps in the hallway. They went around in a circle, then away. Cleverly, he decided to clean up Bootsy's room himself, so he'd look industrious and kindly when Frosty June got back. He wanted to demonstrate he could forgive as well as forget, even though Bootsy had maimed him. She'd been with Bootsy a couple of times. Afterwards she'd said that, although she had plenty of black women friends – she had meant other whores – who she would do just about anything for, she wouldn't trust (quote) *some black asshole just because he's got sad eyes and a pretty dick.* To which Tommy-Tom had responded, "You just don't like it when the guy takes too long, regardless of whether they're paying you, and black guys can do it all night." Frosty June had been offended, and replied, "It's just the shit they've got up their nose." This had intrigued Tommy-Tom, and soon after he had asked Bootsy if this were true, and soon after that Bootsy had started getting friendly with his toot, which was very nice of him.

The pain Tommy-Tom Nolan was now experiencing as he lurched about Bootsy Holloway's room tidying up was excruciating and he began to wonder if cocaine, which he imagined to be similar to Novocain in its chemical make-up, would actually subdue the baby rats tearing at the inside of his throat.

"Is that how you want them?" asked Gilbey's butler. From where he stood, with the row of chairs stretching out before him, Diego Ildefonso appeared to be hovering over the glimmering lake, his feet just touching its surface at the very edge.

"I think we need a trifle more space between them," Diego replied, "otherwise things could get violent."

Clive set about moving the chairs farther apart. Conveniently, the ground was level around the base of the old tree, worn flat by numerous such occasions over the years, and so the chairs sat quite sturdily on their pegged legs.

"Much better," Diego assured him. "Any idea what we can do for music? Something we can stop and start?"

"Cynthia has a music-box, the kind that runs on batteries. It uses *cassettes.*"

"That should do. But what kind of music? I mean, what does she listen to?"

"The usual rubbish. Although, come to think of it, I did give her a rather nice compilation of Satie piano pieces for Christmas. Quite simple, but rhythmic."

"Perfect. Godfather of Les Six."

"Exactly."

"I thought you English couldn't abide the French?"

"Only when it comes to the preparation of beef."

Several yards away, Gilbey was entertaining Roland and little Billy. They were playing with a trick walking stick, one Gilbey had found and been fascinated by in a magic shop in London many years before. The boys had never seen one and were gleefully startled when Gilbey, banging its metal tip smartly on a smooth stone, transformed the stick into a bouquet of flowers.

"Show me, show me," begged Roland, eager to know how it worked, while Billy only looked on, his eyes sparkling with tears of wonder. It was at that moment, as Gilbey elucidated the rudimentary dynamic behind the illusion, that Billy secretly determined to have the walking stick as a gift for his father.

Little Billy stood by the great oak with the cassette-player cradled in his arms. Diego had asked if he would like to be exempted from the game to captain the stopping and starting of the music. This Billy had wanted very much. In fact, Billy was smiling broadly, as he so seldom did. With the exception of Roland, who had agreed to be the first person without a chair, everyone else sat anxiously waiting. Gilbey had insisted that Clive and Cynthia join in, and the two had naturally obliged their employer. While one person sat facing the lake, the next sat facing the house. Diego had placed himself next to his son.

When Billy pressed down the black plastic button and the crystalline piano chimed forth, the players got to their feet and slowly walked around the row of seven gilded chairs. With its oddly disjointed pacing, Satie's composition tempted the players' hands to linger on the chairs' rounded backs. This lingering of the hands in turn tempted the players' bodies to linger also.

"Faster!" cried Gilbey.

"My heels are too high for this nonsense," groaned Nina.

And the music stopped.

Each seat had been claimed, with the exception of Roland's, which had been claimed by two, father and son. But Diego had managed somehow to keep the bulk of his weight balanced on the balls of his feet, saving Roland from any real discomfort.

"Right," declared Gilbey, "it's you two who lose your chair, while...What am I saying?"

"That's how it works," said Diego, and went over to stand beside Billy, who was obviously dazzled by the sight of so many grown-ups behaving so frivolously.

"Mr. Ildefonso, you've forgotten the chair," called the butler.

Roland came to his father's assistance, taking the chair to him. "You can sit on it now, Pop," he said, and scampered back to take his place along the line of players.

Diego glanced at Dolores. Suddenly, startling everyone, Gilbey clapped his hands sharply for more music. Flinging his jacket over the back of the chair, Diego settled himself next to

Billy and nodded for action. Billy pressed down the big black button and again Satie's notes fell upon the players like icy droplets. Round and round they went. But now Gilbey wandered away from the fray. He motioned for Diego Ildefonso to follow.

They slowly made their way across the vast swooping lawn to a distant terrace and the study that resided beyond it. Gilbey unlocked the French doors and the two went inside. The room, its tall windows heavily draped, reminded Diego of an Italian bordello. There had been a problem with damp and the wallpaper, which was red and flocked, had peeled up from the baseboards in great powdery scrolls. The carpet was lime green and altogether inappropriate for the house, and the furniture – Diego counted five huge hairy black sofas – had the look of having been bought secondhand from a bar or perhaps, judging by their flamboyant scale, a gambling casino.

"Nice, isn't it?" said Gilbey, and glanced meaningfully at his guest.

"I like the television," remarked Diego, wondering at the elephantine console in one corner.

"They have even bigger ones now," marvelled Gilbey. "Like a private movie screen to view your nasties on. Have a seat."

They automatically sat side-by-side facing the TV.

"What do you do in here?" asked Diego.

"I come here to think."

"That's all?"

"Well no, not really. I come in here to watch my friends have sex."

Diego stared at Gilbey, who took out a crumpled packet of cigarettes and handed him one.

"Good for your heart," said Gilbey.

They each blew a few lungfuls of mentholated smoke into the room.

"Have you ever had Gus and Babs up here?" asked Diego.

"Once."

"They never said anything about it."

"They wouldn't. Anyway, I couldn't get them to perform. Babs is a bit of a prude."

Diego knew Gus wouldn't go anywhere near this place.

"The Nolans are another matter altogether," said Gilbey. "I especially like Tommy-Tom. He's really wild."

"Yea, he's wild alright."

"He's more than that, he's scary. And Val, she'll do just about anything. I mean, she *used* to do just about anything."

Diego glanced over at Gilbey. He was tittering. Smoking and tittering, like an adolescent girl.

"You don't get it, do you," said Gilbey and shifted over on the sofa so he could tuck his legs up under him. "Like a pajama party. I've had some real studs up here. Black guys. Some real crazy chicks too. And not all of them were hookers. We bring our talent out from Manhattan, mostly. Sometimes we find something good down your way. Like Alicia. What a mouth she had on her."

Diego got up and walked across the room towards the French doors onto the terrace.

"Oh, don't go yet," whined Gilbey. "I haven't told you what you have to be afraid of. Surely you want to hear about that?"

Diego waited.

"Move over, Rover, and let Francis take over!" sang Gilbey.

Diego went back to the sofa and sat down.

"There you go, now check it out." Gilbey's eyes were wide with delight. "Isn't that what you cool guys say?"

"I'm not a cool guy," said Diego.

"No Ildefonso, you're not. Now, imagine we're watching a movie on that great big TV over there. Imagine you're truly interested. Are you imagining?"

Diego could feel the irritation creasing his face.

"Good," whispered Gilbey, sidling closer, and went on whispering, like a tiresome ham actor. "Alicia is sitting on Tommy-Tom's lap at the Fourth of July picnic, with the rest of you looking on. She's only ten years old. But she's something special. New scene. Gus is lying on the cot in Tommy-Tom's workshop while Tommy-Tom sits with little Alicia standing in front of him. She's smiling. Her underpants are in her daddy's pocket. Now the show gets more complicated. Val comes home on a mucky afternoon and catches Tommy-Tom and Alicia, now about thirteen, hurrying from the alleyway outside the basement and into Tommy-Tom's car. Next Val and Tommy-

Tom are in the kitchen arguing. You can see it through the window. Hear the traffic in the street below? Val knows what's going on with her husband and this poor sick kid. The look on Val's face says it all."

"Sometimes these things are better kept to yourself," said Diego.

"What *things?*" asked Gilbey, his delivery loaded with sarcasm.

"Your sick fantasies."

"Why not just let me finish?"

Diego was silent.

"Now you're driving your son and Billy Nolan and Alicia into Manhattan in the Rozzo van. The kids are all excited about going to the Museum of Natural History to see the stuffed animals. Switcheroo, you drop Alicia off at the Stamford Arms instead. And there's your chum Tommy-Tom waiting in the hotel lobby."

"Gus doesn't let anyone drive his van."

"Now for something really amusing. Alicia and Shirlee Simonaire are playing at dress-ups. Naturally, you can't help but wonder how *this* friendship came to be. Oops, there's Gus and Tommy-Tom sitting on the couch in Shirlee's living-room waiting for them to come out in their outfits. Next scene. Now Tommy-Tom and Bootsy Holloway are sitting in The Jewel having a good time. "

The television's lifeless screen, fixed in its ugly cabinet, had fulfilled its purpose as the disgusting images had come flooding into Diego's head. "I don't know anything about Shirlee Simonaire or what's-his-name Holloway."

"Bootsy," Gilbey replied. "And you know an awful lot about Stanley Fischer because I saw you kiss him at a party one time."

"I kissed Stanley Fischer?" Diego had to laugh.

"You certainly did, at the opening party for the new Pretty Feet. I was there. And he – I mean Shirlee – was hanging around with The Cadettes. You thought Shirlee was part of the show. You kissed them all, including that little twat." Gilbey sighed, then anxiously patted his meatless thighs. "So Stanley Fischer lies with *her* face smashed in on the floor of *her* apartment. See, there's Tommy-Tom lurching out onto the landing. And there's Bootsy Holloway running off down Palisade Avenue, with his sleeves trailing blood."

As gently as possible, Diego said, "We're talking about your problem here, not mine. I think we're talking about a problem that you have."

Gilbey ripped Diego's burnt cigarette out of his hand and flung it onto the carpet with his own.

"That's Clive's job," he ranted. "Clive cleans up the messes around here. So why don't you ask Clive to clean up *your* mess? Well? Oh, so you don't think *you* make messes. And that's why Gus Rozzo and his big-titted wife are trying to stick it to you— because *you* don't make messes."

"It sounds to me like you're the one who's trying to stick it to me."

"You? All *you* ever do is go around wiping your friends' asses."

"I don't seem to have much choice."

"You're a real prince." Gilbey took another cigarette from the packet, lit it, and shifted his attention once again to the giant TV in the corner.

Diego hadn't anything to say.

"You've got everything I've always wanted," said Gilbey, bitterly. "Tommy-Tom did too, but he was too stupid to appreciate how well he was loved. What a guy, a real fucking animal."

"Yea, and Gus?"

"At least he knows how to treat his kids – in a fashion. You can't get *no purchase* on Gus, he's the original white nigger."

Diego wished Gilbey were saying this to Gus's face.

"I give them money," Gilbey went on. "How do you think Gus manages to buy all that tacky stuff, like the Jacuzzi he can't be bothered to install? And Tommy-Tom's highly collectible car? He could never afford such a vehicle. I bought that. I did it because he wanted it and there were things I wanted from him. Now there's something I want from you. That's why I'm offering to send you and your family to Italy. That's why I'm willing to give you a job. Not because you deserve it."

The skinny legs now unfurled and the skinny feet in their chestnut red Weejuns were set back down on the floor. A silky-shirted arm was slipped over the back of the sofa, where it lay affectionately across Diego's shoulders.

"So," asked Diego, "what do you want?"

Gilbey nuzzled his face into Diego's shoulder. "I want you and your family to always, always love me. I want you to look after me. You don't like Nina – so I'll get rid of her. She's nothing anyway."

"I don't get it."

"Or do you mean you don't care to get it?"

"What's my family got to do with you?" Diego's ambivalence had turned to hostility.

"We're involved in the same things, with the same people," answered Gilbey, his tone mildly, reprehensibly pleading. "This took a lot of courage on my part. I mean, asking you to understand, and to care. I'm just as afraid of these people as you are. Think about that. What *I* do is really pretty innocent. I don't do any of the really bad stuff. Not me, myself. Believe me, I don't."

"I believe you." But Diego didn't.

"You *can't* say no," murmured Gilbey, handing him another cigarette. "You really can't. Know why?"

Diego waited, seething.

"Because out there on the Hackensack are those oil tanks. They're standing out there waiting for you."

"I'm not pretty like Alicia Rozzo."

"That's a clever thing to say. No, what I mean is – you've already *been* out there – in Gus's van."

"According to who?"

"You went out there to dump Alicia's body. But you made a mess of it, like you always do."

"Who told you to say this?"

"You put a nice big dent in Gus's precious van, didn't you?"

"It was Tommy-Tom, wasn't it?"

"What an unkind thing to say. Tommy-Tom was my friend. But now you're my friend too. And you're going to be a better friend than Tommy-Tom. I'm going to look after you, and protect you. And you're going to do the same for me. We're going to be family, as they say."

"You don't have to lay it on so thick," said Diego.

A little while later, they left the horrible room and went out into the sunlight.

"Musical chairs," remarked Gilbey wistfully, "what a truly splendid idea."

As he walked down the long slope to join his wife and child below the great oak, Diego again remembered his parents being taken away in pieces. There had been lots of sunshine on that day too. All these years he'd been burdened with guilt and self-loathing and he hadn't known why. Now he knew. At last, those responsible would be punished. All of their evil would be concentrated in one man, Francis Gilbey. Diego glanced over at Gilbey, who glanced back and smiled.

With a single pop of plastic, the music stopped. Roland was the first to find himself seated, with Gilbey's maid wriggling in his lap. Removing the unwanted chair, Clive had a brief word with her. The two then strode off purposefully, up the long hill towards the house for refreshments. Everyone had carried on with the game while Diego and Gilbey were away and needed a rest.

"*Andremo a piedi?*" ordered Diego, and little Billy immediately pressed down the button.

The black music-box emitting its fragile tones, Billy Nolan toddled around Francis Gilbey and Roland, the only players remaining. Diego and Dolores and Nina all sat in attendance below the wide branches of the oak tree. Roland, eager to claim the last seat, anticipated the stopping of the music, flinging himself, again and again, down upon his bottom. But Billy steadfastly refused to accommodate his little friend, his thumb remaining poised for that lightning signal from his brain that would leave one player standing in defeat. Initially, Gilbey was only mildly irritated by Roland hopping so often onto the remaining chair. But before too long he took to restraining the lad, clapping hands on him in mid-air. Then Roland did a very clever thing. He wrestled free of Gilbey, waved his hands in the air, and shouted, "Listen!"

Billy was so startled that his thumb came down and the black plastic button came up and the music stopped.

As Gilbey spun on his heels, Roland darted under his flapping arms, and landed squarely on the chair. When Gilbey realized he'd been duped, he began to laugh, and laughed and laughed, until he was nearly weeping. It was in the midst of this absurd display that Dolores leaned gently into Diego and said, "I'll always love you."

Before her husband could respond, Roland had rushed over and was urging them to their feet, panting, "Mom, Billy keeps calling for his dog. I don't know what to tell him. Where *is* Blinky?"

When it got to be dark, around 7:13 by Tommy-Tom's Timex, he began to worry that Frosty June had gone off with his money, never to return. What had happened was Neil Blaine hadn't wanted all of Tommy-Tom's 180 dollars for the three grams of blow, he'd only wanted 120 and a blow-job. Because Blaine had been snorting off and on all day, he couldn't come and had kept Frosty June hanging around waiting for him to get sufficiently hard to have another try. To keep herself occupied, as she'd lounged around Blaine's artist's loft in her underwear, Frosty June had herself consumed one of the grams of blow and a bottle and a half of Korbel Brut.

"Why don't you do my portrait while we're waiting?" she'd said.

"I'm not that kind of artist," he'd replied.

"What kind are you?"

"Take a look around."

No, there weren't any brushes or canvases in Blaine's studio, only a lot of glass jars with different colored liquids in them and several cages full of dyed chicks, the brightly colored kind available at Easter.

"What're you gonna do with the jars and the chickens?" she'd eventually asked.

"Sell them," Blaine had answered, singeing the longer hairs on his testicles with a Bic lighter he'd recently picked up off the street in Cologne.

"I gotta go," Frosty June had apologized. "I'm having a great time but I'm supposed to be getting this shit back to a friend. Well, not exactly a friend."

At the Stamford Arms, Frosty June found Tommy-Tom lying on Bootsy's bed. Blood was seeping into the faded tangerine-colored coverlet from the wound in his throat, which he'd torn at with his long fingernails. Luckily, the coverlet was more like a big bath towel than a regular blanket.

"Now what d'ya want me to do?!" she screeched, then remembered he couldn't talk.

Tommy-Tom patted his throat, then the bed, meaning he wanted the cocaine. How he intended to use it to ease his pain, Frosty June couldn't guess. She lay the two remaining grams on the bed.

"I had to get high with Neil and he made me do my own. We didn't do anything though. I mean, we didn't – you know."

At that particular moment, her relationship with the artist wasn't of much interest to Tommy-Tom, who had managed to flip open one of the tiny packets of folded glossy paper – Blaine always sold his grams wrapped in cleverly cropped Picasso reproductions – and was now smearing the white powder into his wound. Thirty seconds or so passed before he felt anything, or, more correctly, the mildest absence of anything.

"I gotta go down the hall. But only for a minute," Frosty June assured him. "Don't you always feel like you gotta take a dump when you do this shit?"

She was of course referring to the effect the cocaine had on her central nervous system, the spinal cord ending, one was reminded, very near the rectum. But Frosty June wasn't gone for *only* a minute. It was during this interval that Tommy-Tom got the idea to sift the remaining gram of cocaine down his throat. Regrettably, the cocaine fell from the glossy paper to the back of his mouth in a lump and Tommy-Tom gagged. And he went on gagging, and the cocaine never did find its way anywhere near its intended destination, as his wound hemorrhaged, pumping blood into his esophagus and, congruently, his stomach. A cup or so was retched up into his windpipe, then sucked down into his lungs. When Frosty June returned to Bootsy's room, she found Tommy-Tom lying face down, with his head slung over the side of the bed, heaving. Dipping the fingers of his right hand into his bloody mouth, he heroically attempted to scrawl Gus Rozzo's telephone number on the floor.

"Oh fuck, fuck, fuck...*fuck*," shouted Frosty June, and began searching angrily in her purse for a pen to take down the number.

Gus was glancing through *Happiness is a Tadpole called Pete*, one of Dommie's little books, previously Mikie's, when Babs came in to tell him that someone wanted him on the telephone.

"And after that, you can leave," she said.

Where there once had been one Pete the Tadpole on each page, there now were two and sometimes four. It made Gus sad to look at them. They reminded him of his kids: all different, but, when it came to their lot in life, the same.

"My head still hurts," he said, and went from the so-called nursery down into the living-room and picked up the phone. "Yea?"

"Is this 201.222.1212? – cause if it is and you're the guy that lives there, I got Tommy-Tom and he needs to see you, cause he's bleeding all over the fucking place out of his mouth."

"Come again?"

"What're you called?" came through the line.

"Me? I'm Gus Rozzo. You say something about Tommy-Tom? I thought he was in the hospital. He didn't say nothing about leaving."

"I'm standing here where he works. Got it?"

"What, like in the city?"

"Where else? He works here in this hotel. Are you this guy he wants?"

"Yea, OK, I'll drive in," said Gus. "Who're you?"

"Frosty June."

"What're you shitting me?"

"Listen, I'm already sick with this. Tommy-Tom's down the hall in his pal's room – you know, the black dude – so either you get in here from wherever you are, or I'm gonna call emergency or the cops, and I'm outa here."

"I said I was, didn't I?"

With Tommy-Tom needing him, this mess with Babs would just have to wait. That was it for home and family, for a while anyway. And it wasn't just because he felt shat upon. This one was for Tommy-Tom. He'd slept with the guy's wife and this was one way to make up for it. But Gus still felt like a sap.

What will summer be like without Gus? wondered Babs, having removed herself to the bathroom off the living-room. This bathroom used to be the storage shed in the garage, until Gus got the bright idea of breaking through the wall, so that you were actually in the garage, even though you thought you were in the house. There was yellow on the toilet seat. Teddy got this from Gus: never raising the seat. *Who'll go and get the propane tank filled for the barbecue?* she wondered on. *I guess I will, but I'll take Teddy along to carry it. Oh, that's right, he'll have his learner's permit, so he can drive. I hate driving into Jersey City by myself anyways. This is stupid, cause how can Gus be going anywhere? He didn't even know how to stay out on Long Island by himself. He had to come back here to get his stuff – he said. I bet he really wants to stay. Well, he can forget it. For now anyways. I bet that guy Bill Strannard would make a good father. But probably his wife isn't dead, like he said on the fishing boat. I bet he just wants to fuck me. Maybe it would get to be more than that. How can I make up my mind about Gus? I probably shouldn't fuck Bill Strannard, no matter what. Jesus will be there. He always is. What I should be thinking about is – here goes – if Gus doesn't come back right away, who's gonna love me and look after me and my kids? – that's what I should be thinking about.*

Back in the bedroom, with his bad eyesight worsening, Gus was attempting to pack a few things for his trip.

Babs came in and turned the suitcase upside down and shook it. "That's for Teddy to take to college. Find something else."

"How's he going to college?"

"You don't even remember – the church fund, along with that loan you said you could get."

"He's still gotta work this summer, and he don't even have a job lined up yet."

"Don't worry, he'll get one."

"Who's worried." Gus started stuffing his things into the larger, nicer suitcase they'd brought back with them from their romantic holiday at Lido Beach.

"You didn't even empty out my nightie," Babs pointed out, then went across the hall and into the room Theresa shared with the twins. "Here, you can use this knapsack," she called. "Theresa's sick of it, and the twins don't want it – it's got graffiti all over it."

Throwing up his hands, Gus marched across the hall and banged headfirst into the door, which had appeared, due to its multiplicity, to be swinging inward.

"Fuck."

"I'm getting a job," said Babs. "I don't want you to argue. I don't even want to know where you think you're going. Have any idea? I didn't think so. I'm going to make the kids some popcorn. I'm going to think of them and myself now. You can call me from wherever." She thrust the knapsack into Gus's dangling hands. "Who was that on the phone?"

"That's for me to know and you to find out."

"Oh, *wow*," said Babs.

Cracked tiles, filthy tiles, tiles that fall down and shatter and get pulverized under the tires of millions and millions of stupid cars, this was all Gus could think about as he slowly made his way toward the two purple lights – at least, he wasn't seeing four of everything anymore – glowing at the end of the Lincoln Tunnel, its seemingly endless yellow gut dank and deadly. The van rocked and stuttered as Gus refused to shift, as he should at such a snail's pace, from third to second gear.

"Tommy-Tom's bleeding in that jig's room," Gus heard himself say, over the sound of snow tires clicking faster and faster, as the dreary phalanx of vehicles finally moved out. "Who's this bitch on the phone? Frosty fucking *June?* I'll bet he knows what to do with her ass."

Then he ran into the two cars directly in front of him, which was actually only one old Chevrolet driven by an elderly black man named Delon Lee – "My name's Delon Lee, mister, I believe you bumped me," the man said, standing by the van – which was lucky for Gus, because it afforded him the opportunity to tell the guy to go fuck himself.

The extra length of a legal pad had always pleased Leon Huff, even as a boy, before he'd had any real use for one. Now, as Chief of Police for the city of Hoboken, he appreciated the pad's generosity even more. The yellow of the paper was itself pleasing, like the color of a precious female canary, and the fine blue lines had a breeziness to them which reminded him of the seashore on a fine summer day. For Huff, the legal pad was not for scribbling in the margins or drawing little pictures of things, it was for delineating perplexing matters with precision and clarity. This evening however, as his wife Lois and their two kids waited for him outside Headquarters in the family car, hungry for their weekly restaurant dinner and becoming irritable, Huff was having difficulty deciding which course of action to take next, as several were now laid out neatly on the pad before him:

1. Call Wertz, FBI, and get him onto Nolan (have Union City and Newark summarize and update their files to the minute, have Molloy do ours, including condition of dead wife's body, bruises, etc.) - MAKE SURE PHOTOS OF ROZZO GIRL'S VAGINA ASHTRAY GIFT TO NOLAN ARE IN ENVELOPE

2. Bring in Ildefonso and get statement on Friedrich arson

3. Bring in Rozzo and bargain for info on Nolan

4. Question Nolan boy, Ildefonso boy, Rozzo kid(s) on their fathers' questionable activities - how to do this without upsetting their mothers?

5. Hold Ildefonso and Rozzo until they can be charged with something (reckless endangerment, conspiracy to corrupt the morals of a minor, etc.) or until they bring in their lawyers and get themselves released - maybe their lawyers will spill the shit?

Unexpectedly, Lois Huff appeared at the door to her husband's office. When he glanced up, the Chief was overwhelmed by his love for her.

"I'm coming," he said.

Although readily dismissed, the altercation with the old black guy in the Lincoln Tunnel had cost Gus dearly. When he finally found Tommy-Tom, lying half off the bed in Bootsy Holloway's room in the Stamford Arms, there was no such person as Frosty June tending to him, only a dirty gray cat with one eye. Gus however perceived two yellow eyes staring up at him. Ignoring the cat, who resumed licking up Tommy-Tom's blood, Gus had a good look at his friend.

Tommy-Tom was dressed like a fairy, with that long swirly scarf around his neck and flowered shirt and tight slacks. But it was all the blood and whatever was mixed in with it that repulsed Gus most. That, combined with the smell of Chanel No. 5 hanging heavily in the air, made him feel sick. Gus wanted a drink, but instead tried to get Tommy-Tom back onto the bed. This wasn't easy because good ole Tommy-Tom was already dead.

As Gus looked around the room, in a hurry now because he didn't want to be found with Tommy-Tom's corpse, he wished he'd had the chance to tell Tommy-Tom about himself and Val. At first, Gus surmised – through faulty self-psychoanalysis – that his reason for doing this would have been to bring the two men closer together before the end, but then he accepted that, actually, he detested Tommy-Tom, and the thought of such a sentimental scene made him want to puke. On the other hand, telling Tommy-Tom about himself and Val could have really upset the prick, which would have been fine with Gus. It was just as Gus was cherishing this lost opportunity that he found Tommy-Tom's note, addressed to him, sticking out from under a pink ceramic ashtray in the shape of a hand with the middle finger extended upwards. As he stared down at it, Gus noticed that his vision was improving – two sheets of paper were merging into one – but something else was happening at the same time: his field of vision was rapidly telescoping down to a single point of light, like the head of a pin shining in a dark room. Tommy-Tom's note read:

> *Dear Gus,*
> *If I'm not alive if you find me*
> *I want you to know about what*
> *me and Alisa she did things for me*
> *bad things So I did it all.*
> *I'm sorry and not ask to forgive me.*
> *Please let my mom take care*
> *of Billy OK?*
>   *Tommy Nolan*

Gus looked over at Tommy-Tom's corpse, he looked down at the cat, he looked out the window at the building across the street, all of it at the wrong end of the telescope and getting wronger. He sensed these things were the last he would ever see, and asked himself *What were the last things Alicia saw?* and knew the answer: *Tommy-Tom's eyes.* And the world wrapped itself around him in a rush, and everything was so overwhelmingly vivid that he sobbed and shrank away. But his attention was instantly drawn out the window, to the building across the way, and one of its apartments in particular.

Pacing very quickly from room to room was a guy a little younger than Gus. The guy had on a white sailor's uniform and was eating what looked like potato chips out of a large cellophane bag. Gus decided that God had sent this for him to see. He decided that God was trying to tell him something. If Tommy-Tom had lived and Gus hadn't found that note, he and Tommy-Tom would have managed to get on a ship and start off around the world. And Gus would never have known that Tommy-Tom had taken his beautiful daughter away and done what he did to her. Now everything got even brighter, before it went black. It was true, Gus concluded, even though he would have said it was bullshit: *everything does happen for a reason.*

THIRTEEN

Still clamoring to row out into the darkness, Roland and little Billy had eventually been removed from the water's edge and bundled off to bed. It was quiet now, the evening meal having ended without event and pleasantly enough. Dolores waited for Diego in the big chilly bed, warming it with the heat of her body. When he turned to leave the bathroom, he found before him not the tall elegant panels of one of Lakeview's doors but his very own closet door, the one in his office at home, its cheap veneer fraying at the edges. As always, taped to the veneer was the artist's rendering of Vesuvius erupting. Tonight however, this image was no longer a catalyst for the reminiscences he had cherished for so long. The cinders still sparkled in the brooding sky above the volcano's gaping fiery mouth, but they might as well have been fireflies for all Diego Ildefonso knew.

Roland had waded into Hoboken's municipal pool only once, but this didn't stop him from leading little Billy through the darkened halls of Lakeview and back down to the water. Neither did it stop him from urging Billy into their chosen rowboat. Fortunately for Billy, he did know something about swimming, for his mother, who had been an excellent swimmer from an early age, had taken him often to the municipal pool where she'd taught him to do as the dolphins do. And so, Billy hadn't any fear of the water, only, at that late hour, of its darkness, moonlight or no moonlight. Having given up on conquering the oars, the two boys now allowed the boat to drift without guidance across the quiet water.

"Where did those big birds go?" asked Billy.

"Swans. They're called *swans*," whispered Roland.

The arch of the bridge loomed in the distance. It was there that Roland hoped they were heading. If all went well, not only would they be able to secure their boat on one of the iron rings set for that purpose in the stone, but the steps descending to the water's edge from either end of the bridge would naturally afford them a graceful disembarkation. This had been Roland's strategy ever since carefully examining the bridge that afternoon.

"Now put your oar under the seat," Roland ordered Billy.

Billy, who was seated in the stern, did as he was told.

It had taken Gus Rozzo the better part of an hour to find his way down three flights of steps, along three landings crowded with human debris of all kinds, and into the back hallway of the Stamford Arms, where he'd at last felt somewhat safe, sunk low within the arm of a lumpy cushionless sofa.

Tommy-Tom did this was the first thought that came to him as he stared at nothing. *He took her out there and threw her down on those little sharp stones with the stink of oil on them and beat her into sex and then strangled her. She was my girl. He did that. Who was he when I knew him? I don't know who he was who could do that. And I can't ever tell nobody, never. Not after what I told him to tell Huff. I have to take it to my grave all by myself. He did that, Tommy-Tom, he killed her.*

The time passed quickly as Gus's mind reeled on with the immediate potentialities of his life, all dire, the direst being returning home prematurely, humiliated in his blindness. Where was he to go, being blind? If only he could find his way to Val and recover his sanity there, in her arms. Poor Val, gone. No where to be found. Poor him.

"Hey you," said Frosty June, her silhouette against the dim overhead light blacker than the blackness surrounding her. "Why didn't you stay put?"

"How'd you know it's me?"

"Who else would track all that blood down here? Your shoes look like a couple of ketchup bottles."

"I don't know where to go. I'm blind."

"Where the fuck'd I call you anyway?" When Gus hesitated to answer, Frosty June sank down into the sofa too. "Well?"

"Hoboken. I live out there."

"Doing what? Just being blind?"

Gus could tell she was genuinely interested, especially when she also asked, "OK, so how'd you know Tommy-Tom?"

"No, it's OK, I can tell you," said Gus, then added, "You might have to help me out here, I'm not used to this bullshit."

"What *bullshit?*"

Gus could hear it, there was real indignation in her voice. "Being blind, I mean. I only got blind today, er, I mean tonight, after I was looking at Tommy-Tom, and I figured out he was dead."

"He what?" exclaimed Frosty June. "I just went out and got him this bottle of vodka. I got him this ice too. Here, feel it – this – ice, right? We better not hang around here. Not if he's dead."

"I'm sorry," said Gus, even though he obviously wasn't.

"Well, I'm sorry too, but that's different."

Gus liked her voice. It was both womanly and manly at the same time. Comforting, you might say, with a double-edged dimension to it.

"Could you help me out here?" he asked. "I don't know where the fuck to go. And I can't go home. Not yet, anyways."

"So where do you think I'm supposed to take you? – not my place. Where, a hotel or something?"

Now she sounded agitated, like she wanted to get rid of him, and that just wouldn't do. Gus, very quickly, had plans for her.

"Your place sounds good," he said. "How far is it? Can you walk me there, so I can explain everything? Like you said, don't you think we better get the fuck outa here?"

"Yea," said Frosty June, "but not to my place – I got a kid."

"We could just go to a bar," said Gus, and they did, slowly, Gus feeling sick and worried.

Thudding again and again against the damp stones that formed the underbelly of the bridge, the rowboat continued to drift. It was darker now, caught within that chilly passage, however the stretch of water beyond, overshadowed by the woods, was darker still.

"It'll never work," Billy argued, his voice echoing.

But Roland remained stretched out over the glimmering black water, both hands on the iron ring: he no longer had any choice, he hadn't the strength to draw himself back into the boat.

"Yes, it will," he insisted. "Come on, give me your belt."

"It's my one with the Indians on it."

"You'll get it back. You want to just sit here all night, or go back inside, before they find us?"

"How'll I get it back if we go inside?"

Roland sighed with the strain. "That butler guy, he's our friend. Come on, Billy, I've got to tie it..."

"Oops..." Billy froze. Although he weighed less than a moderately large dog, his first step had sent the boat tipping violently leeward.

"What?" shouted Roland, head pivoted hard to his left. "Keep coming. No, take your belt off first!"

"Don't it have a rope? I thought they all had ropes?!"

"I wouldn't be standing here if it had a rope. I untied it at the wrong end. It's back there, where we came from!" Roland, sensing it would be futile to attempt to reason further with Billy, hung his head and moaned.

"I'll take it off," offered Billy, "if we can get Blinky."

"I already told you – my mom says we can get Blinky tomorrow, on our way home."

"Oh yea. I remember."

Billy then unfastened his belt and pulled on it hard, with unselfish determination. But the belt was too wide to slip easily through the loops of his trousers. So Billy pulled harder, and harder still, as Roland watched, hope creasing his brow. Finally, Billy gave a yank, a yank so violent that his sneaker screeched against the wet bottom of the boat. The boat went over and instantly Roland was left hanging from the iron ring, sunk up to his armpits in black water, while Billy was gulped down, into the void.

A cold wind blew through, ruffling Roland's hair. It came hurtling across the lake, over the spindly reeds, and into the hollow of the bridge. Now Roland watched as the hull of the rowboat drifted farther and farther from him, its rigid volume jerking mystifyingly upon the water. But it was Mikie Rozzo and not Billy Nolan who came, in a rush, to occupy Roland's thoughts.

Once again, he felt the little boy's hip brush his own, as Mikie squirmed away from him and rose up on the seat, out from under the chrome restraining bar. Roland had chosen to ignore him, assuming he would quiet himself and snuggle back down in the seat once the Ferris-wheel again began to turn. *The little shit better behave himself,* he'd said to James, and the gondola had lurched forward, with the abrupt engagement of the great wheel's cogs. Mikie had flown backward, into the air, and had plummeted, down, down, down. Now Billy Nolan was equally dead, Roland guessed, lying leadenly at the bottom of Mr. Gilbey's lake, drowned.

Roland's thoughts turned to his own escape, as he sadly calculated the distance between the ring to which he clung and the next, and the next after that, and the next after that, all the way to the steps that shone so brilliantly in the moonlight as they descended to meet the black water.

"Don't frighten yourself," he said, and half-heartedly leapt for the next ring, left hand outstretched, while still holding fast with his right.

Roland's face hit the wall and slid painfully across its mossy surface, and, for the first time, he sank down fully into the lake. Now the sodden weight of his clothes would never allow him to attain his goal. He would always land back where he'd started.

Framed by the arch of the bridge, from Roland's vantage very near the surface of the lake, the enormous house resting on its bluff with the great oak before it reminded him of an illustration from the cumbersome book of designs for the opera his father kept with his tomes on the war. The little boats, all in a row on the sandy shore, only added to the magnificent artificiality of the scene, the moonlight picking out each detail in silvery blue. When Roland turned to peer in the opposite direction, there, captured again within the bridge's arch, was another set, one that was marvellously sinister. The purple tops of the pines meeting the sky's dark luminosity, flecked with wispy pale clouds, and the feathery rays of light shimmering out over the water through the shadowy trunks below, spoke discreetly of intrigue and forbidden romance.

"How beautiful," said Roland. "Now I know what I want to be."

And his little hand fell like a fisherman's sinker into the water, and the mysterious depths gently pulled him down to lie with Billy. But then Billy reached up and took hold of Roland's hand, and flung it over his shoulder, and clasped him round the chest, and swam with him to the waiting steps of the bridge.

"I remember Jack Dempsey," said Gus, feeling better, with two shorts in him and a draft Bud wetting the table. "My ole man had that painting of him bashing the shit outa some other schmuck in his pool room."

"Supposedly a lot of fighters come in here," said Frosty June. "You know, Madison Square Garden is – where? – yea, over that way."

Wanting to get things moving, Gus said, "OK, so here's my proposition," but then waited uncertainly, Frosty June's face an oval of grayish stillness.

Frosty June wasn't partial to short men, and this guy was both short and a wise-ass, a bad combination. Also, she didn't like his clothes, which were woppish – that's right, he was a wop. The way he was sitting in the dark at the back of the Stamford Arms was creepy too. Blind people had always given her the creeps. And, when they'd come into the bar, he'd taken about twenty minutes to wipe the blood off his shoes – blind, no less – and hadn't even bothered to offer her a drink. Lastly, he smiled too much, and when he smiled, his eyes all out of focus, he looked mentally ill.

"So, like what's your proposition?" she said.

"It's what time?" Gus replied.

Without having to look at her Princess, which she'd had since she was twelve, Frosty June said, "A little after two."

"Oh yea, it's Sunday," said Gus, "but I can go to the cash-machine, if you'll press the buttons."

"I can press."

"My plan is to take out some money – I have a lot – and go somewheres nice with you, like Bermuda. You know, with real sunshine and all. How's that?"

"I told you, I got a kid."

"So? Bring it along."

"It's not an *it,* it's a little boy." Now she knew: this guy was fucking crazy. "So, how much money?"

"A lot," said Gus, and drained his glass. "I need another one of these and another Bellows or whatever."

"You'll just have to wait, he's serving somebody. So how much is 'a lot?'"

"Enough probably to pay for everything for a month. Oh yea, and for flying down there."

"That's a lot. But what about after? I work, you know."

"Doing what?"

"What'd you think? Tommy-Tom pays me. He pays me like everybody else, only some are a little more generous. But he's good-looking. At least, *I* think he's good-looking."

"He's dead," said Gus, "and *we* was in there. That's incriminating. So, what's it gonna be, a free trip to Bermuda, or another drink and then kiss-off time? I'm waiting. By the by, I think you sound attractive..."

Now he was acting like a regular little prick. How could a little blind guy act like such a prick? There was something fishy about this guy.

"What'd you say your name was again?" demanded Frosty June wearily.

"I told you – Gus. Do I get more drinks?"

"Show me your cash card. Don't worry, I'll get the drinks in a minute. No, here he comes. Is that your wallet? It looks expensive."

"It is."

Babs had given Gus the wallet for his birthday.

"There's a cash-machine at that big building with the white plastic all over it, a couple of blocks up," said Frosty June.

"Let's have more drinks first." Gus could feel her staring at him. He didn't like it. His tone softening only slightly, he added, "If you want."

The light from the TV suited Babs's mood. *The Star Spangled Banner,* coming after the late movie, had stirred her several hours before and she now leaned on her elbow staring down adoringly at Dommie in the TV's lavender glow. She had used Gus's pillow to make a nest for the infant, the gentle heaving of her bosom obviously bringing great comfort. At last, thankfully, her children were all asleep, the twins, who had earlier been differing over the significance of their father's absence, slumbering down the hall on either side of their grandmother Ruthie.

Wow, think about all the stuff everybody's done, Babs marvelled, *and all of it's right there in little Dommie's head. He's gonna know everything. He won't be like me or his dad. He'll be better than us. He might even be a star on TV, a regular on All My Children, at least until he's old enough to have his own talk show, or maybe even become a politician, although he might get assassinated. Look at his little lips. They're so pretty. He almost looks like a pretty little girl. Gus must of looked like that when he was a baby, only Dommie's gonna keep his beautifulness, like Fabian, or Donovan. I always loved men who looked like that, with big soft eyes and all. Gus used to look like that. Now he looks like a kewpie-doll that's drunk. Some women might like that – having a husband who looks like he's still trying to impress people – but I'm sick of it, even though I love it when he really looks at me. His eyes get all watery, when he's big, and he wants to love me.*

Babs's fingers went to the elastic waist-band of her lollipop briefs and she pulled them down, but only part of the way, so that they creased the tops of her thighs, a feeling she liked: it made her feel even sexier. Her clit felt good, like a gumdrop with feelings, intense feelings. She thought of Bill Strannard, the stranger on the boat, and wondered if he'd call her. It was naughty of her to give him her number, but what if Gus never did come home, or only came home to start acting up again? Then she'd be glad she had a new beau. Babs guessed she'd always call the stranger *Mr. Strannard* in her mind, maybe even to his face, to prolong his strangeness, and the excitement she was now feeling. He had big hands. When he'd been fishing off *Neptune's Slipper,* he'd held the reel with real confidence, manly confidence, like a snake-handler milking the head of a rattler. Bill Strannard was fearless. He would call. And he would come there while the kids were at school and make love to her. She would tell him about Alicia and how Gus had just let it happen. She'd already told him about Mikie, also about the bartender at Sweetie's. Now she would tell him about Gus letting their daughter do anything she wanted. Babs knew Gus had wanted Alicia for himself and had overreacted to other men's attentions, like Tommy-Tom's, but in the negative, by not doing anything to protect their daughter. What Gus did, when he couldn't control what was going on inside himself, was act like nothing mattered. Maybe Gus didn't have a sick thing for Alicia, but you'd never know it by the way he let her hang on him. And she always got her way.

I taught her how to play with Gus, Babs finally admitted to herself, *I taught her how it's done. That's what a woman does, and if she doesn't – well, forget it. Poor Alicia, my little sister. Yea, my little sister. She was going to be my pal. One day, she would of taken me to Europe. I can see her with just the right kind of guy, a lawyer or accountant. I can see them taking me places. I can see Gus telling me I can't go, not by myself. I can see Gus making a real mess of my life, and Alicia's. But all those dreams are over. My little sister's dead now.*

The telephone rang. Babs answered it right away, so Dommie wouldn't wake up. It was Bill Strannard. He was drunk.

"Remember me?"

"Yea," said Babs. "You know what time it is?"

"Late. You alone? I thought I might come over."

"I thought you were married."

"Who said?"

"Nobody. You said you wasn't."

"What, you didn't believe me?"

"I don't usually believe guys when they say things."

"I think I told you I was divorced. I think I told you I was unhappy."

"I don't remember you saying any of that."

"Well, you gave me your number."

"I shouldn't of, because you know I'm married."

"Yea, but you said you were separating."

"Only today. You saw him."

"I saw you pushing him around. Where's he now?"

Babs didn't know what to say, or do: it was all happening too fast, the stranger was forcing himself on her, at least that's how it felt. "You're in a big hurry."

"I never met anyone like you."

"What's that mean?"

"You want me to make pillow-talk, then let me come over."

"I could meet you somewheres, after my mom goes home."
"Uh huh..."
"Even though I don't do that."

He was waiting, wanting her to say more.

"I mean, meet some guy I hardly know."

"So how do you get to know me? Listen, I can promise you, I'm OK. I really and truly am, Babs. You could see that."

Now he was insisting, but warmly.

"Yea, I did. You were nice to me."

"And I can be nicer."

They agreed to meet halfway, as Bill Strannard was out in Queens, which meant they'd rendezvous in Manhattan. They'd meet that evening at the United Nations Plaza Hotel, which had just been built, in the bar in the basement, which was so dark no one could see them, even though no one would know them anyway. Strannard made a kissing sound before he hung up, which Babs thought sounded stupid. She had only just settled back under the covers, index finger distractedly on clit, when twelve-year-old Theresa came into the room in tears and stood over her mother, stifling her sobs with her fists.

"Honey, your hair's all wet," said Babs, and patted the bed for Theresa to sit down.

"I told you I needed it cut," whimpered the angular adolescent, her tiny breasts like water-cooler cups under her nightie.

"Sit down, honey."

Theresa eased down apprehensively onto the mattress, her back to Babs. Babs reached out to draw her daughter's long wet hair back over her shoulders.

"Don't," muttered Theresa.

"What is it? Is it about your daddy?"

The child nodded.

"You think I did a bad thing, don't you?"

"You didn't have to do that. You didn't have to tell him to go away."

"You don't understand. When you're older, you'll understand."

"About what?" Theresa jerked away from her mother.

"About how it is when two people love each other, but how they just can't get along sometimes."

"But isn't it about Alicia?" Theresa turned to stare at Babs in the flickering purple light. "Isn't it about Daddy letting Mr. Nolan take her places, and now she's..."

The child's sobbing began anew, so that Babs couldn't understand the rest of what her daughter said, which was:

"...dead. And who's gonna make her pretty now, when everybody comes to see her. And you and Daddy just went away and didn't go to say good-bye to her or anything. I think we should go find Alicia and love her. Nobody ever loved her, only me."

Gus listened to Frosty June call off the numbers as she entered the identification code for his cash card on the automatic teller's keyboard. He'd entrusted his wallet to her at the Terminal Bar to facilitate the ordering of drinks and she was now most agreeably taking care of the money-gathering for their trip.

"What time is it?" he asked.

"It says here, it's 4:53," answered Frosty June, coolly surveying the computer's glowing numerals. "Now, 4:54."

"It'll be a while before we can get tickets, and what about your kid?"

"We're going over there now. I'm at the Chelsea on West 23rd. You know, where the writers die. So you can stay there, and sleep or whatever, until it's late enough so I can call my friend, like I told you, and order the tickets."

"To St. Bart's, like you said..."

"Yea," said Frosty June, taking two-hundred and fifty dollars from the machine, "where all the fashion people and artists go."

But Frosty June was lying. She hadn't any friend who could conjure up airline tickets on a Sunday morning, neither had she any intention of going to St. Bart's with a drunken blind guy. No, Frosty June intended to hand Tommy-Tom's buddy over to someone who could look after the guy properly, even though she hadn't as yet decided who that might be.

"Let's get a taxi," she said. "Try to look smart."

Diego Ildefonso's eyelashes, so delectably long and black, had enchanted Dolores from the very first moment of their very first encounter. As she lay gazing down at her husband in the dawn light, she recalled that day. She had instantly warmed to his kindness and his maturity as he had taken her mother's hand and helped her onto the bus. This had been the bus into Manhattan, whose last stop before the tunnel stood at the end of Union City's longest street, Palisade Avenue.

Again Dolores watched as the beautiful fat man flicked away the gravel scattered over the pavement with the perfectly buffed toe of his shoe. Unlike any shoes worn by the men she knew, his had a delicacy about them, like those worn by an important person in the theatre or ballet. He seemed preoccupied, although she sensed he was acutely aware of her presence. He smiled, but only ever looked directly at her mother. This she took to be an indication of his shyness. Inexplicably, an exotic world rose to surround the dapper stranger in his dainty shoes and to envelope them both, there at the end of Palisade Avenue. A row of palms hung over the dusty sundrenched street, steepening shadows gathering coolly round their trunks, while a fountain sang in the near distance, its song like tiny brass bells chiming on the breeze. Olive-skinned figures strolled by in fine costumes, the women's hair piled high, combs gleaming, the men's slicked back immaculately to their heads. They entered shops, glinting boxes with opulent bows positioned invitingly in their windows, and churches, their ornate facades draped in shimmering satin. She saw him just that way, a man who had come magically to stand beside her there in the street from a world of such grace. Now she would think twice about marrying any of the young men she knew in Teaneck, some of whom desired her badly.

When she had thanked him for assisting her mother onto the bus, he had offered his hand and said *such a lovely lady as your mother deserves what little comfort I might give,* which had struck Dolores as somehow timeless, like a line from a great play, but timeless too in what his voice, in its intimacy, might awaken and reawaken in her as the years, spent by his side, drifted by.

Dolores now leaned over further in the warm light swelling to fill Francis Gilbey's guest room and pressed her lips to her husband's brow and breathed in the sweet aroma of his hair.

Again, there he stood in the sundrenched street, this time with her by his side, the palms whispering overhead.

But for Diego, eyes still clamped shut, there were no such enchanting reverberations. His waking thoughts were becoming, in a word, *incoherent.* One moment, with unspeakable clarity, he saw Gus Rozzo crouched grinning, burning match in hand, in the rubbish at the back of Friedrich's Auto Body Shop, while the next his friend was once again weeping in his arms as he had the night Mikie died. Similarly, he heard Chief Leon Huff, the man's lips moving evenly over his very white teeth, make some kindly and placating remark while watching him tie his hands together with a length of yellow nylon rope. When he tried to hold firm to an image of the great pink house in which he lay, it collapsed into a slithering pile of chrome noodles.

"How would you know?" Gus asked Frosty June through the shower curtain.

"If a man has a mission in life, he should follow it," she replied, scooping up her cosmetics from the lid of the toilet tank. "You don't know what you're doing, because you don't know what you're doing."

"That's easy for you to say," said Gus, "you can see."

"You only just *got* blind," said Frosty June, as she went back into the bedroom to put on her face. "So that didn't affect how missionless you are."

Gus dropped the soap. "I raised a whole fucking family and now I want to see the world. That's allowed!" he shouted.

"Why's that man shouting?" asked Vincent, Frosty June's little boy.

"Because he can't see and he's angry," she explained.

Crouched in the shower, Gus went on searching for the soap. Eventually, altogether frustrated, he gave up.

Vincent was still in bed. He slept with his mother, because the two-room suites at the Chelsea Hotel only had one bed and a convertible sofa in the adjoining room, ostensibly the sitting-room.

"I saw him walking around last night," whispered Vincent. "He kept saying he wanted to die."

"Oh, he didn't mean that," Frosty June assured him.

As he dried himself, Gus wished he could make his hair look really nice. But doing it by touch wasn't going to be easy. He was excited about their upcoming trip to the Bahamas – or had they decided on Bermuda? – and he wanted to call Babs and tell her all about it. Not to make her feel bad. Just to let her know that he was doing it, even when he was blind. Many great men had done great things even though they were blind. Look at Ray Charles. Maybe Gus's sight would return under the healing rays of the tropical sun. Anything was possible. Gus unconsciously squeezed his penis while feeling around with his other hand for the can of deodorant spray Frosty June had left for him at the back of the sink.

"I feel good, da-da da-da da-da-dat, I knew that I would now," he sang behind the bathroom door, as Frosty June got Vincent up and helped him put his clothes on.

But Gus really didn't feel good. Especially when he remembered he'd given Frosty June his wallet the night before with his license and charge cards and everything else in it. There he was in a cheap hotel with a hooker, who sounded a lot like a man, and her bastard kid, who, as far as he knew, never left the place and cried in his sleep.

"I put your wallet in your jacket," came through the bathroom door. "It's out here by the TV."

"Thanks," called Gus, pissed off with himself for not trusting her. "Planning a vacation can be hard work, unless a guy's got a good secretary!"

No comment came from out in the sunlit darkness.

"Hey, Frosty June?! Wanna be my secretary?!"

"I've already got a job."

"Yea, you're a milklady," said Vincent.

"I'm also an interpreter at the United Nations," said Frosty June, and began combing his hair.

"Is this going to be fun?" he asked his mother.

"Yea, honey, this is going to be fun. It's always fun doing nice things for people."

Diego and Dolores decided to sustain the illusion for Gilbey that they might very well take him up on his offer to give Diego employment in Palermo. It was Dolores who resisted staying on for lunch, saying they now had too many things to do before their departure for Rome on, it was hoped, Tuesday or, at the latest, Wednesday.

In Gilbey's mind, this urgency was due to the threat of Chief Leon Huff detaining Diego for questioning. How they were to arrange all this so quickly Gilbey couldn't imagine.

The three Ildefonsos and little Billy Nolan preceded Gilbey out onto Lakeview's wide front steps. The Cadillac, its chrome brightly signalling departure, waited below them in the gravel roundabout.

"If only we had someone else to do it all for us," Diego wryly suggested, which brought a guffaw from Gilbey.

"Whatever," was Nina's monotonal response. She then offered to sell off the Ildefonsos' possessions, after they had packed up everything they wanted to ship by sea.

"I can't imagine there'll be very much of value," Dolores responded. "Perhaps a few pictures and pieces of crystal."

"The flatware should be worth something," offered Nina, "if you're not having it shipped too."

"I don't believe we have any," said Diego.

This was a fallacy Dolores would immediately put right. "We'll take the silver with us," she said.

Many necessary procedures were tentatively agreed before they finally said good-bye shortly after noon.

"Ildefonso, keep the old chin up," said Gilbey.

To which Diego replied, "Which one?"

And everyone laughed.

Then Billy, clutching the trick cane's golden knob with both hands as if it were fragile as an egg, shyly thanked Gilbey. "I'm gonna give it to my dad," he said.

Even Clive and the maid came out to stand on the steps and wave good-bye as the big convertible lumbered down the lane, Roland and little Billy hanging out over the back, frantically throwing kisses.

Beyond the ever pleasant streets of Nyack, the long empty highway hung high above the Hudson. With Dolores at the wheel, the Cadillac felt refreshingly secure to Diego. In fact, he hadn't felt so secure since leaving Willow Avenue. The two boys slept, legs entangled, on the back seat. Diego could smell the lake's pungent mossiness still lingering in their clothes. The trees parted and there was Manhattan. It sparkled like a pile of tiny rhinestones beyond the haze. Dolores lifted his hand and pressed it to her lips.

"Do you think, in the end, God punishes us for living?" he asked.

Dolores was lost.

"I mean, for living *itself*, rather than for some abominable transgression, or even a lifetime of petty transgressions?"

She tried to concentrate on her driving.

"Unkind or cruel acts," Diego went on. "Thoughtless ones. Anything at all that might harm another living creature. Even living things unlike ourselves. Take for instance someone who hacks down a vine that's roamed into their garden, who just automatically hacks it down, without caring what that *thing* might be feeling."

"We've all done something like that at one time or another, haven't we?"

"That's what I'm saying." But he wasn't, not exactly. He could tell she was still back at Lakeview. "You know what I believe in now – right at this very moment? I believe in protecting ourselves from people like that."

"Like Mr. Gilbey."

"The bastards who are out to rob us of what little dignity we have left. You wait and see, one day schmucks like us will tear down everything, everything that violates that dignity."

"Who'll tear what down?"

"All the useless little people who actually keep things going. When this highway is packed solid with tanks and transports and people running around with weapons, all of it due to the fact that their freedom was stolen from them years ago, we'll be gone. Think about it."

Dolores did, but said nothing.

"I can tell you, that day will come, and God will be very, very pleased."

Dolores now knew they would be leaving anyway, without the old fart's interference.

Seldom had Leon Huff felt quite so elated upon leaving church. It hadn't been the sermon, stirring though it was, or being among the multitude, it had simply been *the truth that surpasseth all understanding* that the Chief had found so uplifting. Usually, while attending Mass, the Chief made a conscious effort to banish any thought of work from his mind, however this Sunday something very special had happened: God had bestowed a new objectivity upon him.

"Did you say your mom was making a roast?" asked the Chief's wife – Lois was looking for something in her handbag.

"Yea, and those potatoes the kids like."

The traffic was getting worse, with so many churches letting out. Luckily, the kids were behaving themselves, looking out the windows of the car and chewing gum. As Chief Huff and his family passed the corner on which the Nolans' apartment building stood, he saw Diego Ildefonso and Billy Nolan lifting the Nolans' dog Blinky into the back seat of a large Cadillac convertible. Dolores Ildefonso was sitting at the wheel of the car, with her son Roland beside her.

"I have to stop here for a minute," said Huff to his wife.

It was fear that most often drove men like Diego Ildefonso to the truth. Ildefonso feared for his family. He would protect his wife and son at any cost. He loved them with the same passion the Chief loved his own family. This was the desperately important thing God had revealed. As the sunlight had streamed down through the towering stained glass windows, Leon Huff had heard the truth. Diego Ildefonso would see Tommy-Tom Nolan and Gus Rozzo rot in hell before allowing his wife and son to be deprived of their happiness, and he knew his presence to be essential to that happiness. His freedom was his most precious possession, and it would have to be taken from him before he understood the miraculous favor the Chief was about to do for him.

Driving a van was new to Frosty June. Gus had wanted to leave the van and take a taxi to the airport, where they would take off for St. Bart's, not the Bahamas, not Bermuda, in less than three hours. Vincent had a whole seat to himself behind them. His mother had promised him a tour of the New Jersey docks if he kept their secret, that they weren't going to the airport but out to Hoboken, where Frosty June would return the blind man to the safety of his family.

"Thanks for checking the limit on my MasterCharge before purchasing those fares," said Gus, using his most masculine and authoritative voice.

He would go on buttering up his date until they got on the plane, when he would entrust her with the all important task of ordering their drinks. It was good there wasn't anything sexual between them yet, so there wasn't any risk of her picking on him.

"I hope you counted your cards," joked Frosty June.

"Oh, they're all there."

It would have been better without the kid, but, hey, if he'd had only one kid he'd want to bring him along too. This was going to be fun. Gus promised himself he would call Babs from the airport. He was already working on what he'd say, which was easier without the distraction of having to see Queens, a place he could do without.

Hi honey, it's me (he'd start). *Sorry I didn't call before, but I've been real busy. I had to take care of Tommy-Tom when he was dying. Yea, he died. But I got to tell you something else. No, about me. I'm going away for a little while, like far away. Maybe even to a foreign country. I'll be a better man when I get back. I'm not so good now cause I still can't see right. Listen, honey, I'm not gonna blame you for that anymore, OK? I think we should just call it an accident. Like what happened to Mikie. God works in funny ways, but there's a reason for everything. I realized that after Tommy-Tom died. No, I wasn't holding him in my arms. It was real sad though, but not for the reason you think. Not because Tommy-Tom's dead. I know, it's pretty heavy. Someday, when I get back, I'll tell you. It's not forever. I don't want you going and getting all upset. You be a good girl now, OK? It's cause I love you Babs. And, like you're always saying, I really, really love the kids too. Our kids. All of them. And, first of importance, I love you.*

That would work. Gus felt around on the dashboard for the pack of cigarettes Frosty June had stuck into the ashtray for them both to use. He took one, found the lighter automatically, and popped it in.

"How much farther?" he asked. "I'm thirsty. You think we'll get there early enough to find the bar?"

"Could be," said Frosty June, "if the traffic stays thin."

She was hoping he wouldn't notice the change in sound when they went into the Lincoln Tunnel.

FOURTEEN

It was a rare moment for Diego Ildefonso. As far as he could remember, he had never been detained by the police before, not in America. And his detention had occurred in such an unorthodox manner, Chief Huff masquerading as a family man on his way from church to his kindly mother's table.

On the street before the Nolans' apartment building Dolores had said, "But Chief Huff, I don't understand, we've cooperated in every way we could."

"I'm doing it this way because I have to. It's best for all concerned," Huff had replied.

"Who?" Dolores had moaned. "Not us?"

The Chief's wife had stuck her head out the window of their car and called to Dolores:

"You don't think I like this, do you?"

Dolores and Roland and little Billy had been obliged to walk home with Blinky. The Chief had driven off with Diego in the rented Cadillac, having first promised to return it to the Hertz lot himself.

Along their way, Dolores had remained silent, until the two boys put their hands in hers, when she began to cry.

Diego's first impulse was to turn on the Cadillac's radio. The Chief immediately turned it off. With the top down, there was a nice summery aspect to the situation and Diego didn't feel at all afraid. They drove back along Washington Street. Up ahead, more and more people were emptying out of Our Lady of Delarosa onto the pavement. There, as was the norm, they stood around in their spring finery talking and laughing among themselves.

"Babs Rozzo and her brood," commented the Chief as they drove by.

Diego had thought he recognized the woman in the shiny blue dress with the large breasts, a pimply adolescent boy hanging on her arm.

"Teddy," said the Chief, "and there're the twins. There's the grandmother too." He kept watching in the rear-view mirror. "I don't see Gus though. You see Gus anywhere?"

The atmosphere in the car was friendly, but there was some unfairness at work.

"I'm glad we have this time alone together," said the Chief. "I thought it best we talk privately before you make a statement. I know it's Sunday and this is awkward for you, but hopefully we'll get a lot accomplished now. Then it'll go easier with Molloy."

Several blocks on, Washington ended. They were obliged to wait at the light before turning west onto Fourth. Down a private access to their right lay a narrow view of the docking basin and Hudson River beyond.

"Warehouses," said Diego.

"What?" said the Chief.

"We burned down the warehouses."

"What warehouses?"

"Rufino Unceta's, by the river."

"Who's he?"

"Munitions. Astra-Unceta. Uncle Isidro insisted they were our friends. He said they were doing us a favor. He would, he's *fascisto*. But there's nothing left."

"'Nothing left' of what?"

"The town. They're mostly dead, except for Uncle Isidro and his family. The glass blew in at his feet. He told me."

"But what about the warehouses? I thought you were talking about *those* warehouses over there." The Chief pointed to the faceless metal structures looming over the river. "I thought you were going to say something about you and Gus and Tommy-Tom...?"

Diego thought on this. "I was going to say we burned them down. The kids were always playing in the rubble. They were a hazard, what was left of them. You could look up right into people's rooms. Sofas standing out in the rain. The walls blown away. Papers scattered everywhere. Clothes too. Not everybody has a basement, you know."

The light changed.

Reluctantly, the Chief was trying to come to terms with this protracted moment of insanity. Either Diego Ildefonso was setting him up for an endless maze of nonsensical answers or the fat man's mind was already rejecting the reality of the situation in which he now found himself, which did happen in some cases when the criminal relied on his psychotic facility for disassociation to enable him to lie without noticing.

"Any idea where we might find Tommy-Tom?" ventured the Chief.

Fourth Street had always perplexed Diego. The way it cut so sharply across town, simply ending Hoboken, never felt right to him. "We're going sideways," he said softly.

"So where's Tommy-Tom?" insisted the Chief.

Diego thought for a moment. "Tommy-Tom?"

The Chief nodded.

"He's at the fair," said Diego. "Everybody's at the fair."

It was extremely annoying to pick up the phone and find Babs Rozzo on the other end when Dolores had assumed the call would have to do with her husband.

"Just a second, Babs," she said.

"Is Billy's dad going to die?" whispered Roland, who had been tagging along beside her for nearly an hour.

"Of course not." Dolores kissed her son on the head. "Why don't you and Billy go down to Mrs. Finkelstein's and see how Blinky likes her garden."

"OK, Mom," Roland mumbled, and went off reluctantly to find his new friend.

"Oh God, it's so hot already and it's only April," groaned Babs. "I got sweat soaked into the armpits of my satin dress – you know, that real pretty blue one – cause there's no air-conditioning on in the church yet and I don't know if I should try to soak it out or just give up and send it to the cleaners."

"You can't soak satin," said Dolores, "the water will ruin it. Babs, I – "

"The kids are doing really great. Mom and the rest of us all went to church together and she was so proud. I could tell by the way she was acting. And that's important. I want my mom to be proud. It looks like Teddy's gonna be our first to go to college. Our Lady's helping to pay for it, most likely. But he's definitely getting a science scholarship this year. And Theresa's thinking about becoming a nun. Can you imagine our Terry as a nun? At least it'll cover up those big ears!" Babs laughed. "She's not interested in boys, not like I was at her age."

"Or Val."

"How do you know? – you didn't even live here then. The twins are pretty smart too. But you know who's gonna be really smart?"

"Gus?"

"Oh *you!*" Again Babs laughed. "I mean Dommie. I just think it's so cool. Little Dominic's got the best of both worlds. Me and Gus's, and all our ancestors too. I probably didn't tell you, but Gus's gone off on a – what'ya call it? – into New York to see about being an efficiency expert or something."

"A what?"

"Something like that."

"I'll tell you what he should be..." Dolores waited, but suddenly Babs hadn't anything to say. "A professional liar."

"*What* did you say?"

"Gus couldn't tell the truth to save his life."

"I don't get it."

"You get it."

"We're going through all this, and doing good too, and you say something like that? I don't *believe* you. Your Roland was with our Mikie. Go ahead, say *so what?* What'd we ever do to you and your family?"

"Babs, before you go on, you should know that Diego's with Chief Huff right now, and it's because of Gus. You can go on talking until you suffocate, but I won't believe otherwise."

A prolonged silence followed. Dolores had the impression that Babs had gone into another room to do something to distract and calm herself before responding, but she was still there, in her brightly colored kitchen, with all those festive faces twinkling at her.

"There's nothing I can do about that," said Babs. "Well, is there? No, I didn't think so. Diego went with him. Whatever they did, it was together. Gus probably just didn't tell it right."

"He told it according to him. Diego knew this was going to happen. He doesn't tell me everything, but he knew."

"*Knew what?*" whined Babs.

"Chief Huff has been visiting with us all along, ever since Mikie fell. He was here again on Thursday evening. He warned Diego about you two, but what was he supposed to do?"

"When Gus gets home, I'll ask him what he wants to do about your husband."

"You do that," said Dolores, but the line had already gone dead.

Chief Huff was in no mood for joking by the time he and Diego arrived at Police Headquarters. He sat himself at Detective Sergeant Molloy's desk and positioned Diego before him on a folding chair.

"I'm not sure you appreciate the gravity of the situation," he said.

Diego gazed up at the fluorescent light hanging from the ceiling. Now the Chief would try to reason with him.

"It's OK, we can plea-bargain you into a nominal sentence. If you cooperate fully."

"I already am," said Diego.

"I mean, like tell us what went on between Tommy-Tom and Gus and Alicia Rozzo." From one of the desk's lower drawers, the Chief extracted a manila envelope and shook out several photographs. He laid them out neatly before Diego. "Recognize these?"

Various angles of the Friedrich Auto Body Shop arson.

"I guess so."

"Well, what are they?"

"I told you before. Astra-Unceta. The factory."

"No, no, no," groaned the Chief, "these – *here*. What are these *here* of?"

"I told you. Unless I'm wrong."

"Of course you're wrong, because you know this is what Rozzo's got on you. He claims *you* set that fire."

Woefully, Diego shook his head. His perspiring hand lay on the photographs. Chief Huff lifted the hand and set it back down on his desk where it wouldn't do any damage.

"Sorry," said Diego.
"Well?"
"Guernica, my town."

"Fine. That's just fine." From the same lower drawer, the Chief extracted another manila envelope. Laying a new photograph on top of the others, he said, "This is Guernica too, I bet." It was Alicia Rozzo, naked, eyes staring. "And what about her?" The Chief now proffered an image of Val Nolan, whose long fine face, in death, appeared to be turned away from the camera in shame.

When Diego had composed himself sufficiently, Chief Huff escorted him down to the men's lavatory in the basement. On the way Huff reached out to Diego, below him on the stairs, and clutched his shoulder. "We're not getting anywhere, are we?" he said. "Why won't you trust me?"

Diego turned to look up at him. "I'm dying."

Huff held his gaze, but what he saw in Ildefonso's eyes was too much for him, and he glanced down at the concrete steps.

"It's OK," said Diego, laying his hand gently on the Chief's.

Four dresses lay spread out on Babs Rozzo's bed. She thought she'd wear the dark yellow one, bordering on gold, with the low neckline, for her first date with Bill Strannard. Her mother was scheduled to return in a little less than an hour to make the kids Sunday dinner as usual, always spaghetti with meatballs, which they adored. Babs was in her bathrobe when the doorbell rang.

"Oh Mom," whined Babs, "you're not supposed to see this!"

Flinging the front door open, Babs found a strange woman standing on her steps. The woman's hair, piled ridiculously high, was the color of unsalted butter, while her lips, just freshly painted, were a lewd shade of magenta. She smiled at Babs, whose eyes instantly went glassy.

"Yoo-hoo, Mrs. Rozzo?" sang Frosty June. "I have a delivery. It's your husband. Want me to bring him in?"

"Gus? Gus Rozzo?"

"Or doesn't he live here anymore?" Frosty June found herself backing away from the buxom woman, who was obviously in a lousy mood.

"That depends."

"On what?"

Babs trod off, back into the gloomy depths of the split-level. "Tell him he's here at a bad time," she called over her shoulder.

"You'll have to help me!" Frosty June called after her. "He's not gonna want to come in. He thinks we're out at Kennedy!"

"Tell him to open his eyes!"

Theresa appeared in the hallway.

"Go finish your homework," said Babs.

Glancing back at the van, Frosty June saw her little boy kneeling on the driver's seat watching her: he didn't like being left in the vehicle with the blind man, who was loudly singing along to an eight-track of old dance tunes, currently *The Bristol Stomp*. Frosty June ventured into the house.

The selection of dresses sparkling maddeningly before her, Babs slammed the bedroom door. Theresa saw her chance and ran down the hallway and into the stranger's arms. The woman's heavily made-up face was like those of the elegant women *and* men Theresa had seen in a library book on the French Revolution. "Where's my dad?" she whispered. "I'll help you..."

Gus protested only as long as it took him to realize that it was Theresa reaching into the van to touch him.

"Daddy, please," she begged. "This nice lady says you're blind. She wants you to come with us."

Eventually, Gus found himself collapsed on the sofa he'd fallen asleep on countless times before when everyone but his drink had abandoned him. It felt good. "You better get a taxi," he said, reaching into his back pocket. "Frosty June?" He felt around in the air for her. "Here, take some money to get you and the kid back into town. Take enough." Gus remembered the two-hundred and fifty dollars in cash Frosty June had got from the cash-machine the night before, but he wasn't about to lower himself by bringing that up. All he said was, "I thought we were pals..."

"I'm going to find your wife," was Frosty June's response. "Going to a party or something?" she said, when Babs came out of the bathroom with the dark yellow dress on.

"Am I supposed to thank you, or what?" Babs replied.

"Mind if I sit down for a minute?" Frosty June cocked her thumb in the direction of the bed.

"What for?"

Ignoring her belligerence, Frosty June went and sat in the space left by the dark yellow dress. "I don't know what's going on here but something's fucked up. You probably don't wanna know but I found your husband at the back of the Stamford, where he knows Tommy-Tom Nolan, and he's just sitting there in the dark. Who sits in the dark like that except a blind guy?"

Babs couldn't quite believe the insolence of this woman, with her tawdry clothes and painted face.

Frosty June went on. "He says he wants me to take him to Bermuda. Basically, I want nothing to do with the mother. But, he's blind, right? So I play along – basically, he's like totally out of fucking control. And where's he supposed to sleep, huh? So I take him to my place. My kid's there – that's fucked up. Don't worry, he wasn't interested in me."

"I wish he was."

"No you don't." Frosty June had to make this quick: she wanted to call a taxi immediately so she wouldn't have to bring Vincent into this house. "OK, you've got kids, right?"

Babs caught sight of her frown in the mirror on the closet door.

"Pay attention," snapped Frosty June. "What you do is, you take your nice big tits and your blow-job mouth and you go out and get a fucking job. Or, you go and get a welfare check, right? Like decent people, who *really* can't work. You don't sit around here picking out dresses to go out God-knows-fucking-where, to do God-knows-fucking-what on a Sunday night. Your husband may be a dickhead, but he's blind. And, from what he told me, *you* wanted the babies. Babies, babies, and more babies." As she got up to leave, Frosty June remembered one more thing. "Oh yea, and don't forget to see about workman's comp for your hubbie. That could help."

"Wait," said Babs, and skipped after her. "Are you married?"

"Do I look like I'm married?"

"Well, I was supposed to have a date with a guy at the U.N. Plaza Hotel tonight, at the bar. You know, that new hotel right near the U.N.? He's a really neat guy. You might like to meet him. I think he's kinda lonely, and I don't think I oughta just stand him up. He's too nice."

Babs was it, as far as Frosty June was concerned: *the ultimate pussy.* What more could a man want, a brain?

"What time was your date?"

"Eight-thirty," Babs pertly replied.

"What's the guy's name?"

"Bill, Bill Strannard. He'll probably be wearing a nice big grin. He's a grinner."

"I may or may not get over there," lied Frosty June, knowing she couldn't pass up a possible new trick.

"Well, thanks in advance if you do."

Frosty June headed for the stairway.

"And thanks for being our friend," Babs persisted.

In the living-room, Frosty June glanced at Gus, asleep on the sofa. His daughter sat on the carpet beside him with her head laid tenderly against his thigh.

Seated once more at Molloy's desk, Diego Ildefonso and Chief Leon Huff regarded each other across its considerable width. The fat man had a hopeless look about him. The Chief detested what he was obliged to do next. If Molloy had been there, the Chief would have had him do it. After all, this particular part of the process was his job. But it was Sunday and Molloy was no doubt ensconced in a bar somewhere throwing darts and drinking beer. From the same drawer from which he'd taken the envelope with the photos the Chief now extracted a sheet of paper in a clear plastic sleeve. Diego examined it carefully: a sheet of paper from a small note-pad, with something scrawled in ball-point. It meant nothing to him, he couldn't even read the handwriting.

"Do you see your name there?" asked the Chief. "It appears twice. Look at the very bottom. Here, allow me. It says – I'll correct the bad English – 'Alicia, I left her with Diego. He knows Bootsy, who tried to kill Shirlee. Diego will tell you he doesn't know, or that I did it. *Diego lies.*' What do you make of that?"

"I can't make anything of it. I don't know who wrote it."

"One of your pals."

"Oh."

"Not Gus, the other one."

Diego shrugged.

Chief Huff stared at him blankly. He would retire early, he decided. That was easy, and he'd struggled with the idea for nearly a year. "Do you want to call your wife, or shall I?"

"Can she come get me now?"

"You don't get it, do you?"

Diego waited.

"We have no choice but to charge you as an accessory to the murder of Alicia Rozzo."

As soon as Babs Rozzo's mother had arrived and got going on dinner, Babs got Gus up and took him to the hospital. On the ride across town in the van, Babs felt like a new woman.

I'm gonna remember this, Babs promised herself. *Always and always. Today I got my husband back and, even though he's blind, he could turn into a different person, a better, nicer person. Miracles happen a lot in funny places, like poor villages in the desert, where people only fish and drink out of wells. But they can happen in modern times too. Today, I also learned from a new friend how I can sacrifice, like other people do who care so much, and even don't have as much as I do. I'm pretty, and I'm smart, and I don't know how I do it – maybe it's because He's always watching me – but I meet life's worst things head-on. Don't I? You sure do, Barbara. That's my Mom talking, always giving me confidence. She knows I'm special, and she tells me. And that's nice of her, although she'd say that's just what she's there for. Mom would say, What could be worse than your husband going into New York to help a pal and coming home blind? I know I didn't do that. I just know it. My instincts are to protect my family. Like I was doing just before that woman showed up. I was going out to see what I could do to keep us marching forward, like with God's banner going on before. That's exactly what I was doing. I wasn't going out to meet some guy just for the fun of it, I was going out to partake of all the fruit in the garden. That's why God put it there, for good people to partake. People who are bad don't even know where to look. I offer all my precious bounty to my loved ones. That's how you should do it.*

Gus reached over and lay a facial tissue in Babs's lap, because she was sniffling so hard with tears of joy. This gesture in itself demonstrated a new kindness on her husband's part, and it was a truly welcome relief.

Chief Huff had gone on by taxi to Sunday dinner with his mother and family. Diego Ildefonso would be arraigned in the morning, sometime after ten when the courtroom down the block was open for business. The Chief would then send Molloy out to the Sunoco plant to see if he could find any tire tracks or scratched-off paint that matched the Rozzo van. He himself would go over to the development and pick up the little bastard for questioning.

Around four o'clock that afternoon, Officer Carl Durks looked in on the fat man, lying on his bunk. Though he appeared to be sleeping, his huge chest steadily rising and falling, his eyes were open.

How to find Dr. Herbert on a Sunday afternoon? Dolores didn't know where to begin. As she and everyone else knew, Christian Herbert and his wife were about to separate, if they hadn't already, so it was unlikely he would be at home. Not knowing precisely what was ailing her husband worried her desperately. Whatever the problem, it was affecting his perception of the world – his behavior at Gilbey's had, at moments, been disconcertingly peculiar. It was essential that Chief Huff know that her husband was unwell.

As luck would have it, Dolores hadn't any need to speculate on the whereabouts of Dr. Herbert. He was on his way to Willow Avenue at that very moment, with an excruciating hangover. He was hungover for a very good reason: his girlfriend had demanded a meeting, under threat of revealing her pregnancy to his wife: they would settle the matter of their future, either together or apart, once and for all. At two in the morning, while Mrs. Herbert slept, Dr. Herbert had slipped from the house and gone to the Lambeth Hotel where his lover had been drinking since eleven. There she had insisted upon an exorbitant sum to abort the fetus, which she referred to as *Jean Claude*. Although he seriously doubted the existence of the miraculous love-child, Dr. Herbert had agreed a more modest figure and they had gone off drunkenly to make love just once more in Manhattan.

Dolores was sitting slumped in the living-room watching Roland and little Billy bathe Blinky in the bathroom when she heard someone trip and swear in the front hallway. When she opened the door, she found Dr. Herbert standing with his back to her tucking his shirttails into his trousers.

"I can't believe you're here." The relief caught in Dolores's throat. "I've been trying – please, please come in and sit down. Can I get you anything?"

"You don't have a beer, or anything alcoholic?" Dr. Herbert stumbled into the room and sank sideways onto the sofa. "Oh, Jesus," he groaned.

There were a few cans of beer left in the case in the back hallway. "Why don't I open a bottle of champagne?" she offered. "Diego always keeps one cold at the bottom of the fridge."

"Yea sure, absolutely, if you insist." When he had drunk one flute very quickly and was anxiously accepting another, feeling immensely more like himself, Dr. Herbert said "What's the occasion?"

No response.

Mrs. Ildefonso, as Dr. Herbert had always known her, had situated herself next to him on the sofa with the bottle of champagne resting in her lap. He was somewhat dismayed to notice that she hadn't taken a glass for herself. Now he noticed the boys in the bathroom with the wet dog, which appeared to be, if it were possible, a cross between a spaniel and setter, blotched brown and gray.

"Distinctive coloring," he commented.

"Tell me about Diego," said Dolores.

"What did he tell you? Anything?"

"No, you tell me," she gently insisted.

Leaning into her, so that the two boys couldn't possibly hear what he was saying, Dr. Herbert began, "I owe you both an apology. No, more than an apology, I owe you an explanation." He searched for some way to continue.

"It's OK. Just tell me."

"Well, I did stop by here yesterday after my half-day at the clinic, but there wasn't anybody home."

"We were visiting friends."

"I should have called. I mean, I really should have called right away." Dr. Herbert took the bottle of champagne from Dolores and poured yet another flute. "Here," he said, offering it to her, "have a sip. It's really very good."

She did as she was asked, and watched as he rested the cold sweating bottle against the inside of his thigh. When she had lowered the flute and was pressing the back of her hand to the mist of champagne dampening her upper lip, he said, "I've consulted with a specialist, an old college chum of mine, Jim Heinemann. Actually, I've consulted with him twice now on Diego's case."

"Case?"

"On his *condition,* if you will."

First, the blotchy dog bounded from the bathroom. Then the two little boys came dashing after it. Dolores got up and went into the kitchen to urge them all down the back stairs.

"Sorry," she said, returning to her place beside Dr. Herbert.

"We think now we can get it out of there," he said.

Apparently, Dr. Herbert had gone on talking to Dolores in his thoughts. But she grasped immediately what he was alluding to – a tumor. Her mother had dreaded cancer all her life and so Dolores was familiar with its many ingenious varieties.

"Radiation," she said, "cobalt treatments."

"And then chemo. That's what Heinemann wants."

The sound of the boys shouting in the back yard, coming dimly up from the street, drew Dolores to the window. There, for what seemed to Dr. Herbert an interval verging on the melodramatic, she stood staring out at the pigeons fluttering about on the sills across the way.

"What is it?" he asked, wanting to escape to a dark and soothing corner of some nearby bar.

"Would you mind very much taking me over to the police station? Diego's in jail."

"In jail? What'd he do?" Dr. Herbert couldn't picture Diego Ildefonso in such circumstances.

"Nothing," said Dolores, on her way into the bedroom to get a sweater and to telephone Mrs. Finkelstein. "I'll explain in the car."

"Mind if we take what's left of the champagne along?" called Dr. Herbert.

"Not at all," Dolores called back. "I just wouldn't take it into the station."

On the way home from his mother's house, Lois and the kids listing sleepily against one another in the back of the car, Chief Huff decided to look in on Diego – it wouldn't take but a minute or two – and ask him if he minded being tested for drugs. Felix, who ran the lab, was usually at home on Sunday and could be over in a flash. While waiting for Felix to return his call, the Chief decided to resort to intimacy with the inscrutable Spaniard.

"Do you love your wife?" he asked.

The beautiful fat man gazed dopily out through the bars, apparently at the blank wall behind the Chief.

"Your son?"

No answer.

"Tell me, what price would you pay to guarantee them happiness?"

"Anything," Diego replied without hesitation.

"Right. So, what would you give this very moment to insure their peace and security?"

"Anything," Diego repeated.

"Then would you sign something for me?"

"Is it a check?"

"Not exactly."

"I feel tired. I think I'd like to take a nice hot shower and then lie down and rest for a while."

"How about signing this first?"

"If you're returning your purchases, *you* have to sign."

"No, Ildefonso, *you* have to sign."

"Whatever it is, shouldn't I read it first?"

"What's the point, it won't make any sense to you anyway."

"Listen, it's not that I don't trust you – I mean that – it's just that I never sign anything without reading it first."

"You're a wise fellow."

"I guess that's why I'm here." Diego took the document, which was in triplicate, and began reading. About five minutes later he sensed Chief Huff was growing impatient. "I just have one more paragraph to go."

"Take your time."

Diego finally handed the document back to Chief Huff.

"Proximity?" said the Chief.

"What?"

"How close were we? I mean, to what actually happened?"

"Not close at all."

Huff simply hadn't the patience for any more of Ildefonso's nonsense. "Just fucking sign it, OK?"

"You've never been rude before."

"Sorry."

"You're missing someone," Diego began.

Blinky was steadfastly chewing one of Mr. Finkelstein's old galoshes he'd found in the shed.

"I know lots about your dad," said Roland, "like he wanted me to eat one of those meat pies he makes, the ones with all the hair."

The green eyes stared back at him, unafraid. "You wouldn't even be here if it wasn't for me," said Billy. "You'd be drowned, you fairy."

"Sure. And I guess you wouldn't be here if it wasn't for my mom and dad? They know everything about what goes on in your house. Like your dad plays with his *thingy* all the time."

"Oh yea, prove it, you fuck-shit!"

Mrs. Finkelstein ran from her kitchen and came to stand between the two boys.

"How do you know to speak to each other this way?" she demanded. "You think because you know so much about baseball you don't have to play fair?"

"We're not playing baseball," said Roland.

"We're not even playing," added Billy.

"Then what's this ugly shouting?" demanded Mrs. Finkelstein.

"A difference of opinion," said Roland.

"Now, hug yourselves and say *I love you.* And do it nice," said Mrs. Finkelstein, and reached down and plucked her husband's galosh from between Blinky's two front paws.

"I don't want to," said Roland.

"Why not?" asked Billy.

"*Because*," whispered Roland.

"You hold my hand when we sleep and your mom sees it."

"How do you know?"

"I saw her." Billy looked up at the old woman. She was smiling down at him, and at Roland. "She comes in and looks at us and cries."

"She loves you," said Mrs. Finkelstein.

They all turned to stare up at the windows of the Ildefonsos' apartment. The telephone was ringing. Roland bounded up the back steps and lifted the receiver just as Babs Rozzo was about to hang up, there in the lobby of St. Mary's hospital.

"Is your mommy home, sweetheart?"

"No, Mrs. Rozzo, she went away with Pop's doctor, about an hour ago."

"I hope it's nothing serious. Not like *our* daddy."

"Whose daddy?" Roland had often found Mrs. Rozzo's patter unintelligible.

"Mr. Rozzo. I thought your mommy oughta know – he's blind. So we're not having it so easy ourself. I know what it's like now, with Gus blind. Your mom and I have a lot to share. Like both of our husbands stand up for what they believe."

"Mrs. Rozzo," said Roland, "is there anything you really want to tell her? I have a number."

"OK. Then you call her and tell her *I'm sorry,* about your dad and all. And tell her I – this is important, Roland – "

"I'm listening."

"Tell her Chief Huff should come to the hospital and see Gus. He should talk to him about Tommy-Tom."

This woman was not the slightest like his mother, Roland decided, this woman was not like a mother at all.

"You're quite a gal," said Roland. "You want me to tell her? You got it."

When Babs returned to Gus's bedside, she pulled the curtain closed around them, unbuttoned her blouse and allowed him to suckle her breast. Now and again, his blind eyes peered up at her, like a newborn kitten's.

Later that night, Leon Huff lay in bed next to his sleeping wife, staring at the badge on his hat. It glinted in the darkness on the top of his dresser – he and Lois each had their own, matching mahogany ones. His uniform, freshly cleaned and pressed, waited in its polyethylene bag draped over the chair by the door. Now it was all so obvious. Diego Ildefonso was a decent guy who had gotten mixed up with the wrong people. Huff savored the moment once more. He had cranked the pages down into Detective Sergeant Molloy's machine and his nerves had tingled with satisfaction and relief. Again the voices came to fill his head, all of them rendered by Diego Ildefonso, and they weren't about to go away.

"I want you'se to suck me, like at Christmas," Tommy-Tom had said, smiling over his shoulder at the girl.

Alicia Rozzo had been in the back seat, Diego Ildefonso holding her hand.

"No way! Suck it yourself!" she laughed.

"Hear that," whispered Gilbey to Tommy-Tom, "the way she said *it* – the way she said the word *it* – I'm getting hard."

"I told you," Tommy-Tom whispered back.

"I'm going to college," announced Alicia. "One with a nice campus. I get good grades, I bet none of you did."

"Ildefonso got good grades, didn't you?" insisted Gilbey.

"Yea, but I got a good job," howled Tommy-Tom, "a good blow-job!"

"Oh, Tommy-Tom, you're so crude," said Alicia.

"Crude as wood," Tommy-Tom sassed her back.

"You're a poet, Mr. Nolan," said Gilbey. "Almost as good as Carl Sanburg."

"More like Sam and Dave," remarked Alicia, and everyone laughed.

Pushing a lever at his elbow, Diego lowered his window. Outside, beyond the narrow bridge over the Hackensack, the landscape was empty. Then he heard a noise. It was in the car. It sounded like a length of pipe in a woollen sock being thumped repeatedly against the steering wheel. Then, in the light drifting in from the refinery, he saw the color of the thing. It was Tommy-Tom's erect penis.

"Dear boy," murmured Gilbey, "my plumbing's about to spring a leak."

The raspberry red Pontiac Bonneville skidded off the road onto the loose gravel and as it did Alicia pitched forward, glimpsing the spectacle in the front seat. Wrenching free of Diego, she threw open her door and ran shrieking mockingly from the car.

"Not that old thing again!" she called.

"It only *looks* old!" Gilbey called after her. His urine went streaming over the debris littering the flattened rushes at his feet.

Leering at Diego in the darkness of the back seat, Tommy-Tom said, "I'm gonna come twice tonight, which ain't like me."

Later, for a short while, there was more shrieking. Alicia's wrists were tied and she was forced to the ground. Without her fake-leather skirt and panties, her belly and thighs shone starkly white against the shiny black stones at the base of the tank.

"Rather pretty," said Gilbey. "But she can't talk with her mouth like that. I want to talk to her."

"And say what?" laughed Tommy-Tom.

"Fuck-talk," answered Gilbey. "Come on, my man..."

"Cool," said Tommy-Tom. "Talk that talk."

And Gilbey did, with Alicia Rozzo hefted up onto a large feed-pipe, her knees up around her ears, toes pointing at the moon, held in Tommy-Tom's vice-like grip. But Tommy-Tom had decided not to remove the electrician's tape he'd wrapped around her head and, in the end, Gilbey had ceased his complaining.

"You gotta know how to fuckin do it," Gilbey grunted, eyes locked on Tommy-Tom's. A warm breeze, heavy with sulfur, blew in from the river.

Now Tommy-Tom let out a sickening whine, like an electric guitar, and sang *"Move over, Rover, and let Tommy-Tom take over!"*

"Oh, my man!" Gilbey shouted, and did his best to help Tommy-Tom lower the girl onto the ground.

Diego Ildefonso had only listened, he said. He had walked from the car to stand by the stagnant water just beyond the tall metal fence, listening. Sickened, he had walked on a ways further. When he returned he found Tommy-Tom lying on top of the girl in a ditch on the other side of one of the fuel tanks. Gilbey was standing nearby, watching.

Lifting his head, still partially hidden in her hair, Tommy-Tom said, "I fucked up."

"Not good..." said Gilbey. Alicia Rozzo was choking groggily on her own blood. Her wrists were broken and her hands lay on either side of her head like withered lettuce leaves.

Tommy-Tom got up and just stood there.

"What a mess you've made now," said Gilbey, and knelt down and took Alicia's throat in his hands and squeezed.

He then stripped her naked, to keep anyone from identifying her, and with Tommy-Tom's help laid her under a piece of black plastic between the two tanks, the kind, Ildefonso said, that move up and down so slowly you never notice. He couldn't recall what Gilbey had done with her clothes. Huff had had to fill that one in: they'd gone into a chopped-off oil drum full of rainwater and bits of burnt black crap. But Huff had done some embellishing of his own, adding that it had been Gilbey who had tied them around a discarded hunk of cast iron, part of a dismantled lathe, to weight them down.

That was it. Ildefonso said that he and Francis Gilbey got back into the Pontiac. Tommy-Tom Nolan hit the gas, and they were gone.

The Chief rolled over and looked at his wife. As usual, Lois was sleeping with her mouth open. Her breath smelled sweet, like a child's. The Chief got up and went down the hall to the bathroom. He fidgeted around for a while then decided to clip his toenails.

The beleaguered shoe salesman had wept at only one point in his confession, strangely enough when he mentioned how lonely it was out there in the marshes. It was then the Chief knew he hadn't been there: his grief had plainly been for Alicia Rozzo, not for himself. Real criminals cried only for themselves. How Ildefonso had conjured up the crime so vividly the Chief couldn't possibly say, but he would find out. The truth, or something very like the truth, had, uncannily, flowed from the beautiful fat man's lips.

On Monday, the Chief would have Ildefonso's doctor's file. Supposedly, he was gravely ill. Failing a court order, he would remain in the basement of the Hoboken police station. He would continue to lie staring at the ceiling with his great wet eyes fastened on someone, or something, no one else could see. Tomorrow the Chief's real work would begin. First, before having Francis Gilbey picked up, he would have Molloy call the FBI to see if they had anything on him. Then the Chief would go into New York and have a look around the Stamford Arms. Perhaps Tommy-Tom Nolan had stupidly left some clue as to where he might be headed.

Bootsy Holloway still couldn't believe his good fortune. How could anyone love another so immediately? He'd wondered this off and on throughout the night, with the beautiful girl lying chastely by his side, her parents lying not so chastely inside their trailer less than twenty yards away. He could only accept that certain things – miracles, more exactly – were inexplicable. Sometimes things just happened, things that had the power to change everything, or nearly everything. He and Esther Estrada would be married momentarily, there on Henry Moore's fishing boat, with Uncle Tookus as Bootsy's best man.

Mrs. Estrada had proudly provided her daughter with her own wedding dress. It had a crinoline skirt with little yellow ribbons fastened at the hem. Mrs. Estrada had worn the dress less than seventeen years before while carrying Esther. The urgency of the occasion – the bride and groom intended to embark for their Haitian honeymoon just as soon as the festivities had ended that evening – made the scene livelier perhaps than it might ordinarily have been. Music played constantly, and loudly, the drinking having begun among Mr. Estrada's friends long before they'd gotten into their cars and headed east for the village of Engelhard.

At this late hour of the morning, Engelhard in its glaring whiteness was nearly indistinguishable from the great piles of blistering oyster shells piled everywhere along the pine-studded shores. As the newly married couple posed in the stern of

Henry Moore's boat wrapped in each other's arms, Bootsy's father's old brown suit looking more rakish than out-of-date, flashbulbs popping, Uncle Tookus raised his glass and called, "Here's to the young lovers! Here's to love!" And Bootsy wondered what his new life with Esther would be like, but he wasn't worried, because she gave him strength. He sensed there would be a baby before very long – he hoped their first would be a boy – and began to see how they might live quite contentedly without very much at all. Bootsy could barely remember what Tommy-Tom Nolan looked like, and the white man's law – well, it probably wasn't any better or any worse than the black man's, so he would just do his best to keep his nose clean.